OHIO SALT

FRANK C. DUPUY

Copyright © 2002 by Agincourt Publishing, LLC

All rights reserved. No part of this book may be reproduced in any form or by any electronic or mechanical means, including information storage and retrieval systems, without permission in writing from the publisher, except by a reviewer who may quote brief passages in a review.

First Edition

This is a work of fiction. Names, characters, places and incidents are either the product of the author's imagination or are used fictitiously, and any resemblance to actual persons, living or dead, business establishments, events or locales is entirely coincidental.

Library of Congress Control Number: 2002111595

ISBN 0-9723852-0-7

Cover designed by: Nate Jordan
                   Sarah Norgren

Printed in the United States of America

In memory of my friend Lee G. Feathers, private investigator and polygraph examiner extraordinaire.

I miss you, pal.

salt: to enrich (as a mine) artificially by secretly placing valuable minerals in some of the working places.

OHIO
SALT

Prolog

Washington, D.C.
August, 1939

     Ponderous, lead colored clouds hovered over the city, sucking the vitality out of it. The stale, sultry air being disturbed by the ceiling fans in the Polish embassy did little to alleviate the suffering of the building's occupants. A weary courier carried his heavy dispatch case to the office of the military attaché. He knocked on the door.
     "Enter."
     The courier set his case on the desk, extracted a key from his pocket, and, after unlocking the chain that secured the case to his wrist, stepped back and saluted. The man behind the desk returned the salute.
     "I have only now arrived, sir," stated the courier formally, "I came straight to your office."
     The man at the desk examined the seals on the case. They appeared to be intact.
     "Thank you, Lieutenant. You may go."
     The lieutenant executed a precise about face before marching out of the office.
     The man sighed as he watched the earnest, youthful officer depart, wondering if he had ever been that green, or naive.
     Someone drummed his fingernails on the frosted glass panel of his office door. It was the Ambassador's trademark.
     "Come in, please."
     The Ambassador, in his shirt sleeves, stepped into the office.
     "I understand that the courier brought you another shipment, Colonel."

Frank C. Dupuy

"Yes, the last one, I'm afraid. We have almost run out of time."

The two men considered each other in silent commiseration. Both knew they were powerless to influence the events about to engulf their country.

"When do you return?" The Ambassador finally asked.

"In three days. I am to be given command of an armored unit." He shook his head. "We have so few tanks – antiques compared to what the Germans possess."

"How long?"

The Colonel grew thoughtful. "At the most, three months. The Germans will attack before winter sets in. Hitler is not a patient man; he has nothing to gain by waiting until spring."

The Ambassador nodded glumly as he contemplated the case on the Colonel's desk. He felt like crying.

Dallas, Texas
November 22, 1963

The man standing by the railroad fence near the grassy knoll glanced at his watch. The motorcade was behind schedule. Carefully, he scanned the street to make certain he could still pick out the zero point. He hoped that the flake in the building would wait until the car reached the exact spot. If he did, they would fire together.

Camelot, that's what the press liked to call the administration. The man spat. It was too bad that none of those dipshit reporters had ever bothered to read a book; otherwise, they would have known what was in store for Camelot.

He thought about the months of planning that had gone into his mission. Everything would have been perfect if it hadn't been for that goddamn Guzman. He had been silenced, but not quickly enough. Those jerks from Cleveland only thought they knew something; still, they were an inconvenience that would have to be dealt with.

He caught the faint shout of a distant bystander.

"Here they come!"

The man extracted a scoped rifle from its tan case. The case

Ohio Salt

almost matched his DPS uniform. Pulling up on the bolt handle, he drew the bolt back less than half an inch; just enough to assure himself that there was a round in the chamber. The lead sedan in the motorcade came into view. He lifted the rifle to his shoulder as he had done hundreds of times in practice. The zero point was clearly visible in his scope. He shifted his sights. The head of the youngest man ever to be elected president of the United States was centered in the cross hairs. The front bumper of the black Lincoln sedan crossed the zero point.

Frank C. Dupuy

1

"Remember, pal, nobody ever tells you the entire truth"

Lee G. Feathers
Polygraph Examiner

April, 1994
Tuesday

Your time's up, I thought. The woman sitting before me was starting to repeat herself. She wanted me to confirm what she already knew, and was willing to pay me $2,000 to do it. She had the cash in her purse. I sighed, knowing that I wasn't going to accept her money.

"Mrs. Grey, I appreciate your confidence in my abilities, but I have already explained to you that I do not accept domestic cases. I'll be happy to refer you to a competent investigator who specializes in your situation."

Her expression hardened sufficiently to express that she was not accustomed to being turned down. "Mr. LeBlanc, when we met, I told you that I had been referred to you by my attorney. That wasn't true. I don't have an attorney, yet."

My features remained parked in polite neutral.

Seeing that I wasn't going to reply, she continued. "Actually, I was referred by a close, personal friend, Ted Meyers."

My expression did not waiver, though I swore silently. Ted Meyers was a valued client who had sent a lot of work my way over the years. A successful entrepreneur who owned several manufacturing companies, he dined with the rich and famous, and slept with

Frank C. Dupuy

their wives and girl friends. His flamboyant lifestyle had made the scandal rags often enough to make him a minor celebrity. If Meyers liked you, his generosity was legend; if you were on his shit list, life could be unpleasant.

I stood up. "Will you excuse me for a moment, Mrs. Grey?"

She nodded, smiling brightly. "Grey is my maiden name. My married name is Lipscomb." Her dazzling teeth were only slightly marred by the lipstick on them.

I stepped into my secretary's office, shutting the door behind me. "Karen, get Ted Meyers on the phone, will you?" Karen twirled her Rolodex, located the number, dialed it and handed me the receiver. His secretary put me through immediately.

"Adrian, how are you?" Meyers enthused, then continued before I could answer. "I was expecting your call. It seems Julie is in need of a top-notch private eye, so naturally, I thought of you."

"I'm flattered, Ted." I replied, choosing my words carefully, "You do know that I don't handle divorce work?"

"Who said anything about divorce? Julie has a problem she needs handled discreetly. Since you're the best in the business at keeping a secret, I insisted on her calling you. You weren't seriously thinking about not helping her were you?" I could still hear the smile in his voice, but his teeth were showing.

"Any friend of yours is a friend of mine."

"Splendid. I knew you wouldn't let me down."

"By the bye, Ted, what's her husband's first name?"

"Harold."

"As in Harold Lipscomb of Newport Industries?"

"I believe so, now that you mention it."

"You believe so? Ted, I thought you and Lipscomb were mortal enemies."

"Don't be so dramatic. Harold and I are businessmen who occasionally chase after the same piece of business."

"Uh huh."

"Anyway, Julie is an old and dear friend. I would take it as a personal favor if you would help her out."

"Consider it done."

"Good. Give me a call in a few days – we'll do lunch."

I returned the receiver to Karen. "How much did I make off

Ohio Salt

of Ted Meyers last year?

"Counting referrals, over $50,000."

"In that case, we have a new client."

"Ms. Snooty?"

"That's Mrs. Lipscomb to you. She'll be leaving my office in about five minutes. Find out what she's driving."

"Can do. I'll leave now." With that, Karen stood up and slipped into the corridor.

Julie Lipscomb was peering into her compact mirror when I reentered my office. I estimated her to be in her early thirties, though she could pass for younger. Her well-rounded body was encased in a tightly tailored, high-priced, dark-red suit trimmed in black. It was not quite tacky. Her dark hair was expensively cut, as was the large diamond on her left hand. The woman was attractive, and knew it. It was a good bet she made the most of her looks when it came to getting her way. Sweet and innocent were not words I would use to describe my new client. No, I decided, pain in the ass suited her perfectly.

"Mrs. Lipscomb," I articulated as I sat down at my desk, "would you please tell me exactly what you want me to do for you?" Her expression was both relieved and triumphant.

"I thought I was clear. I want you to gather evidence that Harold is having an affair. As I told you, he is going to be at our cottage tonight with – that woman." Her stricken mien did not have the effect on me she was probably hoping for. Julie Lipscomb extracted an envelope from her purse and placed it on my desk. "I have a map for you with directions to the cottage. About a quarter of a mile from our cottage is an abandoned house that burned last year. You can leave your car there." She went on to detail exactly where I should station myself for the best view of the cottage and the best shots of people entering and leaving it. I wondered how long she had been planning this.

"Mrs. Lipscomb, how do you know that your husband is going to show up tonight?"

She smiled a tight, conspiratorial smile. "Harold is such an organized man. He wrote it in his appointment book. I made copies of it night before last. It reads "GH, the cottage, 7:00". GH is Gwen Hiltie, his current slut. She works for him."

Frank C. Dupuy

My new client rummaged in her purse again before ferreting out a bank envelope. "There's $2,000 in there, Mr. LeBlanc. Ted told me you charge a thousand dollars a day. I wish to retain your services for two days." She frowned as I counted the money. There were twenty crisp one hundred bills in the envelope.

"My secretary had to leave. Would you like me to write you a receipt now, or mail one to you?"

"Oh, there's no need for that, Mr. LeBlanc. I trust you," she breathed, gazing into my eyes. I stifled an impulse to reach for my billfold to assure myself that it was still there.

"When I'm finished tonight, how do I contact you?"

"I will call you in the morning. You see, I can't risk Harold finding out that I'm having him investigated."

Julie Lipscomb rose, then dramatically extended her hand. "Thank you, Mr. LeBlanc. I knew I could count on you." Her handshake was quick and firm. I noticed that she was missing a button on her right sleeve. I also noticed the ample swell of her chest as she inhaled. I wondered how long she had been married and how long she and Ted Meyers had been old and dear friends.

I was sitting with my feet resting on my desk when Karen rapped on my door.

"Well?" I inquired.

"She was driving a year old Lexus. I ran the plate through BMV. The car is registered to Ontario Enterprises, Inc., which has its offices over on Detroit Avenue."

I pondered that information. "You ever hear of them?"

"Never."

I pondered some more. Karen Koenig is a wealth of information. She is a fifty-three year old Cleveland native who has lived and worked in the Cleveland area all of her life. She had been the executive secretary for the owner of a long established machining firm that was liquidated when he died of a heart attack. I hired her four years ago and have come to depend on her judgment.

"What did you think of Julie Lipscomb?"

"If Harold Lipscomb is really her husband, he doesn't give her a very generous clothing allowance," Madam Koenig pronounced.

"Oh?"

Ohio Salt

"That outfit may have cost a lot of money, but it was at least three years old and missing a button on one sleeve."
"What else?"

"Her civilized veneer is paper thin, probably only recently acquired. That woman grew up in a rough neighborhood and is trying to put on airs."

"You don't think she graduated from a posh finishing school?"

"I don't think she finished high school."

"I wonder what Lipscomb saw in her?" I mused innocently.

"Ha!" Karen snorted. "I just bet you do. Her manners may be phony, but the rest is all real."

"So's her money. For $2,000, plus Ted's not so subtle arm twisting, I guess I can go take pictures of hubby escorting Ms. GH to the cottage."

Karen Koenig pursed her lips. "Adrian, that woman is trouble. You had better watch yourself tonight."

"Fear not, fair damsel. Ace Investigator LeBlanc is eternally vigilant." As it turned out, Ace Investigator LeBlanc was eternally stupid.

Frank C. Dupuy

2

My intercom buzzed as I contemplated excuses I could use to weasel out of going to Harold Lipscomb's love cottage.

"Do you want to speak with Louie Kolakowski?" Karen inquired. "He says it's urgent."

Karen added the urgent because she knows damn well that I duck Louie whenever I can. Louie is a character I had the misfortune to meet at a private investigators' conference about five years ago. He specializes in sleazy divorce work, skip tracing and process serving. What few ethics he has are questionable. Unfortunately, he regards me as a friend, and I have never been able to dissuade him of that misperception. With Louie, urgent could be anything from needing a fifty dollar loan to wanting to share a hot tip on a lame nag.

"Sure, Karen, put him on. He's probably going to send some more divorce work my way." I lifted the receiver.

"Hey, Adrian. It's lucky for me you were in. You're one hard guy to get hold of."

I didn't reply.

"I, uh, got a small problem. I need a secure place to stash some, er, ah, sensitive documents." Before I could tell him to go pound salt, Louie hurried on. "I'm on to something big, Adrian, really big. If things are a little slow with you, I could cut you in." I quailed at the prospect. "You remember me telling you about the Polish gold that disappeared in World War II? I got a line on it." Now, I was really on my guard. Louie has been chasing fairy stories for as long as I have known him. He could go on for hours about lost treasures, conspiracies and mysterious strangers with maps who were begging him to help find elusive loot. I cut him short.

"Louie, I would love to help you; unfortunately, I have an important investigation that will have me tied up for awhile."

Frank C. Dupuy

"You after a big embezzler?"

"I'd tell you, but then I'd have to kill you."

Louie laughed. "That's what I like about you, Adrian. You always play 'em close to your vest. I understand. You and me operate alike."

Cringing, I was about to make a polite excuse to hang up when Louie continued.

"Can I leave the package with you? I don't feel safe leaving it with anybody else."

"Sure, Louie. Drop it off. I won't be here, but Mrs. Koenig will. I'll give her strict instructions to place it with our other top secret documents."

"Thanks, Adrian. It's good to have a friend I can count on."

We hung up. I stepped into Karen's office.

"Louie Kolakowski is coming by in a little while to drop off a package of important documents. I won't be here."

Karen correctly interpreted my expression. "Is it racing forms?"

"Who knows? He claims it has something to do with the deed to a Polish gold mine. Anyway, on the off chance his stuff is important, drop it off at the bank."

"I'll take care of it. You know, boss, you're too hard on Mr. Kolakowski. He is always so pleasant, and he really is entertaining." Karen has taken to Louie ever since he asked her if she was still modeling for fashion magazines.

"So are trained ferrets. While he's here, don't leave him alone for a second, and make sure to count the paper clips after he leaves."

Karen's frown indicated that she considered me callous.

My office is next door to an older bank that has a massive safe-deposit vault. I maintain three large boxes there on the theory that it is cheaper and a lot more secure than a safe. My wife and Karen Koenig are the only people who know about the boxes. So far, nothing I have put in them has ever been tampered with.

Louie Kolakowski is in his early thirties, which makes me his senior by about a dozen years. If you can believe him, his father was an officer in the Polish army in World War II, who escaped from the blitzkrieg by fleeing to England, where he served with distinction in

Ohio Salt

a Polish brigade attached to the British army. The senior Kolakowski immigrated to Canada, married a refugee from Lithuania, then proceeded to the U.S. where he and Mrs. Kolakowski produced several children, including Louie. His father died a few years after Louie was born. How do I know so much about Louie Kolakowski? It's because he corralled me one night after his second wife left him and poured his heart out to me at a bar; a bar in which he ran up a considerable tab that I ended up paying.

Louie read too many cheap detective novels as a boy. His attempts to emulate the hard bitten P.I.s of the fifties would have been comical, if he had not been so pathetic. His favorite costume is a black suit, black fedora, black gloves and a black trench coat. He can never figure out why he is spotted every time he goes out on a surveillance. To his credit, Louie is one of the best con men on the telephone I have ever listened to. That one skill helps him earn a modest living locating deadbeats, serving subpoenas and pursuing errant spouses. He is 5'10" and weighs all of 130 pounds fully clothed. Although he claims his hands are registered weapons, I happen to know that he was beat up by both of his ex-wives. I have tried to convince him that his fascination with big women is unhealthy, but he is a glutton for punishment.

If that were all there was to Louie, he would be bad enough, however, he is a conspiracy nut who has purchased every crackpot book ever written about the Kennedy assassination, alien abductions and lost treasures. At least twice a year he claims to be involved in some search for a missing fortune. It only bothers me when he manages to defeat my ability to dodge him, then tells me all about it in excruciating detail.

Louie likes me, though I don't know why. Karen claims it is a case of hero worship, that I represent a father figure. I believe it has more to do with my being the proverbial soft touch.

Thinking about Louie was more fun than thinking about Julie Lipscomb's problem. I sighed, deciding that a man could do worse than humoring a harmless nut who likes to indulge in missing gold fantasies. That was my second mistake in less than an hour.

Frank C. Dupuy

3

The unseasonably early spring was in full glory as I drove east on Interstate 90. It was a shame that Harold Lipscomb would look back on this day only to remember it as the time he was photographed at the cottage with Gwen Hiltie. Another of life's lessons: If you are going to philander, do not leave your appointment book where your wife can find it. Speaking of philandering, I wondered how long Ted Meyers had known Julie Lipscomb. I was willing to bet that their relationship had been more than platonic at one time.

I let my mind drift as I soaked up the sunshine. Harold Lipscomb had been born into money. His grandfather was a blacksmith who had developed an interest in forgings, ending up with one of the largest forging operations in Ohio. Lipscomb's father had expanded the business, diversified into manufacturing and machining operations. Harold sold most of the older companies at premium prices shortly before the Great Lakes economy crashed in 1981, then reinvested in real estate and high-tech industries. He had a reputation as an astute businessman and sat on several boards. Unlike Ted Meyers, Lipscomb's lifestyle never made headlines.

In the last decade, Meyers and Lipscomb had butted heads over real estate deals. Both accused the other of underhanded practices; it was a well known fact that they despised one another. So, I wondered, for the umpteenth time, how had Ted Meyers and Julie Lipscomb become friends? Helping your worst enemy's wife set him up for adultery was low, even for Ted Meyers.

I exited the freeway onto Route 45 and headed south. The heavily wooded area I was driving through was resplendent with bright-green newly emerging leaves. Julie Lipscomb had told me

Frank C. Dupuy

that Harold's grandfather built the cottage as a place to take his family in the summer. It sat on fifty or so acres that bordered the Grand River a few miles south of Austinburg. I slowed as I searched for the gravel road that would take me to the burned house, found it, and after driving several hundred yards, spotted the charred remains next to an overgrown driveway that led to what had been a detached garage by some large maple trees. After parking my pickup as far under the trees as I could, I shouldered my backpack and pocketed Julie's map before heading into the woods.

    I located a trail that Julie claimed would lead to the cottage. The ground was still spongy from the rains that had fallen a few days ago. I was glad I had worn hiking boots. After fifteen minutes, I stepped onto a well maintained gravel driveway that curved through the woods. According to the map, the cottage was located about 300 yards off of the main road. A few minutes later, I spotted the "cottage", although Hansel and Gretel would have never called it that. A two-story, stone, slate roofed mansion with rustic, exposed wood beams hunkered on a hill overlooking the Grand River. Empty stables and a caretaker's house in matching stone were located nearby. Julie assured me that no one had lived in the caretaker's house for years and that the kitchen would be a perfect vantage point for taking incriminating photos. She had even made certain that the caretaker's house would be unlocked. All I had to do was let myself in, snap the photographs of the happy couple arriving and leaving, then wait for Julie Lipscomb to call me. It seemed too simple. With all of her preparation, my client could have hired any competent P.I. to shoot the pictures for one hell of a lot less than she had paid me. I reminded myself that she had selected me because of her old and dear friend's recommendation.

    As the evening shadows lengthened, I zipped up my jacket, then consulted my watch. 5:36. Sitting down at the edge of the woods, I removed my binoculars from my backpack and scanned the area. There was no sign of life or movement. I waited another fifteen minutes to satisfy myself that no one was lurking behind the shrubbery before heading over to the caretaker's house. The rich, I mused, have a funny way of perceiving the world. They call a rustic stone mansion a cottage and the caretaker's tiny cottage a house. I guess it eases their conscience.

Ohio Salt

Instead of walking across the open, I ambled along the edge of the trees until I was as close to the house as possible. Years of experience have taught me to be cautious. I deposited my backpack behind a tree, in case I ran into somebody. I didn't want to have to explain a camera fitted with a night vision lens to Mr. Lipscomb or one of his employees on the off chance that someone was taking a siesta in the caretaker's house.

Two stone steps led up to the small porch that sheltered the back door. Several muddy shoe prints were on the steps. After pausing for a moment, I decided that they probably belonged to Julie Lipscomb, or whomever she had unlock the back door. Just to be on the safe side, I knocked. No one answered. Cautiously, I tested the door knob. It turned easily. Peering through the open door, I could not discern anything that appeared out of place, so, with a shrug, I stepped into the house and walked to the kitchen. A loud pop sounded milliseconds before I felt a sting. I lost control of my body as a figure in a ski mask zapped me with 20,000 volts of electricity.

Frank C. Dupuy

4

My body convulsed with a tremendous spasm, forcing the contents of my stomach to spew into the atmosphere.

"God dammit!" rasped a voice next to me.

I opened my eyes, but they wouldn't focus. Everything was spinning. Shutting my eyes, I retched again.

"Shit! Hurry up will you?"

I felt myself being pulled and shoved into an upright position. Vaguely, I was aware that something was terribly wrong. My head lolled forward on my chest; I would have fallen over except for the strap. Forcing my eyes open, I had a feeling of familiarity. I was in my truck. Someone reached across me. The engine started. We were moving forward. We hit a bump, more bumps. We were gathering speed. The door beside me slammed shut. Big bump. The truck was free falling. The mother of all jolts slammed my head into the headrest. I was mashed against my seat belt as the truck tried to stand on its nose. Then water as cold as liquid nitrogen cascaded through the open windows.

Instinct, luck, or maybe my guardian angel caused me to take a deep breath. Seconds later, I was under water. Panic. I fumbled for the seat belt release. It was jammed. My eyes were open, but I couldn't see anything. It was pitch black. The truck stopped moving. It occurred to me that I was about to die. I quit straining against the seat belt, then carefully pulled on the shoulder strap. It gave a few inches, enough for me to slide it over my head. I grabbed the edge of the window, pulling and wiggling for all I was worth. I desperately needed to breathe. My shoulders were through, then my legs and feet as they slid free of the lap belt. An eternity later, my head found the surface, and air. Gasping, I inhaled deeply, then choked as I sucked in air and water. I was sinking. I ceased thrash-

Frank C. Dupuy

ing, concentrated on floating. Something was wrong. I was dizzy, my eyes weren't cooperating, nor would my hands and feet move the way they were supposed to. I was cold. I dimly comprehended that spring or not, the water was icy as hell and if I didn't reach land soon, I would be fish bait. Part of my visual problems stemmed from the fact that it was dark. The moon produced enough light for me to take in its reflection on the water. I could discern the blurry outline of trees. Although I wasn't too far from the shore, it was moving past me. Current. I was in a river. Laboriously, I managed a breast stroke that kept me afloat, and, using the current, pushed me to shore.

Mud. My feet were in mud. A branch poked my face. I grabbed it. Pulling and crawling, I inched my way out of the water. The ground was shaking. No, I was. If I didn't get moving, I would die. I made it to my knees before nausea took hold. I heaved, then heaved again. I had nothing left to give. Pulling myself up with the help of a tree, I took a step, tripped and fell down. Vertigo seemed to be a permanent condition. Another helpful tree and I was up again. Concentrate, one foot in front of the other. I think I can, I think I can. My head hurt, my stomach was in turmoil; I discovered that my groin ached as though I had been kicked in the cojones by a soccer player with an unpronounceable last name.

I must have stumbled around in the woods for an hour before I wandered onto a gravel road. The moon provided sufficient light for me to avoid toppling into the bigger pot holes. I realized that most of the blurriness was gone. My coordination was improving, although that may not have been saying a lot. Even though my brain was still pretty foggy, one thought penetrated the mist. Some son of a bitch had tried to kill me.

I had been lurching down the gravel road for ten minutes when I noticed a vaguely familiar clearing. It took me a few moments to realize that it was the burned-out house where I had parked my truck. My mind was beginning focus. I had left my backpack in the woods by the caretaker's house. If the asshole who tried to drown me hadn't found it, I could make a telephone call. Besides my camera with the night vision lens, I had my cellular telephone in it. There was no way I was going to stumble through the woods at night hoping that I could find the driveway. No, this time I would go in

Ohio Salt

through the front.

Another fifteen minutes of determined, slightly weaving, walking brought me to Harold Lipscomb's driveway. It was flanked by two massive stone pillars that supported wrought iron gates. The gates were open. I recalled Dante's cheery greeting as I passed through them.

Staying in the center of the drive, I attempted to listen for any telltale sounds that would alert me to the presence of the people who had endeavored to drown me. My hearing was impaired by the demon who was working my head over with a mallet. Even though I felt awful, my balance and eye sight were almost back to normal.

The cottage grounds were peacefully illuminated by the soft moonlight. No vehicles or hoodlums were readily apparent, but then, I hadn't seen anyone the last time, either. With that blithe reflection, I skirted the treeline to the caretaker's house, then spent several minutes searching for my backpack. Ha! The bad guys weren't so smart after all. Before retrieving my cellular phone, I examined the cottage again. Something was out of place. It took a minute before I realized that the front door was open. The old gray matter was really perking tonight. Slowly, I circled the grounds, keeping to the trees. A light was shining from a second story window in the back of cottage. I concentrated on the window. Several panes of glass had been broken out of it.

What I should have done, had I been thinking on all four cylinders, was to call the police and let them deal with the mystery of the open front door and the broken window. As you may have guessed, my brain was not at its optimum and, anyway, I was developing a serious grudge against whoever had driven me and my truck into the river. Rummaging in my pack, I retrieved a small, but powerful, black aluminum flashlight, though its beam seemed inadequate as I passed through the front door.

I was standing in a huge den with a flagstone floor and walls with rustic oak and maple accents. A massive stone fireplace dominated one wall. To my right was a curved staircase I could have driven my truck up, if it hadn't been sitting in the river. Cautiously, I ascended the stairs, unconsciously holding my breath lest I tread on a loose board. The stairs were solid and the house was as quiet as the proverbial tomb. As I reached the top of the stairs, I could see light

Frank C. Dupuy

peeking through a slightly opened door in the hallway. I turned off my flashlight and waited. Nothing. I was almost tiptoeing as I approached the door. I pushed it open with my foot.

The bedroom, illuminated by an overturned table lamp, was a shambles. Two end tables on either side of a massive four poster bed were knocked over, and the mattress was pulled off of the bed. The mirror of an ornately carved dressing table was shattered; everything that had been on it, was on the floor. A torn, dark-red skirt lay crumpled on the floor at the foot of the bed. It was the same shade as the black trimmed jacket the corpse was wearing. The jacket and the blood-soaked, white blouse beneath it were ripped open, exposing the woman's breasts. She was lying on her back with her legs spread. She wasn't wearing any panties. The woman's expression was difficult to read because her face was missing. Actually, parts of it may have been there, though it was difficult to be certain. The face had been obliterated by a shotgun blast, maybe more than one. Three empty, blue shotgun shells lay on the floor by the woman's feet.

I forced myself to look at the body. The arms were extended over the head; the hands were tied together with what I guessed was wire. It was hard to tell because the hands and wrists had been pulverized by multiple discharges from a shotgun. The pellets had gouged a crimson crater in the carpet exposing mangled floor boards. Bits of flesh and bone had been forced into the fabric and the wood.

The woman had lived long enough to have been beaten and tortured. Bruises had formed on her breasts and torso. At least a dozen burn marks scarred her chest and stomach.

I fought down the urge to vomit, forcing myself to stand perfectly still, before examining the room. A bottle of Makers Mark bourbon was on the floor by the dressing table, its contents almost totally consumed. There was something under the corpse's right shoulder – my billfold. Oh, did I mention that she was missing a button on her right sleeve? A surprisingly large pool of blood had collected beneath the remnants of the corpse's head, surprising, because so much of it had splattered on the walls and furniture.

Carefully, I backed out of the room, located a light switch in the hall and flipped it. Lights. I examined the hall carpet. There were no signs of blood. As I made my way to the stairs, I turned on every light I could find. In the den an old fashioned rotary dial telephone was on a table near the front door. I lifted the receiver and dialed 911.

"Nine one one, what is the nature of your emergency?"

"My name is Adrian LeBlanc, I am a private investigator. I have been attacked; a woman has been murdered. Someone shot her in the face with a shotgun. I have been drugged and have survived an attempt to drown me. I am at Harold Lipscomb's cottage on Old River Road, just south of Austinburg. I don't know the house number. Tell the Sheriff's deputies that they need to bring detectives and someone from forensics here as soon as possible."

I won't go into the annoying questions that the pinhead operator asked me, but we did not like each other by the time I hung up. I made another call.

"Hello," intoned a pleasant female voice.

"Hello, this is Adrian LeBlanc. I need to speak to Collin Yates. Tell him it's an emergency."

"One moment, please. I will see if Mr. Yates is available."

I cursed under my breath. Collin Yates is one of the best defense attorneys I know, and he prides himself on being hard to get hold of. Calls to his house are usually screened by his housekeeper or his companion du jour.

"Yates here. What's going on, Adrian?" he demanded in a no nonsense tone. Evidently, I had his attention.

"Collin, I'm at Harold Lipscomb's cottage near Austinburg. That's Lipscomb as in Newport Industries. His wife hired me today to take pictures of him cheating on her. When I arrived, I was zapped, drugged and driven into the river in my truck. I escaped, came back to the house and found what's left of Julie Lipscomb. Julie is the wife. Her face was blown off with a shotgun. Everything was staged to make it look like I tortured, raped and murdered her."

Collin made a clicking noise with his tongue. "Have you called the police?"

"Yeah, I called 911 just before I called you. The Ashtabula Sheriff's Department has jurisdiction."

"OK, I'm on my way. Try not to piss off the cops, but say as little as possible until I get there."

Frank C. Dupuy

Swell, I thought, as I sat down to wait. I'm being framed and the best my hotshot attorney can come up with is try not to piss off the cops.

5

The emergency room doctor was young; not as young as Doogie Howser, but young enough not to inspire confidence. He had neatly trimmed dark hair, pressed tan slacks, a blue oxford cloth shirt and a Donald Duck tie that coordinated nicely with his mint-green doctor's coat. The gray eyes peering at me through his gold frame designer glasses at least appeared intelligent.

"Hmm," he pronounced as he rubbed his chin between thumb and forefinger. Collin Yates and Ashtabula County Sheriff's Detectives Yuhas and Kules shifted their attention to him. Wearing only a hospital gown, I was not comfortable being on display, especially when one of the detectives was female.

"Well, those two puncture wounds and the burns around them are consistent with injuries caused when someone has been shot with a Taser. I've treated several people who were subdued with those things." Dr. Donatto was referring to the two painful areas on the middle left side of my ribs. "We won't have the blood analysis until tomorrow, but I think that at least part of what you were given was plain, old-fashioned alcohol."

I didn't comment. I had already told Yates and the detectives that I had not had a thing to drink in over two days.

"Mr. LeBlanc's testicles are swollen, plus there are abrasions on his penis. These type of injuries are not consistent with rape. In fact, I would say that he was roughly manipulated by someone."

I blushed crimson. I might as well have been a side of cheap beef for all the people in the room cared.

"The cuts and scratches on his hands and face were probably caused by branches and brambles. I removed several small thorns," Donatto continued as he pointed to a small plastic tray containing the remnants of his handy work.

Frank C. Dupuy

"Can I get dressed?" I demanded. Enough was enough.

"Certainly," Donatto replied as though this were something I should have done a long time ago. I moved behind a screen and pulled on a sweat shirt and sweat pants that Collin had been thoughtful enough to bring. They draped on me, but not as badly as his shirt and slacks would have. Yates is at least 6'2" and is starting to put on a few pounds. I, on the other hand, am 5'8" on good day, weighing all of 160 pounds. Somebody in the hospital had found me a cheap pair of dorky, foam slippers – they were better than going barefoot. The cops had kept my clothes.

When I emerged from behind the screen, Ashtabula County Sheriff's Detective Sally Yuhas was giving me a seriously hostile once-over. She had no doubts that I had brutally murdered Julie Lipscomb. In her early to mid-thirties, Yuhas was a big-boned woman who didn't carry a lot of fat and who didn't have much use for men. Even in her flat-heeled, sensible shoes, Yuhas was at least 5'9". She was wearing green slacks, a tannish blouse and a brown tweed jacket. Her dishwater blond hair was pulled back in a tight bun. No make up and no jewelry completed the picture of a tough woman with an attitude. I didn't like her either.

Fred Kules (pronounced Koo' les) was a laid back, slightly rumpled man who provided the impression that he would rather be out casing doughnut shops. His thinning dark hair was combed straight back, cut by a barber who was more proficient in discussing sports than in barbering. Kules was in his early fifties, carrying about thirty pounds too many. If he hadn't slouched, he would have been six feet tall. His brown sports coat and brown slacks would have benefitted from a trip to the dry cleaners. Kules's most notable features were his tired, basset hound eyes which missed nothing. It didn't appear that he particularly enjoyed being with Sally Yuhas.

"You got anything else for us, Doc?" Detective Kules inquired.

"No, that's it. The lab results will be in tomorrow."

"How about Mr. LeBlanc? Does he need anymore treatment?"

"No, he's free to go." Dr. Donatto focused on me. "You've had a rough evening. I suggest you go home and get some rest."

"Thanks, Doctor. I will," I replied.

Ohio Salt

Kules's features were noncommittal. He at least was willing to give me the benefit of the doubt. "You mind coming with me? We got an office we can use down the way."

I turned to Collin Yates. He nodded.

"Sure."

We trooped down the hall to a bank of elevators with Kules leading the way while Yuhas hovered behind me in case I tried to make a break. The pastel colors of the hospital made me uneasy. I have an abiding conviction that hospitals are places where people go to die. We stood around in awkward silence until the elevator car arrived. Kules pushed a button. We shuffled out on the second floor, then proceeded into an administrative area. Kules stopped in front of an office with an open door. He knocked anyway.

"Come in," urged a voice. As I entered the office, I recognized Jeremiah Cotsworth Jensen, the number two man in the Ashtabula County prosecutor's office. Jensen prefers to be called J.C.; he is alleged to have started the rumor that his initials stand for Jesus Christ. I met J.C. six years ago when he handled the prosecution of an embezzlement case I had investigated. He is an aggressive prosecutor with a first rate legal mind. We exchange Christmas cards and maintain a professional respect for each other. I wondered if he was going to cut me any slack.

Jensen was clad in baggy, pleated cotton pants, a Kelly green Lands' End cotton sweater and cordovan loafers without socks. He is almost forty and should know better, but he hasn't gotten over the expensive prep school he never attended. You'd never know by looking at him that his mother worked two jobs in order to have enough money to keep J.C. and his younger brother fed. He attended a Catholic high school on a scholarship, joined the Navy, then used the G.I. bill to get through college. Jensen is not known to be sympathetic to people who rape and murder.

Our eyes met before he extended his hand.

"How are you, Adrian?" J.C. inquired evenly.

"I've been better, thank you." I was wondering who had called J.C., and why he had come out personally.

"Collin phoned me while he was on his way to see you. It's not every evening that I receive a call from a famous defense attorney, especially one representing a P.I. who, on the face of it, raped, tortured, and murdered the wife of a millionaire, a millionaire who contributed generously to my boss's campaign." Jensen paused as he considered me quizzically. "You told me that you never accept divorce cases. Why did you take this one?"

"I was pressured by a client who was friends with Mrs. Lipscomb."

J.C. nodded. "Yeah, Ted Meyers, the millionaire playboy who hates Lipscomb's guts."

I didn't try to hide my surprise.

"I spoke to your secretary while you were in the E.R.. Lucky for you she corroborated everything you told the detectives, especially since the dead woman isn't Julie Lipscomb."

"Huh?" I responded brightly.

"That's right. Harold Lipscomb is on his way back from Sandusky as we speak. He was there on business and was spending the night in a hotel. When Mrs. Julie Lipscomb spoke with a deputy from her home, she assured him she is very much alive."

"Then who is the woman in the cottage?"

"Good question. I was hoping you could tell me."

Collin Yates spoke. "J.C., my client has already told you he knew the woman as Julie Lipscomb."

"That's what he said. I want to know if he has any ideas as to who she really is."

"Look," I blurted, "Why don't you call Ted Meyers? He's the one who sent Julie Lipscomb, or whoever the woman is, to see me."

"We tried that. He is not at his house or on his boat; his people don't know where he is. Supposedly, they are trying to locate him. Oh, two items of interest. First, they pulled your truck out of the river. There was a 12 gauge shotgun behind the seat with an empty shell in the chamber. The shell matched the ones found on the floor of the bedroom. Second, the driver's seat belt buckle was jammed shut with a piece of metal, which explains why we are talking rather than having you arrested."

"That doesn't prove a thing. LeBlanc probably did it himself before he pushed his truck in the river," Sally Yuhas spouted. Her scowl had been growing ever since we had stepped into the room. She was not pleased to see J.C. Jensen.

"Thank you for that insight, Detective Yuhas. Now, I want to

Ohio Salt

ask Mr. LeBlanc some questions. If you can be quiet, and not interrupt, you may stay. Otherwise, leave the room." J.C.'s words were colder than the river water I had been swimming in. Yuhas shut up and moved to a corner of the room. I wondered which charm school she had graduated from. Fred Kules avoided eye contact with everyone as he tried to fade into the woodwork.

"Collin, Adrian, please have a seat." Jensen perched on the edge of the desk as he motioned to a couple of chairs. We sat down.

"Collin, I want to ask Adrian some questions. Is that alright with you?"

Yates nodded. "Normally, I would advise my client to say nothing until you were prepared to take a formal statement. However, neither the situation nor my client are normal." Collin Yates's noble features radiated his disapproval . "He insisted on talking with the Sheriff's detectives, and he has insisted on giving blood samples for analysis. With one or two stipulations, he has advised me that he will submit to a polygraph examination."

J.C. tugged his lower lip as he regarded me. "LeBlanc," he declared at last, "You certainly manage to involve yourself in some interesting messes. Right now, your situation is as messy as they come. Start at the beginning, and tell me everything, every last detail."

"All right. I received a call this morning from a woman who called herself Julie Grey. She said she had been referred by an attorney, and that she had to see me in person because the matter was too sensitive to discuss over the phone. At about 10:30, she arrived at the office. She told me about her husband and his girl friend, claiming she knew when and where they were going to meet for their tryst; all I had to do was be there to take pictures. She also mentioned that she had $2,000 in cash in her purse as a retainer. When I explained that I didn't accept divorce work, she informed me she was an old and dear friend of Ted Meyers, and that he was the person who recommended me. She then confided that Grey was her maiden name and that her married name was Lipscomb.

"I telephoned Meyers. He was waiting for my call. He told me he and Julie were old chums, then leaned on me, politely, to take the case. When I asked, he admitted that Julie was Harold Lipscomb's wife. He tried to downplay the fact that he and Lipscomb hate each other.

"Julie Lipscomb had a map and instructions on how to locate the cottage. That's what she called that stone mansion. She said that after going through Harold's appointment book, she learned that he was going to be at the cottage at 7:00 tonight with GH. GH is Gwen Hiltie, who supposedly works for Lipscomb. Julie was adamant that I should take the pictures from the kitchen window in the caretaker's house. She informed me that the door would be unlocked when I arrived. She also gave me $2,000 in hundred dollar bills.

"My secretary noted that the dress Julie was wearing was about three years old and was missing a button on the right sleeve. Karen's comment was that Lipscomb wasn't too generous with his wife's clothing allowance.

"To be on the safe side, I arrived at the cottage at about 5:30. I parked my truck by a burned-down house on a gravel road near the estate and walked through the woods to the driveway. I looked the place over for about fifteen minutes before proceeding to the caretaker's house. I left my pack with my camera in it by the trees in case I ran into someone. I noticed muddy footprints on the steps by the back door, but figured that they belonged to whoever had unlocked the house. Anyway, I knocked, waited, then entered the house. I heard a bang and something hit me in the side. As I collapsed, I saw a guy in a dark ski mask standing near me. I started to move and he zapped me again. A few seconds later, someone clamped a rag over my face. That's all I remember until I came to when the truck was being driven into the river."

Jensen had been sitting on the desk with his hands in his pockets listening intently as I spoke. He stood up, then paced behind the desk for almost a minute before speaking. "What happened to the map the woman gave you?"

"I put it in my jacket pocket. It should still be in there."

Jensen directed his attention to Fred Kules. "Well?"

"We found a soggy map and directions in his jacket."

Jensen sat down on the desk again. "Go ahead," he commanded, "Finish the story."

I did. I stopped talking after I got to the part about calling 911. Jensen resumed pacing. When he stopped, he addressed Kules. "Times," he demanded.

Ohio Salt

Kules pulled a small wire bound notebook from inside his jacket. "According to LeBlanc, he arrived at the Lipscomb estate about 5:30. He was hit with the Taser at around 5:45. 911 received a call from a male who identified himself as Adrian LeBlanc at 1958 hours. Deputy Alex Norton arrived on the scene at 2016 hours." Kules started to put his book away, then flipped a page. "Dispatch received a call at 1833 hours from a woman who identified herself as Julie Lipscomb of 1788 Old River Road in Austinburg Township, complaining about a possible prowler. She stated it wasn't an emergency, but that she would like someone to come by to check things out when they had a chance."

"Did they?" asked J.C., standing absolutely still.

"No, sir." Kules's face was blank.

"Why not?"

"Patrol is shorthanded. Right after they received the call, a tanker hauling chemicals hit a car on I-90. Because there were injuries and a possible spill, all available units were working the accident. No one called back; the report was, uh, never followed up on." Kules and everyone in the room knew that someone was going to catch hell for not responding to the report of a prowler.

Jensen focused his attention on me. "When did you call your attorney?"

"Right after I called 911."

"Why?"

"See here, J.C.," Collin Yates interrupted before I could speak, "Everyone has the right to legal counsel; that my client sought to exercise that right should in no way be prejudicial to his situation."

Jensen stifled a retort. "I understand that perfectly, Collin. What I want to know is what your client was thinking when he called you."

"It's alright, Collin," I interjected before he and J.C. had time to mix it up. "I called Collin because it was obvious I was being framed for murder. First, I never killed anybody. Someone had gone to a lot of trouble to make sure the body would be found. The front door was open, the only light in the house was in the bedroom and the bedroom window had been broken out. When I saw my billfold tucked under her shoulder, I knew I had been set up. Not only that, I wasn't supposed to have survived the dip in the river.

"Think about it. The cops find a mutilated, raped corpse lying on my billfold, and an empty booze bottle, probably with my fingerprints all over it. A day or two later, my truck is fished from the river with the murder weapon in it, not to mention my corpse with a humongous blood alcohol level. End of story, case closed. I screwed up the scenario by surviving.

"The other complication is that the Sheriff's Department didn't send a car out as planned. If they had, then they would have found the open door, the broken window and the corpse before I called.

"J.C., I was set up. They were waiting for me in the caretaker's house when I got there."

I shut up, waiting to see if Jensen would ask the obvious question. He did.

"Let's say you were set up. Who set you up, and why?"

"I have no idea. You told me that the body in the cottage is not Julie Lipscomb. Well, the only reason I accepted the case was because Ted Meyers pressured me to do it. I've done work for Ted for at least five years. We aren't bosom buddies, but we get along fine. As far as I know, he has no ax to grind with me, and, certainly, no damn reason to kill me.

"Ted Meyers is my only link to this woman. I never saw or heard of her before this morning."

"That's what your secretary said."

Detective Sally Yuhas could no longer contain herself. "Surely, you don't believe him, do you? This cheap gumshoe was setting up a scam to shake down Lipscomb. Something went wrong, he got drunk and blew it. You can't let him go just because he's your friend and bought himself a big name lawyer."

The four men in the room gawked at Yuhas. I couldn't believe what I was hearing. Apparently, neither could J.C. Jensen.

"Lady, you are way off base. Before I tell you to get the hell out of here, I want you to know that whatever you think of Adrian LeBlanc, he is one clever, devious son of a bitch. He may stretch the law every now and again, but he would never pull a stunt as sloppy and ill conceived as this."

Yuhas glared defiantly at him. "You just wait until the media gets hold of this. They'll crucify you."

Fred Kules blanched. "Shut the hell up, Sally. Are you crazy?"

J.C. lifted the telephone receiver, then punched in a number. "Hello, Ben? Sorry to call you at home, but we have a situation here. One of your detectives, Sally Yuhas, has taken issue with the way I am conducting a murder investigation; she has threatened to crucify me in the media. What's that? Yes, Detective Kules is here as well. No, I don't think he shares her views." J.C. put his hand over the receiver. "You don't, do you?"

Kules stood up straight with no hint of a slouch. "No, sir, I don't."

"He says he doesn't. Just a minute." J.C. handed the receiver to Kules.

Kules accepted the instrument as though it might bite him, placing it gingerly against his ear. Evidently, there was no problem with the volume because I could hear muffled shouts emanating from it ten feet away. Kules confined his answers to short "Yes, Sirs" and "No, Sirs". He was sweating freely by the time he handed the receiver back to J.C.. Jensen spoke briefly before replacing the receiver in the cradle.

He pointed a finger at Fred Kules. "Tell her," he snapped.

Kules was as uncomfortable as a man could ever be. "Sally, you're suspended as of right now. The Sheriff wants me to take your pistol, badge and I.D.. We have a meeting with him in his office in the morning at 8:00."

Silently, Sally Yuhas opened her purse, removed a black I.D. case with a badge pinned to it and dropped it on the desk. Reaching under her coat, she unclipped a nylon holster containing a black automatic pistol, placing it next to her badge. Before she could walk away, J.C. Jensen addressed her in frigid, controlled tones.

"Detective Yuhas, I do not care what you think of me; however, know this. I have never let my personal feelings stand in the way of fulfilling my professional obligations to the state. Yes, I do know and respect Mr. LeBlanc; that knowledge has played a part in helping me evaluate the facts in this case. He has agreed to submit to a polygraph examination and, as far as I am concerned, he has cooperated fully. Unless other evidence is forthcoming, I believe that he is as much of a victim as the woman who was murdered. The investigation has just begun. I do not care what your personal agenda is. However, if you jeopardize this investigation because of some immature, selfish reason, I will come down on you so hard that you will regret you ever drew breath. Do you understand me?"

J.C. had not raise his voice, yet his words penetrated like daggers. His gray eyes were narrowed and harsh.

Some of the fight had gone out of Sally Yuhas. Her eyes met Jensen's. "I understand," she affirmed, then turned and walked stiffly out of the room.

6

The ride back with Collin Yates allowed me time to think, and for the reaction to set in. Somebody had tried to kill me and frame me for the murder of an attractive woman I had known for all of twenty-five minutes. I discovered that I was gripping the door handle of Yates's Mercedes a hell of a lot harder than the German engineers had intended. It didn't break. Collin groused at me for not listening to him. I promised to do better in the future. Then he started to ask questions.

"Adrian, anything you tell me is protected. If you want me to represent you, you must tell me everything you know, including why you are a target."

"Collin, for the record, I did not kill that woman. I told J.C. everything I know. Well, almost everything. I had my secretary, Karen Koenig, follow Julie to find out what she was driving. It was a '93 Lexus registered to Ontario Enterprises. Ever hear of them?"

"Doesn't sound familiar."

"Karen told me they have their offices somewhere on Detroit Avenue. First thing in the morning, I'm going to go over there, right after I have a conversation with Ted Meyers."

Yates pursed his lips. "That is a bad plan. Simply because you weren't arrested and charged tonight, does not mean that you won't be. My advice is to keep a low profile; let the Sheriff's office conduct the investigation."

"Get real. If you were in my position, would you put your fate in the hands of detectives Yuhas and Kules?" The more I thought about Sally Yuhas, the more upset I had become. The woman was a man-hating psycho.

Yates sighed, "You have a point; on the other hand, if I am going to represent you, I insist on being kept informed."

Frank C. Dupuy

"I won't do anything rash without consulting you. Speaking of which, how much is this going to cost? I called you because you're the best, Collin, and because I know you; however, I'm not made of money." I had been worrying about how much Yates was going to cost me for the last hour. I knew Collin charged at least $400 an hour. The thought of telling my wife that I had retained a $400 an hour attorney was not pleasant.

"How much do you charge my firm?"

"A thousand a day, plus expenses."

"Then, that's how much I'll charge you."

I stared at him. I could make out the outline of his face from the instrument lights. Collin's features were relaxed as he watched the road.

"That's a hell of a deal, Collin."

"I owe you. You saved my bacon on that Murphy case; besides, this is the most convoluted thing I have ever been involved in. I'm dying to know what is going on."

"You and me both." I relaxed against the leather seat as I reflected that Collin Yates was a class act. The Murphy case he referred to, had involved a contested will, in which the senior Murphy, a godzillionaire, had changed his will several months before his death leaving everything to his live-in nurse. I had nosed around, discovering that A, the nurse was using an assumed identity, and that B, she had a history of patients changing their wills just prior to their deaths. The woman could have lived a life of total luxury on the cabbage old man Murphy had left her. Unfortunately for her, my inquiries prompted an exhumation, leading to the discovery that Murphy had been helped along to meet his maker by a rather hard-to-trace, esoteric drug that was missed in the first autopsy. The nurse was convicted of murder; the family, represented by Yates, inherited. Collin had made a bundle on that deal, so I guess I didn't feel too badly about accepting his largess.

Collin drove me to my house. As I opened the car door, he said, "If I were you, I would think hard about why someone wants me dead. It might save your life if he is prepared to try a second time."

With that jovial reflection, we said good night.

7

The clock in the kitchen informed me that it was almost 1:00 a.m. I thought about having a drink and almost threw up. I'd had enough booze for one day. I opted for Alka-Seltzer and a hot shower instead.

My wife Jeannie was in bed, fast asleep. I had told her I had an assignment and might be late. After seventeen years of marriage, she is used to my weird hours. Trying to make as little noise as possible, I discarded the sweat clothes Collin had loaned me before stepping into the shower. The hot water stung as it hit my various abrasions. My crotch was the worst. I wasn't certain what had been done to me, but I was willing to bet that the coroner would find traces of my semen on the corpse. I promised myself, for the umpteenth time, that some son of a bitch was going to pay.

I crawled into bed wearing my typical sleep attire, a T-shirt and shorts. Jeannie instinctively turned on her side as I slid under the sheets. I snuggled next to her. "I love you," I told her. A muffled grunt was her acknowledgment. Then she propped herself up on an elbow.

"You're supposed to call Karen. She tried paging you, but you never answered. She said it didn't matter how late it was."

"Oh yeah, my pager is on the blink. It got drowned tonight along with my watch and my truck."

Jeannie, her message delivered, flopped back down on her pillow. "Well, you should be more careful," she muttered and promptly went back to sleep.

Shaking my head, I stumbled into the room we euphemistically call the study when we have guests. At all other times it is referred to as the junk room. I sat down at the desk and dialed Karen's number. She answered on the third ring.

"Where have you been? I've been paging you for hours."

"I was avoiding being drowned by murdering maniacs."

"Very funny. Anyway, Louie Kolakowski called. He says he's in trouble and needs your help."

"How much does he need?" This was turning into a very expensive day.

"No, it's not money. He says he has a lead on some gold the Polish government sent to the U.S. just before the Germans invaded. Well, he's been looking for it in some old buildings. A few days ago, he was chased out of one by some guards. He thinks he has been followed ever since then."

"That's it?" I asked incredulously. "Louie gets chased by a couple of security guards when he was trespassing and now believes the boogie man is out to get him? For crying out loud, Karen, that's no reason to call me at home." My volume control was tweaked by exasperation.

"You don't have to shout. There's more. Louie's apartment was broken into and trashed this evening. He thinks it was right after someone tried to shoot him."

"Huh?"

"He said someone tried to shoot him when he was walking down the street. A bullet passed through his coat; two more hit the wall next to him. He said when he ducked behind a parked car, they fired at him six more times before driving off."

"Is he OK?"

"He's a little shook up, but he's OK."

"Did he call the police?"

"Yes, but they're treating it as a random drive-by incident. Louie said they didn't want to hear about the gold he was looking for."

I groaned. "Where is he?"

"He's at a cheap hotel in Cleveland. He wants you to pick him up at the corner of East 9th and Bolivar at 10:45 tomorrow morning."

"Any particular reason why?"

"He didn't say. He did tell me it was important."

I groaned again.

Ohio Salt

"Oh, I think you should call the Ashtabula D.A.'s office in the morning. A J.C. Jensen called me at home, asking a lot of questions about Julie Lipscomb. I think they must be investigating her for something."

"I already spoke to him. Karen, can you pick me up at my house at 7:30?"

"Sure. What's up?"

"I need you to take me to a car rental agency in the morning."

"Why?"

"Because I need to rent a car, that's why."

"Where's your truck?"

"It fell into the river."

"Well, you should be more careful."

Stifling an impulse to scream, I hung up. Damn and blast, I thought as I dragged my abused body back into bed. At least nothing else could go wrong tonight.

The Hudson police called me at 2:45 a.m.

Frank C. Dupuy

Wednesday

"Good morning, boss," Karen greeted me cheerfully as I fastened my seat belt.

"Good morning," I grumbled.

"My, didn't we get up on the wrong side of the bed?"

I started to snap a rejoinder, but thought better of it. "Karen, I got about two hours sleep. The Hudson cops called me in the wee hours to inform me that our alarm had gone off. It seems that someone broke into our offices last night."

Karen became serious. "No kidding? Did they take anything?"

"I couldn't tell. Evidently, whoever broke in wasn't expecting an alarm and, for once, the cops were right on top of things. They arrived within two minutes of being notified. The door had been forced open with a crowbar which was found lying on the ground by the door. They're guessing that the burglar dropped it when the alarm went off.

"I want you to go through all of our files thoroughly. If anything is missing, let me know. Now, I have a number of things for you to do today. First, call our insurance agent and report the break-in, then report that my truck went into the river last night. It's in the Ashtabula Sheriff's Department's impound lot. Tell him that I was in the truck, but had been drugged by people who were trying to kill me. He can call Detective Kules. Tell him that under no circumstances is he to contact a wacko detective named Yuhas.

"Second, call Matt Unser to fix the door. Tell him to install an extra deadbolt on each door. Oh, set up the pin hole camera in the reception area. I want to get a picture of our burglar if he returns."

Frank C. Dupuy

"Third, order a new pager for me. The old one drowned last night." I was silent for a few moments as I gathered my thoughts. I knew that Karen would remember everything I told her. She has that kind of mind.

"Send Collin Yates a retainer check for $5,000. Then I want you to find out everything you can on Ontario Enterprises."

Karen turned into the parking lot of the car rental agency. She shut off the engine before turning to face me. "Adrian, what is going on?" She pushed her glasses up on her nose as she examined my face. "Were you in a fight last night? If you won, I'd hate to see the other guy."

Reader's Digest has nothing on me. Within four minutes I gave her a full account of my adventures. To Karen's credit, she did not gape or make silly comments. Instead, she merely asked one question.

"So, what are we going to do about it?"

"We are going to find out what in the hell in going on with Ted Meyers, then we are going to try to learn the identity of the woman who came to our office yesterday. Start with Ontario Enterprises."

"I have my cellular telephone. Call me if you need me," I remarked as I climbed out of her car.

"Oh wait a minute. Do you know a Joseph Jablonski?"

"No. Why?"

"He called the answering service around six last night. They paged you to call him. He kept calling back saying that he had to talk to you. Finally, they paged me. When I called him, he sounded pretty upset. He said he had to talk to you right away, that it was important. I told him that you were on an assignment and would be in the office this morning. The guy has a foreign accent; he sounded ancient. He wouldn't tell me why he wanted to talk to you. I told him he could call you then or come to the office. He griped some before he hung up."

"Well, if he comes in, find out what he wants and call me. I don't have time for foreign geriatrics this morning."

The rental car agency was able to give me a decent weekly rate on a Ford Taurus. I figured that my car insurance would cover most of my rental expenses once they determined how to classify my

Ohio Salt

claim. Collin Yates had persuaded J.C. Jensen to intercede with Detective Kules so that I could at least retrieve my driver's license and credit cards from my billfold. Thanks to Collin, I could rent a car.

The drive into Cleveland was uneventful, which gave me time to think. Why had Meyers set me up, and why had someone broken into my office? Over the years, I have investigated hundreds of cases that involved criminal charges being filed. My specialty is white-collar crime, a discipline that places me in contact with a variety of morally weak middle class and upper class thieves. Most of them are not violent; I could not think of anyone who had a real grudge against me. Nothing made any sense.

I reminded myself that I would take my wife out to dinner this evening to explain everything to her. I had left a note on the front door, asking her not to make any plans for this evening. Painful experience has taught me that mornings are not a good time to conduct lengthy conversations with the light of my life.

Jeannie is a realtor who is very good at her job because she relates well to both men and women. She received her MBA from Loyola, but was turned off by large corporations. She claims she likes the freedom of being a realtor, although lately she has started to question the meaning of life or, at least, her life. I think this has something to do with our fifteen-year-old son, Jules, who is having problems in school, not to mention the universe in general. Neither he nor Jeannie are morning people, a trait which has often led to daybreak shouting matches. Jeannie recently informed me she admires female praying mantises because they devour their young.

Northeast Ohio, I reflected, is a hell of a long way from Louisiana, my native state. Jeannie and I had moved north when I took a job as the security manager for an aerospace company. One thing led to another; I ended up as the Director of Loss Prevention for what was then the second largest bank in Ohio. About six years ago I went nuts and opened my own agency, a move I have almost never regretted.

We purchased a house in Hudson in 1982 because it was a quaint, almost rural area, with a separate township and village. The two eventually merged and, thanks to the developers and realtors, Hudson has lost much of its small town charm. Whenever I accuse

Frank C. Dupuy

Jeannie of being on the team of the Anti-Christ, she merely refers to the substantial commission checks that provide us with a healthy portfolio. As a card carrying member of the Sierra Club, I once referred to our relationship as "sleeping with the enemy," receiving a solid punch in the ribs for my attempted humor.

Ted Meyers's office is located in an industrial development near West 150th and I-480 in Cleveland. He owns several manufacturing companies that produce parts for the automotive industry. In the last ten years, Meyers has aggressively branched out into real estate development. It is this endeavor that placed him at odds with Harold Lipscomb on several occasions. Ted's reputation as an aggressive, ruthless competitor is well deserved.

When he cares to be, Meyers is charm personified. Although in his early fifties, Ted maintains his leading man looks by working out regularly with his personal trainer, frequent trips to his Hollywood dentist and periodic touch ups by the same plastic surgeon Cher patronizes. He has several mirrors in his office which he is not shy about using. Ted makes no secret that he employs his looks, money and influence to bed as many women as possible. I have sometimes wondered if he ever had aspirations to be the governor of Arkansas.

I noted that Meyers's parking spot was empty as I pulled into one of the spaces reserved for visitors. The building that houses his umbrella company, The Meyers Group, Ltd., is a cinder-block manufacturing complex with an attached chrome and glass, two story administrative area that was added about eight years ago. Ted's office, which occupies half of the second floor, is used to house his collection of awards and pictures of himself with movers and shakers.

The cute brunette receptionist recognized me as I entered the gleaming, ultramodern lobby. "Good morning, Mr. LeBlanc," she smiled from behind a partition. "How are you?"

"Super, Peggy, simply super. How about yourself?" Peggy and I exchanged pleasantries for a few minutes. She was exactly like all of the female staff at The Meyers Group, attractive, polite and efficient. Ted once confided that he could not abide having an ugly woman work for him. It is a marvel that no one has ever filed a sexual harassment suit against the man.

Finally, I got down to the reason for my visit. "Is Ted in?" I

Ohio Salt

inquired politely.

"No, he isn't. He hasn't been in all morning. Was he expecting you?"

"No, he wasn't. How about Les Fazio? Is he in?"

"He's here. Let me see if he is in a meeting." Peggy punched several buttons on her console.

Lester Fazio is Ted's brilliant chief financial officer who serves as a buffer between Ted and the rest of the operations. He is also Ted's extremely efficient hatchet man. Fazio is a CPA with a law degree whose scruples and values are dictated by his boss. He has the charm of an iguana.

"Mr. Fazio is extremely busy. His secretary asked if you could schedule an appointment with him later in the week." Peggy informed me apologetically.

"Would you put me through to his secretary, please?"

"Certainly. You can use the telephone on the table. When it rings, just pick it up."

I sat down on a black leather couch next to a low glass and chrome table that supported the telephone. The phone rang. I picked it up.

"Mr. LeBlanc, this is Betty Knowles, Mr. Fazio's executive assistant. His schedule is very tight for the next two days. If you could tell me what you wish to see him about, perhaps I can schedule an appointment." Betty Knowles had a condescending manner, one she had employed countless times to brush off inconsequential "little people." She irritated the hell out of me.

"That is so kind of you, Betty," I said sweetly. "Tell your fat-assed boss that Ted Meyers is an accessory to murder, and that if he doesn't listen to what I have to say, Ted will fire him as soon as he gets back. You have exactly one minute to find him and schedule an immediate appointment."

I hung up the telephone, then checked my watch. The second hand had not ticked off fifty-five seconds before the intercom buzzed on Peggy's desk. She lifted the receiver, listened, then replaced it. "Mr. Fazio will see you now, Mr. LeBlanc. Do you know the way to his office?"

I nodded.

Peggy pressed a button that released the electric lock on the door that protected the administrative offices from the outside world. I turned left and ascended the wide, polished stairs that led to the executive suites. At the top of the stairs, I scanned an ample expanse of tastefully decorated open area. A peroxide blond in a tight-fitting, gray pinstripe suit was waiting for me. Her expression fluctuated between shocked and wrathful. "This way, please, Mr. LeBlanc," Betty Knowles grated. I followed, observing that she had nice legs when she was angry. Knowles ushered me into a large office dominated by a bulky man behind a massive desk. Lester Fazio did not stand up nor did he offer to shake hands.

I gestured to Betty Knowles. "Bring me a cup of coffee, please. Black will be fine. You care for anything, Les?" I inquired solicitously. He shook his large, balding head. After his executive assistant stalked out, I closed the door behind her. Uninvited, I sat down in a chair in front of his desk. We scrutinized each other for thirty seconds. Fazio broke first.

"Alright, LeBlanc, what in the hell did you tell Betty that upset her?"

"I'm not sure. It may have been the part about Ted's being an accessory to murder, or it might have been the part about your getting fired if you didn't talk to me." I diplomatically omitted my remark about his fat ass.

Over the years I have dealt with Les Fazio on a half dozen occasions. He is in his early forties, a big framed man about 6'4", gone to flab, who weighs at least 280 pounds. His pouchy face supports a round lump of a nose that would look ludicrous on a smaller man. A few strands of dark hair cover his shiny scalp. The backs of his massive hands are covered with black tufts of hair that match the ones protruding from his nostrils. Fazio is totally dedicated to his job, putting in seventy hour weeks. We have never cared for each other. For my part, I simply do not admire bullies.

"We can start with this accessory to murder crap." Fazio was eyeing me intently. Although he had himself under control, I could swear that he was as nervous as hell.

"Let's." We were interrupted by a knock at the door. Betty Knowles set a heavy mug of steaming, black coffee in front of me on the desk, then departed in cold silence. I wondered if she had sprinkled hemlock in it. I took a sip, decided she hadn't, and collected my

Ohio Salt

thoughts.

"Yesterday morning, I interviewed a woman who identified herself as Julie Lipscomb, the wife of Harold Lipscomb. She wanted me to take pictures of Harold and his latest romance at his cottage in Ashtabula County. When I declined, she informed me she was an old and dear friend of Ted's. I called him. Ted told me he had referred the wife of his worst enemy to me and that they were friends. He then leaned on me to take the case. Like a dummy, I did.

"When I went to the Lipscomb estate, somebody zapped me, filled me full of booze, propped me in my truck and drove me into the river where I was supposed to have drowned. As you can tell, I didn't. I went back to the house where I found what was left of Julie Lipscomb. She had been tortured; her hands and face were blasted into jelly by a shotgun. We have several problems here. First, the woman is not Julie Lipscomb. The real Mrs. Lipscomb is alive and well. Second, the shotgun in question was found in my truck, and third, my billfold was left under the corpse."

I drank some more coffee to give me time to calm down. I was starting to get pissed off which was not going to help me. Every time I blinked, I could see the mutilated remains of what had been an attractive woman.

"You see, Les, if I had died, there would be no story. I would have been the scapegoat and the case would have been closed. As you can imagine, I am just the tiniest bit upset with your boss."

Les Fazio was wide eyed. Whatever he had been expecting me to say, this wasn't it. A thin film of sweat was sprouting on his head and face. I leaned back in my chair, waiting.

"Christ, LeBlanc. You can't expect me to believe that fairy tale."

"Nice try, Les. I'm certain that a Detective Kules of the Ashtabula County Sheriff's department has been trying to locate Ted this morning. Detective Kules is more circumspect than I am. He probably didn't say why he wanted to talk to Ted. Now you know why the cops are so very interested in your boss."

"You can't prove anything, LeBlanc," Fazio blustered. "You keep this up and we'll file a libel suit against you that will bury you."

"Super. The tape of my conversation with Ted is quite good, actually. He is going to have a dandy time explaining that away," I lied, wishing like hell I had taped the conversation.

"What do you want?"

"I want to talk to Ted to find out what's going on. I want to know who the woman was he sent to my office, why I was set up, and the name of the son of a bitch who tried to kill me."

Fazio mopped his face with a wad of tissues he had yanked from a box on his desk. He was perspiring heavily. Damp patches were starting to show through his starched, white shirt.

"Look, LeBlanc, there has been some kind of horrible mistake here. I'm sure Ted knows nothing about this."

"Bullshit. Let me tell you what I'm going to do, Les – I'm going to start digging like I have never dug before. The cops don't know how to dig like I do. Something is totally wrong here, and I am going to find out every last detail."

Lester Fazio's flabby face resembled a sweaty, pale cheese. He closed his eyes for a moment, reached a decision, then opened them.

"LeBlanc, you have no idea what you're getting into. You stay the fuck out of our business. You hear me? You mess around in this and you're gonna get hurt."

"What'cha gonna do, Les? Kill me? Frame me for murder? You got a free shot the first time. I liked and trusted Meyers. Now I don't. It won't be so easy the second time around."

I stood up. "Give Ted my regards. Ask him to call me. Maybe we can do lunch."

Fazio spoke as my hand touched the door. "Jesus, LeBlanc, listen to me. I have not seen or talked to Ted since yesterday afternoon. We've been trying to reach him all morning, ever since the cops started calling. There's been some kind of horrible mistake here. Ted didn't try to kill you, I swear it."

"Who was the woman, Les? Give me her name."

Lester Fazio considered the top of his desk. "I, I can't tell you that. Look, I promise I'll have Ted call you the minute I hear from him. I swear." I had never heard Fazio plead before.

"All right, I'll wait for his call."

Betty Knowles was seated at her desk when I walked out. "Thanks for the coffee." I actually felt her glare on the back of my neck as I negotiated the stairs.

9

I called Collin Yates from a pay phone. Too many snoopers have scanners these days for me to have faith in the privacy of cellular calls. I briefly told him about my conversation with Les Fazio.

"So, what do you think is transpiring at The Meyers Group?" he asked.

"Something rotten. When I told Les his boss was an accessory to murder, he was verging on panic. However, when I delivered my story about the late, bogus Julie Lipscomb, he wasn't so much panicked as shocked. I really touched a nerve when I threatened to start digging into The Meyers Group. I've never seen Fazio shaken up."

"What are you going to do?"

"Start digging. Whatever Ted Meyers is up to, Fazio is in it up to his ass. He knows who the murdered woman is, or was," I amended.

I could hear Yates breathing, so I knew he was alive. I probably only imagined that I could hear his brain cells clicking. Finally, he spoke. "I don't suppose it would do any good to tell you not to investigate The Meyers Group?"

"None at all."

"So be it," he sighed. "I'll see what my sources can tell me about Meyers. Oh, I almost forgot, we have an appointment with a polygraph examiner tomorrow morning. J.C. Jensen has you scheduled with Robert Hodas at 9:00 in Hodas's office. I assume he is acceptable?"

"Yes, Hodas is one of the best. He's a good choice."

"Do you know where his office is?"

"Yes."

Frank C. Dupuy

"Good. Meet me at the Denny's restaurant near his office at 8:00. We can formulate the relevant questions during breakfast."

After I hung up, my spirits lifted a little. Bob Hodas is a retired cop who is one of the best polygraph examiners I know. The couple of times I'd used him, he was an impartial, thorough professional. He would be fair, which was all I wanted.

My mood deteriorated slightly as I remembered my meeting with Louie Kolakowski. I wondered what that bone head had gotten himself into this time. It was exactly 10:44 when I cruised slowly up to the corner of East 9th and Bolivar in downtown Cleveland. Sure enough, my black clad, cadaverous-looking colleague was standing in a doorway peering nervously about. Since he was the only person on the street wearing a black fedora, black suit, black leather gloves, and a black trench coat, he stuck out like the proverbial sore thumb. He didn't recognize the rental car. When I blew the horn, Louie almost hopped out of his trench coat. Finally, he spotted me, ran over to the car and jumped into the passenger seat.

"Jesus Christ, Adrian, you almost scared me to death." Louie's normally pale face was whiter than ever. Judging from the dark circles under his eyes, he hadn't slept well.

"What the hell, Louie, I drove up the street in this battleship as slowly as I could. What do you want, flashing lights?"

"No, it's OK. I'm a little edgy, ya know, cause of gettin' shot at. I was looking for your truck." He paused a moment as he examined the inside of the Taurus. "Not bad. I guess I should've known that you would change cars. Clever, Adrian, real clever. That's what I like about you, always thinking. I bet you learned this trick when you were in the Border Patrol, huh?"

Louie was alluding to the organization I had spent four years in before discovering that federal and law enforcement are not synonymous. Louie, who has seen too many movies, believes that I led a life of glorious adventure on the southern border. I ignored his last comment.

"Louie," I declared at last, "tell me what the devil you've been up to that has people shooting at you. And stop fidgeting, it makes me nervous." Kolakowski was squirming in his seat like a three year old with a full bladder.

"Huh? Oh sorry, Adrian. Just making sure we weren't tailed.

Ohio Salt

Uh, you know I've told you a lot of stories about looking for lost treasures?" I nodded. "Well, I realize they were mostly just wild tales, but I enjoy that kind of stuff." He paused to perceive how I reacted to this revelation. I didn't. "Anyway, this is different. You know how I told you that my father was a hero in World War II?"

"Yes."

"It's all true. My father got the DSM from the Brits, that's the Distinguished Service Medal. He got it for valor. My mom's got the medal and the papers. He was a true Polish patriot. Mom told me how he loved Poland and hated the Communists. He'd have been killed if he had gone back after the war. Anyway, my father belonged to a Polish veterans' group. The members had all fought in Polish units under the British. After the war, most of the Polish veterans stayed in England, or immigrated to the U.S. and Canada because the Commies were running Poland. There weren't a lot of his old outfit in Cleveland, maybe a dozen or so, but they all kept in touch with their buddies across the country. My dad was looked up to in the group on account of he was an officer and a hero. They used to hold meetings to plan how they were going to overthrow the Communists. They raised money to support people who spoke out against the Polish government. Some of Dad's friends made broadcasts for Radio Free Europe or wrote books which were smuggled into Poland. Mom says it breaks her heart to think that my father died before the Solidarity movement pushed the Commies out of power."

I drove slowly, as I guided the Ford toward Cleveland's west side. I had no idea where Louie's story was leading. So far, I had heard everything on previous occasions.

"There was a colonel in the Polish army who was really sharp. He had it figured out that the Germans were going to invade Poland a few years before it happened. This guy tried to convince the Polish Generals to modernize the army, to buy better fighter planes, tanks and anti-tank weapons, but they didn't listen to him."

"What was the colonel's name?" I asked in spite of myself.

"Count Stanislas Petrowski. He was a nobleman as well as a colonel, ya know. He formed an association of senior officers and noblemen who made plans to carry on the fight if the Germans invaded. All of the members were sworn to secrecy. They started con-

Frank C. Dupuy

verting private funds to gold, then moved it out of the country to pay for resistance forces if it became necessary."

"Alright, Louie, the Germans invaded. Get to the point."

"Hey, let me tell it in my own way, will ya? The problem was that most of the secret society was killed during the Blitzkrieg, or arrested by the Nazis within a few weeks. It only took the Germans a month to overrun Poland. Even though Count Petrowski was severely wounded, he managed to escape to England. He was worried that Germany was going to invade England, so he came to the U.S. where he had about 4,000 pounds of gold. That's over $22,000,000 on today's market."

"Wait a damn minute. How did a wounded Polish soldier transport two tons of gold into the U.S. during war time?" Louie can only stretch my credibility so far.

"I told you this guy was a sharp planner. He pulled some strings to get himself stationed as the military attaché at the Polish embassy in Washington in 1938; he brought all that gold in as part of diplomatic shipments. The ambassador was a secret society pal of his."

I did my best not to roll my eyes. For a minute, I had started to half believe my ditsy passenger might actually be on to something. Long experience with Louie's brand of story telling caused me to resign myself to a drawn-out narration.

"Well, the Count took a long time to recover on account of he had lost a leg in the fighting. He was in pretty good shape by the time the Japs attacked Pearl Harbor. With the U.S. officially in the war, Petrowski gets in good with army intelligence and wangles a commission, even though he's only got one leg. Pretty good, huh?"

"Super," I agreed.

"Petrowski was real upset with the Americans and the British when he found out that they were gonna let the Russians keep Poland after the war. What the Communists did to the Poles was just as bad as the Nazis, see? This guy decides there ain't ever gonna be a free Poland in his lifetime if he sits around waiting for the West to do something, 'cause the Poles were sold out by the allies. Now, we got an upset Polish patriot with two tons of gold, but no country. Most guys would have used the loot to live like a king. Not Petrowski. He finds a few of the members of his secret society who survived

Ohio Salt

the war, then helps set them up in businesses around the world. He makes them interest free loans."

"Louie, Franklin Roosevelt outlawed the private ownership of gold in this country in the 1930s. Possessing gold was illegal until about 1971. How did he convert that much gold to cash without the IRS and the rest of the Treasury Department raising hell with him?"

Louie's eyes narrowed as he endeavored to assume his inscrutable mien. "That's real good, Adrian. Most people wouldn't think of that. You and Count Petrowski are a lot alike. What he did was order several of his people to immigrate to Cuba. It was easy back then to get Cuban officials to cooperate if you gave them a little juice, if ya know what I mean. He smuggled gold into Cuba, had his boys convert it to cash and invested it. Well, by 1948, these guys had their own bank in Cuba, plus a couple of branches in the Caribbean. They did real good. Members of the secret society established businesses in the U.S., Europe and Latin America. Their goal was to keep the flame of Polish independence alive and never to have to rely on any-one but Poles for anything. They knew that only Poles would ever be loyal to Poles.

"The other thing these guys did was to revenge themselves on traitors. You know, the ones who sold out to the Communists and the Germans. They had an organization to track the Judases – that's what they called them. They hired and trained Judas teams who identified then liquidated traitors who traveled outside of Poland. Most of the time, they made it look like accidents."

"Are you telling me that a one-legged Pollack smuggled in two tons of gold to the U.S., then smuggled it out again to set up a millionaire Polish hit squad?" I hoped my eyes weren't bulging too badly.

"Yeah. You got it. They did lots of other things to mess with the Commies in Poland, things like my old man was involved with. Propaganda and stuff."

"Dare I ask what happened to this secret society?"

"It's still around, kind of. Most of the original members are dead, or old as hell. When Castro took over Cuba, it broke things up, even though Petrowski was smart enough to move the bank's money off the island before the Commies could get their mitts on it. By the sixties, most of the original members were mellowing. Their

Judas squads had killed over a dozen traitors and frightened the hell out of the rest. I think they were tired of killing, and they weren't successful in recruiting younger people who shared their dreams. In the end, it all turned into a wealthy Pollack's club.

"Petrowski was the heart of the organization, the pusher. He had a falling out with some of the secret society members right after Castro chased them out of Cuba. When he disappeared, nobody felt like being the leader."

"What happened to Count Petrowski?"

Louie Kolakowski's face grew as thoughtful as I had ever seen it. "That's a real good question, Adrian, real good. Count Petrowski and my dad both disappeared on November 21, 1963."

10

10124 Detroit Avenue, suite 210, was the address of Ontario Enterprises, according to the Ohio Bureau of Motor Vehicles. At least it was the address that had come back to the license plate on the car the bogus Julie Lipscomb had been driving yesterday morning. Karen Koenig had checked with the Ohio Secretary of State's office, learning that Ontario Enterprises had been incorporated in 1992 by a J.B. Johnson. Johnson was the president and treasurer. No other officers were listed. The incorporating agent was Thomas Tolliver. According to the telephone directory, Tolliver had a law practice in North Olmsted, a Cleveland suburb.

"What are we doing here?" Louie inquired as I pulled into a pitted parking lot which was shared by a half dozen small, glass-fronted businesses that appeared as though they barely produced enough income to pay the rent. The oxidized aluminum window frames coordinated nicely with the faded, peeling paint trim. A modest, molded plastic sign informed the public that 10124 housed Reliable Office Services, a firm that, according to the flyers taped to the plate glass windows, offered secretarial, facsimile and copying services at reasonable rates.

"Making discreet inquiries. Sit tight and don't let anyone steal the car."

A bell tinkled when I opened the front door, heralding my presence to the aging Formica topped counter that protected the office area from customers. Noises were emanating from a large copying machine set against one wall. Peering over the barrier I spotted a spiky head of bottle-blond hair. The hair belonged to a woman who managed to squat near the base of the copier in spite of her tight black slacks. She was glaring at the guts of the machine. The female with the glare was in her late forties. She was trying to

Frank C. Dupuy

wipe black smudges off of her fingers with a wad of paper towels. Her blouse was also smudged.

"Good morning," I announced.

"Maybe for some people. You know anything about copiers?" she queried hopefully. Her eyebrows and eyelashes were the beneficiaries of generous applications of Maybelline.

"Yes. Stay away from them unless you want to smear toner all over your hands."

She smiled ruefully. "Where were you when I needed that advice twenty minutes ago? I should have waited for the repairman, but he takes an hour or two to get here. Oh, well. Is there something I can do for you?" As the woman tottered upright on crimson high-heeled pumps, she tossed the paper towels into a trash can. The shoes matched her blouse, lipstick and nail polish.

"Maybe. Now that I'm working out of my house, I occasionally need secretarial services. I stopped by to see what you offer."

"I'm Lou Ann Blevins and we offer a full line of services." She foraged under the counter for a few seconds before presenting me with a pink 8 ½ by 11 sheet of paper listing the options available from Reliable Office Services. I noted the flyer proclaimed an answering service and a business address service.

"What's a business address service?"

"Some of our customers don't want people to know that they don't have an office, so we accept their mail at our address." Lou Ann motioned toward a rack of numbered pigeonholes on the wall opposite the defunct copier. "You might be interested in that service yourself, Mr...."

"Nelson, Oliver Nelson. I just might. How much does it cost?"

"If you don't receive too much mail, $20 a month."

I could see that pigeon hole 210 had several pieces of mail stuck in it.

"That's reasonable," I lied. She was merely $200 a year more expensive than the Post Office. I noticed that only three of the eighteen pigeonholes contained mail. "You mentioned an answering service. Where are the operators?"

Lou Ann hooked a thumb over her shoulder. "In the back. I have a girl who answers the phones from eight in the morning un-

Ohio Salt

til 5:30. After that, each line transfers to an answering machine."

"If I receive a call, how do you contact me?"

"It's up to you. You can rent a pager or call in for your messages."

"I see. How much does this service cost?"

Lou Ann Blevins eyed me speculatively. "Thirty dollars a month. If you receive over sixty calls, we charge fifty cents for each additional call." She must have read my expression. "Our operators are very professional. When they answer the phone, the people calling you think they have reached your office. When combined with our business address service, your clients will believe you have an expensive office and staff."

"Gee, that's pretty slick. How many people are using your services?"

Lou Ann evaded my eyes. "Oh, three or four dozen. It just depends."

Yeah, I thought, it depends on whether or not pigs fly. Instead I remarked, "That's pretty impressive. Are you certain you could handle an additional client?"

"Oh yes, we have plenty of room for expansion." Her bright response did not disguise an underlying desperation. Business must have been slower than I thought.

"Let me have one of your flyers. It'll take me a couple of days to decide what I want to put on my business cards."

Lou Ann handed me a business card and another flyer. Her eyes did not reflect her forced smile. She knew she would never see me again. "Call me as soon as you decide."

"Will do," I answered as I strolled out the door.

I was relieved to see that my rented ride was still in one piece. Louie Kolakowski was slouched down in the front seat sound asleep. I slammed my palm on the car roof as I opened my door.

"Jesus Christ!" my now awake passenger yelled. "You try'n to give me a heart attack?"

"Nope. I was simply checking your reflexes. You pass."

Louie glowered before slumping into a pout. He gave me the silent treatment for about ninety seconds. "I ain't been sleeping too good, you know. This getting shot at by strangers is a scary thing."

I stopped for a red light and contemplated my passenger. To

Frank C. Dupuy

hear Louie admit to fear was a first. His dark eyes were circled by gray smudges that complemented his hollow cheeks. "When's the last time you ate?"

"Yesterday morning. Those guys tried to kill me right before dinner. I've been keeping out of public places since then. That flea trap I stayed in last night didn't offer room service."

The golden arches of one of America's favorite cholesterol palaces was visible about a block and a half down the street. I considered using the drive through window before deciding that having my car smell like essence of fast food for the rest of the day was not appealing. We were waited on by a woman who would rather have spent her golden years some place else; some place where her boss did not remind her of her grandson. Louie ordered two Big Macs, extra large fries and a large chocolate shake. At least he still had his appetite. I contented myself with a cup of coffee and a cheeseburger.

Louie devoured both of his hamburgers before I had finished mine. He was halfway through his French fries when I interrupted his concentration on his food. "Louie, will you tell me exactly what happened to you yesterday?"

His cheeks contracted as he sucked a generous quantity of chocolate shake through his straw. "I was coming back from your office. I had given my stuff to Karen to lock up. Anyway, I parked my car about a block from my office on account of the spaces all being taken up in front of the building. When I came around the corner, I heard an engine start up. I don't know why, but I looked over my shoulder. There was this big, ugly guy hanging out the window of a Buick with a pistol in his hand. He was pointing it at me. I was ducking behind a car when he started shooting. He fired three times. I think it was his first shot that went through my overcoat. The other two shots hit the wall behind me."

"Then what?"

"Then I almost shit in my pants when I see the Buick back up. I got nowhere to run so I try to crawl under the car I was hiding behind. Fortunate for me, the shooter don't get out of the Buick. They just pulled up close, then the son of a bitch blasts at me at least six more times. He shot out the windshield and side window of the car I was under. Christ, you shoulda seen it. Glass was all over the place. Anyway, the driver burns rubber and they get the hell out of there."

"What time did this happen?"

"About 4:45."

"Anybody else see anything?"

"Yeah, four people, including the little old lady who owns the car that got shot up. She almost had a heart attack when the shooting started. Then, when the cops finally get there, she wants them to arrest me because I picked her car to hide behind. She finally settled on telling me that her son knows an attorney who will sue me for damages. Jeez, what a pain in the ass she was."

"Besides being a pain in the ass, did she get a license number?"

"No, but a guy down the street did. He's a retired fireman. He wrote down the license number and gave the cops a description of the driver. He said from what he could see, the driver was a black guy who had a skinny face with a moustache and a goatee. The driver was wearing shades and a knit cap. The fireman said his skin was light for a black – he might have been Puerto Rican."

"Were both men black?"

"No. The shooter was a white guy. He wasn't wearing a hat. I could see he had kind of long, greasy hair. He had a scraggly beard and moustache, kind of like a hard-core biker. His neck was thick. I got the impression he was big."

"Anybody else see anything?"

"Yeah, but they couldn't add any details. The Buick was dark green. When the cops ran the license number, it came back to a car that was reported stolen the night before. Oh, the cops think the pistol was a 9mm. I could only tell that it was a silver-looking automatic."

"What did the police do?"

Louie's expression clouded. "Not much. I gave the patrolmen who responded all my information, then I followed them to the Fourth District office where I talked to a couple of dumb detectives. They asked me why anyone would want to shoot at me. I told them that I had been chased out of a couple of buildings when I had been looking for this gold from World War II. I figured I must have upset some people, so they hired these guys to kill me."

I stifled a groan. "What did the detectives do?"

Frank C. Dupuy

"They acted like they were dealing with a nut. They told me they would look into the matter and get back to me. I know when I'm getting the brush off, so I go back to my office taking my time to see if I'm being followed. I cruise around the neighborhood a few times, but I don't see nothing suspicious. This time I find a spot in front of the building. When I get to my office, I can see the door frame's been busted. I ease the door open and look in. The place is a disaster; they trashed everything. My files and my desk drawers had been taken out and dumped; all my stuff in my closet had been tossed on the floor. The bed was pulled apart. I'm telling you, Adrian, my place had been gone over by some real heavies."

I have actually been in Louie's office/apartment on two occasions. He has a two office suite in an old office building on Fleet Street in Slavic Village. An understanding landlord had installed a toilet and shower so Louie could use the back office as an apartment. Besides the indoor plumbing, his one room apartment had a Murphy bed, a two-burner hot plate and a toaster oven. Louie claims he likes to live "light."

"Did they take anything?"

"Nothing I could see. I didn't stick around too long to find out. I called my landlord. Told him I'd had a break in and asked him to fix the door. I called you, talked to Karen and then split."

"Did you call the police?"

"Nah. Why bother? Those two assholes would just file the break-in report with the shooting report."

I considered Louie's story. It certainly appeared that someone had tried to assassinate him, plus whoever had tossed his office was looking for something. Then it hit me.

"Louie," I entreated in my gentlest voice, "Did you tell anyone you were going to store those documents with me? The ones you gave to Karen?"

"Huh? No, not a word, I swear. I didn't tell anyone about that."

I slowed as I turned into a convenient parking lot. I stopped the car. "What have you done, Louie? Someone tried to break into my office last night. Do you think they might have been looking for something, something that they couldn't find in your office?"

He avoided my eyes.

Ohio Salt

"Talk to me, Louie. Who did you tell?"

"No one. I didn't tell no one."

"Then tell me what you did do, Louie. What did you do that caused someone to look in my office for your stuff?"

"I uh, might have given your card to one of the guys who chased me off from one of the buildings."

"What?" My voice cracked as I stifled an impulse to grab my passenger by his skinny, conniving neck.

"You're gettin' upset with me, aren't cha?

"No," I lied, "I'm not getting upset. Just tell me what happened."

"Well, I'd been poking around the basement of this old building and was on my way out when I was spotted by a security guard, which was kind of funny now that I think about it."

"Life's just one big yuk, sometimes," I grated.

"No, not that kind of funny. I mean it was funny that someone would hire a security guard to watch over a deserted heap of brick. Anyway, the guy hollers at me, so I run. He had a limp; the bozo would have never caught me except that I ran right into his supervisor who had stopped by to pick up a report. Just my luck. The supervisor was coming around a corner and I run smack into him. He holds me until the guard catches up. They ask me what I'm doing; I didn't say nothing, so they tell me that they're gonna call the cops to arrest me for trespassing. I tell them they better not mess with me 'cause I'm working a big case for you, and that their boss will regret messing with you. I gave them one of your cards."

My hands tightened on the steering wheel. "Louie, why in the hell did you involve me?"

He blushed and looked away. "Adrian, you're a big shot detective. I'm a nobody. I figured if I told them I was working for you, they'd let me go. It worked."

I cursed silently. This was typical Louie Kolakowski. He has the mistaken notion that my name is a household word in northeastern Ohio. It's not. Other than a two line listing in the Yellow Pages, I don't advertise, and I make it a point to avoid the news media like the plague.

"Uh huh. How many of my cards did you hand out?"

"None, I didn't have any more. When I ran into a guard at

another place, I just told him I was working with you."

"Louie, did you tell any of the security guards you were looking for World War II gold?"

"Heck, no. You think I'm crazy? All I told those bozos was that I was on a confidential investigation."

None of what Louie had told me made sense, yet I was convinced that the break-ins of our offices were connected. I was also convinced that the break-ins had nothing to do with his search for mythical gold. Figuring this out would have to wait. I had other priorities.

Louie cocked his head at me as I pulled into the parking lot at Great Northern Mall. "What are we doing here?" he asked.

"Going into part one of trying to keep you alive. C'mon, it's time to change your image."

Forty minutes later, a thoroughly disgruntled Louie Kolakowski and I emerged from the mall. "I can't believe you're making me do this," he whined.

"Believe it. If you want to make certain that the guys who are trying to kill you have an easy time of it, keep wearing that undertaker costume. Trust me, you look fine."

Louie contemplated his refection in a car window, and groaned. He was wearing a navy blue windbreaker over a maroon cotton sweater. His tan Dockers and white Nike running shoes completed the ensemble. His trench coat, suit, shoes and fedora were in a large plastic bag which I tossed in the trunk. I would have been more sympathetic if his new duds had not been charged to my credit card.

We were on the freeway headed toward my office when I called Karen Koenig on my car phone. She answered on the second ring.

"What's up, boss?"

"Who does your hair?"

"Huh?"

"I said who does your hair?"

"Margie Jacobs. Why?"

"Call her and make an emergency appointment for Louie. Tell her that you are going to bring him in as soon as possible."

"OK." Karen's short answer indicated that she had a thousand questions, yet knew better than to ask them.

Ohio Salt

"Good. Louie and I will be at the office in about fifteen minutes." I hung up.

"What's going on, Adrian?" Louie demanded.

"Part two of trying to keep you alive."

"You said something about a hair appointment."

"Yep." I eyed Louie's dark brown hair. "Blondes have more fun, especially blondes with very short hair."

He touched his hair with a protective gesture. "Bullshit! You ain't gonna lay a finger on my hair."

"You're right. Margie Jacobs is." Before Louie could protest, I cut him off. "If you want me to help you, you are going to do exactly what I tell you to do. I have a few minor concerns of my own that I have to deal with at the moment. If you give me any shit, I'll dump you on the side of the road right now." The edge in my voice was sharper than I had intended.

Louie Kolakowski squinted at me. "You OK, Adrian?"

"No, I'm not. I've got a lot on my plate which I don't have time to explain to you. When I get a free minute, you and I will sit down to figure out why someone tried to kill you. Until then, let's concentrate on keeping you in one piece. All right?"

"All right." Louie's curiosity was burning, however, he had enough sense not to push.

My cell phone buzzed.

"Hello."

"Boss, you have a message from Collin Yates. He wants to talk to you immediately. Also a reporter from Channel 4 called. He wants to talk to you about the murder at the Harold Lipscomb cottage. I told him you were out of town."

I groaned, wondering what the press had been told and by whom. The image of a vengeful Detective Sally Yuhas flashed through my mind. "Great. If any more reporters call, tell them I'm still out of town."

"Will do. That Joseph Jablonski called again. He said he was coming to the office this morning, but he never showed."

"I guess he decided he didn't have an emergency after all. Anything else?"

"Oh, I have your new pager."

I thanked my lucky star for Karen Koenig, then called Collin

Yates from my cell phone. I was too tired to bother with a pay phone. I glanced at Louie as he pretended not to listen to my conversation.

"Adrian, how are you?"

"Fine, Collin. What's up?"

"The Ashtabula Sheriff's department has issued a statement to the press. They said that the body of an unidentified female was discovered by private investigator Adrian LeBlanc last night at a vacant vacation home off of Old River Road. The Sheriff stressed the fact that you are not a suspect and are assisting in the investigation."

"That's it?"

"Essentially. They went out of their way to avoid any mention of Harold Lipscomb, which means he has exerted some influence. The county is trying to keep everything as quiet as possible, so we probably have until tomorrow morning before all hell breaks loose."

"Wonderful. A reporter from Channel 4 called my office a few minutes ago."

"Oh? Tell me you didn't talk to him."

"I did not. Karen has been instructed to tell all reporters that I am out of town."

"Good," he announced. "Stay away from the press. Call me tonight at my house." He hung up.

Wonderful, I thought. Now the press is involved. I wondered what else could possibly make my day brighter.

The cell phone buzzed. It was Karen.

"Adrian, you are not going to believe who just called."

I braced myself. "Who called?"

"Harold Lipscomb. He wants you to call him right away."

11

Though it was not ostentatious, 1049 Parkhurst appeared as though it had cost someone a sizeable chunk of change. The dark-red brick home perched on about two acres of perfectly landscaped, wooded land that bordered Lake Erie. I guessed that the house had been built in the late thirties, though it apparently had been expensively refurbished within the last few years. A late model, dark-blue Lincoln Towncar was parked in front of a detached four car garage. I remembered reading somewhere that Harold Lipscomb would only purchase American automobiles. His taste in cars was probably influenced more by his business connections with the big three auto makers than with his patriotism.

I parked next to the Lincoln, then walked cautiously to the front door. I didn't really expect to be mugged by a goon in a ski mask, but I had not expected that yesterday, either. The doorbell button was housed in a polished brass plate. When I pushed it, I could hear chimes announce my presence. A man I judged to be in his mid fifties opened the door. He was a few inches over six feet tall and looked like he played tennis about once a week even though his waistline suggested that he should have done a few more sit-ups. I assumed he was not a butler since most butlers do not wear expensive boat shoes, starched khaki trousers and forest green, cashmere sweaters.

"Mr. LeBlanc?" the man inquired.

"Yes, indeed." I handed him my card. He inspected it carefully before placing it in his trousers pocket.

"I am Harold Lipscomb." He did not offer to shake hands. "Come in, please."

Lipscomb shut the door behind me. I followed him to a spacious room with a magnificent view of the lake. He went to a small

Frank C. Dupuy

bar, opened an ice bucket and, using tongs, dropped three ice cubes into a cut crystal tumbler. He carefully poured a generous slug of single malt Scotch over the ice. Lipscomb's manners got the better of him.

"Would you care for something to drink?"

"Sure. I'll have whatever you're having," I replied, hoping that he wouldn't poison his own bottle.

He handed me my drink, then motioned me to a leather wingback chair near the huge picture window. Lipscomb settled himself in a matching chair across from me. He did not touch his drink. Instead, he scrutinized me for almost a minute. The man was having trouble making up his mind.

"Mr. LeBlanc, I have a problem. You may or may not be part of it. I would like you to tell me exactly what happened yesterday at the cottage."

"Mr. Lipscomb, I'm not sure I can do that. At the moment, I may be a suspect in a homicide. Until I know for certain that the authorities have cleared me, the less I say the better."

"You are not a suspect."

"Oh? Care to share your source of information?"

Lipscomb swallowed some of his Scotch, before setting his glass on an end table. His gray eyes met mine and held them. "I met with John Wright, J.C. Jensen and Ben Marston this morning. They gave me all of the details of the investigation. As far as they are concerned, you were set up. They don't believe that you had anything to do with the murder."

John Wright is the Ashtabula County D.A., and Ben Marston is the Sheriff. I wondered how much clout Lipscomb had with the locals. He correctly interpreted my expression.

"LeBlanc, I am a powerful man who contributes generously to the elected officials in a five county area. I called in a lot of favors this morning. Jensen speaks highly of you, as do the other people I checked with today. I have some difficult decisions to make, and before I do, I want you to tell me everything you know about what went on at the cottage yesterday." Lipscomb's jaw was set defiantly. He had stopped just short of ordering me to tell him about the murder of the fake Julie Lipscomb.

Although my host was doing his best to control himself, it was apparent he was upset. When we had spoken on the telephone, Lipscomb had asked me to meet him at his house as soon as possible, stating he did not want to discuss the matter over the telephone. I agreed to meet with him because, frankly, I was curious about why he wanted to talk to the man who had been hired to photograph him cheating on his wife.

"Mr. Lipscomb, we are in an awkward situation. I was hired by a woman I thought was your wife to take pictures of you committing adultery. She was murdered at your cottage. Somebody tried to kill me and frame me for her murder. Besides being stupid, I have done nothing wrong. You, on the other hand, are questionable. For all I know, you could have found out about the set up, killed the fake Julie Lipscomb and framed me."

Lipscomb met my gaze. "I could have, but I didn't. I was in Sandusky at the time of the murder. The Sheriff's Office has checked on that."

"Yeah, like those hotshot detectives are infallible." I watched Lipscomb carefully, confirming that I still couldn't read minds, or tell a murderer by his expression. Well, being rash is one of my more highly developed qualities, so I plunged in.

"Alright, Mr. Lipscomb, I'll tell you everything I know. I've already told it to the detectives, and you were given all of the reports by the D.A. and the Sheriff. Since you're a generous political contributor, I'm going to assume that they didn't grill you too hard about what you knew. You probably haven't told them who the dead woman really is."

Lipscomb's mouth tightened. He tapped his fingers against the arms of his chair. "You are correct. I didn't."

I nodded, then proceeded to tell him everything I knew about Julie Lipscomb, Ted Meyers and yesterday's events. He listened intently without interrupting. When I had finished, he stood up and carried both of our glasses to the bar where he poured us more Scotch. After handing me my drink, Lipscomb sat down and crossed his legs.

"Mr. LeBlanc, you have a reputation for being clever. Tell me what you think happened at my cottage."

"I don't know what happened, except that a woman was brutally murdered after having been tortured for some time. Whether the killer wanted information, or is simply a sadist is anybody's guess. One conclusion regarding the destroyed face and hands is that the killer did not want the woman identified; however, he could have just as easily hidden the body in the woods or sunk it in Lake Erie. Instead, the killer went to a lot of trouble to implicate me before calling the cops with a bogus prowler report to make certain the body was discovered.

"Whoever killed her knew I was going to the caretaker's house because they were waiting for me. I say they, because at least two people pushed my truck into the river.

"I'm going to assume that you and the killers both knew the woman, and that she and Ted Meyers were setting you up for blackmail. My guess is, you and the dead woman were having an affair, something you do not want to become public knowledge." I paused before deciding I had no more brilliant deductions to impart.

Lipscomb's features betrayed less emotion than an IRS auditor. "Do you think I murdered the woman?"

I contemplated his question for a few moments before answering. "Probably not. If you wanted to conceal that you were having an affair, I doubt that you would have gone through this elaborate set up. It doesn't take a genius to know that the cops will identify the body within a few days. Her murder probably had nothing to do with keeping your affair a secret; in fact, the killers likely wanted it made public to muddy the waters. A hell of a lot of pieces are still missing. Besides the woman's identity, what else haven't you shared with the detectives?"

Lipscomb did not answer immediately. He walked to the picture window where he stared at the lake. I noticed that his thinning, gray hair did not cover the bald patch on the back of his head. He spoke without turning around.

"Mr. LeBlanc, I wish to hire you."

"To do what?"

"To find out who murdered my mistress, Gwen Hiltie."

12

I called my wife on my way home. "Did you get my note?"
"About what?"
"About having dinner with me."
"When?"
"Tonight."
"What?"
"Jeannie," I explained with infinite patience, "I left a note for you on the front door this morning, telling you that we were going out for dinner. I need to talk to you."
"Well, I have class tonight. We can talk when I get home. Oh, I'm leaving money with Jules so he can order a pizza. I'll be home at 9:30."
I shook my head as I flipped closed my cell phone. For the last four months, I had barely seen my wife because of conflicting schedules and her classes. Realtors often show homes in the evenings and on weekends. When a realtor also takes night classes, it leaves very little time to spend with her. I was not certain what kind of classes Jeannie was attending because she was being secretive about them. Our son, Jules, had tipped me off that his mom had been purchasing camping items which she was storing in a locked trunk in the basement. She was also receiving outdoor adventure and survivalist magazines at her office. Jules had found them in one of her desk drawers while waiting for her one afternoon. This had me entirely puzzled since Jeannie's idea of camping out is a Holiday Inn.
  She was gone by the time I arrived at the house. The loud music I could hear from the driveway was a clue that my son was determined to permanently damage his hearing before he was eighteen. Pushing open the front door, I was greeted by thunderous

heavy metal lyrics performed by a band that could have benefitted from a music appreciation course. I strode into the den and turned the stereo volume down to a bearable level.

"Hey! I was listening to that," came an aggrieved bellow from a lump on the couch.

"What's that?" I asked cupping my hand to my ear.

"I said I was listening to the music."

"Huh?"

"I said I was... Oh, very funny."

"I'm sorry my hearing was damaged by a blast of noise when I entered the house."

Jules glanced up from the book he was reading long enough to scowl at me. The cover depicted a muscular man brandishing a sword at an alien monster while a scantily clad, buxom babe watched admiringly.

"Studying our geography assignment, are we?" Jules's grades have been an issue for the last year. He is bright and capable, but has an aversion to completing his homework assignments. Counseling and taking away privileges have done little to correct his refusal to turn in his assignments. His mother and I may become prematurely gray before he graduates from high school.

"I already finished my homework."

"Good. Show it to me."

"I put it away."

"Son, let me be perfectly clear. You either show me your homework, or you haul your dead rear-end up to your room right now and finish it."

I have become indifferent to sullen expressions, so one more didn't bother me. Glowering, Jules slouched off to his room.

"What kind of pizza do you want?" I yelled up the stairs.

"I'm not hungry," came the martyred reply.

I called the pizza shop, placing an order for a cheese only medium pizza and a pepperoni and mushroom medium pizza, the same order I always make when ordering for Jules. The kid on the other end of the line promised to have the pizzas delivered in thirty minutes.

I sat down on the couch to read the newspaper and promptly dozed off. The door bell woke me. I paid the delivery girl, giving her a $2.00 tip which she accepted without any expression before driving on to her next customer. I was momentarily depressed by the thought that generation X will be running the country when I am in my dotage.

By the time Jeannie came home, Jules had managed unobtrusively to slip into the kitchen and demolish both pizzas. I had feasted on a salad and a cold turkey sandwich.

"How was your class?"

"Fine."

"What are you studying?"

"It's a kind of nature appreciation course."

"Oh? Sounds like something I might be interested in."

"Maybe. You can sign up for the fall class at the end of the summer."

So much for techniques of interrogation. I sighed as I plopped down in my favorite leather chair.

"Jeannie, I need to tell you about what happened last night." Without any further ado, I launched into my tale. By this time, I was getting pretty good at telling it. When I had finished,
she was watching me with shocked concern.

"Oh, Adrian. Are you alright?"

"Pretty much."

"What are you going to do?"

"Well, tomorrow I'm going to see Bob Hodas to take a polygraph exam. Once he gives the results to the D.A., I should be in the clear. After that, I am going to find Ted Meyers and rip his throat out, but not before he tells me what in the hell is going on."

Jeannie was giving me her best "I don't think you are being smart" look. "Why don't you let the police handle this?"

"Because too much is going on. I don't think the Sheriff's department has the horsepower to handle it properly. Not only that, one of the detectives is a psycho-bitch who wants to hang me by my manhood."

"She would have to be awfully determined to do that," my mate observed innocently.

"Cute, Jeannie, real cute," I responded. We both smiled; I relaxed for the first time in two days. Then my pager went off.

Frank C. Dupuy

13

The lady at my answering service informed me that a Mr. M. Theodore wanted me to call him immediately. He said it was urgent.

I dialed M. Theodore's number. The telephone was picked up on the first ring. I could hear the sound of automobile traffic in the background.

"Hello," someone answered in a muffled voice.

"Hello, Ted. Take your handkerchief off the telephone."

"OK. I'm just being careful," Ted Meyers stated in a much clearer voice.

"You call to send me some more divorce work, or are you merely lonely?"

"Adrian, this is no time to be funny. I'm in serious trouble."

"Not yet you're not, you low life son of a bitch. However, you will be as soon as I get my hands on you."

"Please, Adrian, listen to me. I had nothing to do with what happened to you."

"Really? Then who was it who pressured me into taking a divorce case for an old and dear friend who turns out to be as phony as you are?"

"OK, I admit I sent a woman to see you, but I didn't have anything to do with killing her or hurting you."

"Her name, Ted. Tell me her name."

"Gwen Hiltie. She and I were friends. Taking the pictures was just business, that's all, just business."

"I don't know how to break this to you, Ted, but blackmail is against the law in most states, including this one."

"Yeah, well only if you get caught." Meyers paused. "Les Fazio told me you made some threats when you came to see him. Adrian, for your own good, don't mess around in my business affairs.

Frank C. Dupuy

I'd hate to see anything happen to you," he hesitated, "or to your family."

Before his last comment, I had only been seriously pissed off at Ted Meyers; now I was totally furious. My hand convulsed on the receiver until my knuckles creaked.

"You base born bastard," I stated as calmly as I could, "You just made the biggest fucking mistake of your life."

Meyers started to say something else as I crashed the receiver into the cradle. Jeannie was staring at me.

"What in the world was that all about?"

"That was Ted Meyers, the man who started all of this. He called to tell me he hadn't done anything wrong, then threatened me and my family."

"Is he serious?"

"I don't know. I've never known him to use strong arm tactics, but then no one has ever tried to pin a murder on me, either." I slowly exhaled, slumping down in my chair. "Sometimes your husband isn't too bright; I didn't handle Ted very well."

"No shit, Sherlock," Jeannie declared, using one of my favorite phrases against me. "So, what are you going to do about Ted Meyers?"

Good question. I rubbed my eyes and sat up. "The first thing is to get you and Jules out of town until I can resolve this. Tomorrow is Thursday. Why don't you take Jules out of school for a couple of days. Kentucky is nice this time of year."

My wife skewered me with a cold stare. "Just like that? You want me to leave at a moment's notice while you stay here and let people try to drown you in rivers? How about my job? I have appointments scheduled for the next three days. You think you can simply wave your hand and order me out of town at your convenience?" Jeannie's features had acquired that set, determined quality which has always reminded me of a mule with an attitude.

"Sweetheart," I implored patiently, "We are dealing with bad people who tortured and killed a woman before trying to kill me. I don't think they would let the fact that you are busy stop them from hurting you. If I wasn't sincerely worried about you and Jules, I wouldn't have said anything. Jeannie," I pleaded, "please believe me when I tell you that the best way to ensure your safety is to get you out of town for a few days."

My eloquence must have had some effect. Jeannie's expression eased from mulish to sullen.

"Oh, all right. I can get Carla Porelli to handle my appointments. I suppose you won't be coming with us?"

"Yep."

"When Jules and I return, you and I need to have a serious talk about your double standard and," Jeannie averted her eyes, "a few other things."

Sometimes, when I am on an assignment that goes seriously off track, I develop a hollow, almost sick feeling, exactly like I had now. In our seventeen years of marriage, Jeannie and I have always talked out our differences, but she had never used the ominous, cold "and a few other things" on me.

"You care to discuss the other things now?"

"No." She stood up. "I don't have time. I have to pack." With that, the light of my life marched out of the room.

A lesser man might have been driven to find solace in whisky. I, on the other hand, am made of sterner stuff. On the bottom shelf of the pantry, I retrieved a bottle of merlot which I promptly opened. Walking back into the den required too much effort, so I sat on a stool at the kitchen counter, focusing on my glass of wine.

Why, I asked myself, had Ted Meyers called me? Because, dummy, you threatened Les Fazio that you were going to start digging into the affairs of the Meyers Group, Ltd., if you didn't get some answers. Meyers called to give me some answers and to ask me not to involve myself in his business. OK. So, what had he actually told me? That the woman he sent to my office was Gwen Hiltie and that he had nothing to do with killing Hiltie or hurting me. Well, Harold Lipscomb had told me the same thing. I thought back to our meeting when Lipscomb had informed me that he wanted to hire me.

"Your mistress?" I asked.

He turned from the window to face me. "Gwen and I have been lovers for three months. I guess mistress is an old-fashioned term, but then I am old-fashioned."

I didn't comment.

Frank C. Dupuy

"I was married for nineteen years to a wonderful woman. Sharon died in an automobile accident in 1979. I loved her and never once was unfaithful to her. When she died, I was devastated. Everyone handles grief differently. Work was my therapy, Mr. LeBlanc, long hours of work. It helped me not to think. Foolishly, I resolved never to let myself get close to another woman because I believed that I could never love anyone as much as I had loved Sharon.

"In 1986, I was in Toronto on business. Based on new information I had received in a morning meeting, I had a number of proposals that needed to be amended immediately. My customer was kind enough to provide me with an office and a secretary. She and I worked until eight that night before everything was revised. The secretary, Julie Grey, was a pleasant, efficient woman. On impulse, I invited her to share a late dinner with me. She accepted. That evening, I learned that Julie was a widow who was putting her daughter through college. I told her about Sharon, about myself and my businesses. It was the first time I had enjoyed a relaxed conversation with a woman since Sharon's death. We said goodnight at the restaurant. When I returned to my office the next week, I found a simple, old-fashioned thank you note from Julie in my mail. I was touched in a manner I cannot describe. I called Julie at her office; we talked. When she gave me her home number, I called her several times a week simply to talk. I hadn't realized how lonesome I had been.

"A few weeks later, I finally summoned the courage to ask her to have dinner with me again; she accepted. One thing led to another; after a year's courtship, we were married. Julie and I bought this house and completely remodeled it together. Mr. LeBlanc, for the last seven years I have been happily married to a kind and gentle woman who has made me content."

"As content as Gwen Hiltie?" I asked.

My host winced, then became thoughtful. "No, it's not, wasn't, the same at all. Julie is an attractive, caring companion. Gwen was an addiction. Do you know what it is like to have a young, gorgeous, sensuous woman offer herself to you without any reservations? To tell you how much she admires you, how much you stimulate her in bed?"

Ohio Salt

I shook my head. Lipscomb had me there. Not too many gorgeous women were throwing themselves at me these days.

Lipscomb was gazing out of the window again. "Gwen was hired as an administrative assistant in our marketing department in late October. My company hosts an annual golf outing in Florida the first week in December. We fly our guests in, covering all expenses. Gwen was asked to help co-ordinate the events on the golf course and at the hotel reception because she was in the marketing department, and because she was attractive. Well, the outing was a complete success, thanks in large part to Gwen's efforts. She was incredibly efficient and completely charmed our customers.

"On the last night, we held a dinner dance. Some of the females who attended were hired from an escort service. The rule is that the girls are not supposed to look like hookers or accept money from our guests. Our people make certain they are well compensated for their time. The point is, Mr. LeBlanc, that if one of our customers wants to get laid, we provide the opportunity; however, it doesn't have the taint of crass prostitution."

I nodded understandingly, wondering how many contracts Lipscomb had acquired as the direct result of the girls from the escort service.

"That night, Gwen danced with all of the customers in a friendly, but not flirtatious manner. She had a way about her that let men know pleasantly, yet firmly, that there was a line they could not cross. She and I danced several times, including the last dance. She told me her only regret was that she hadn't gotten to go on a single boat the entire time she had been in Florida. My boat was in the hotel marina, since I leave it in Florida during the winter. Though I should have known better, I invited Gwen to my boat after the dance. It was the most incredible evening of my life."

Lipscomb lost himself in his reverie for a moment. I wondered what kind of incredible things Gwen Hiltie had done to him.

"Have you ever fantasized about beautiful women, Mr. LeBlanc?" he inquired softly.

"Sure, I'm human."

"The sad part about fantasy is that it can never measure up to reality. At least that's what I thought before I met Gwen. She was more intense, more pleasurable, than any fantasy I had ever imagin-

Frank C. Dupuy

ed. In bed she was a sensuous, imaginative, uninhibited animal. She did things to me that caused incredible pleasure, things I had never even dreamed about. And then she taught me how to do things to her." He stared wistfully at a spot about a foot over my head. "The strange thing is that with Gwen, I never felt guilty afterwards. She made it clear that she was fascinated by me, but that she did not want a long term relationship. One day at a time, she used to tell me. We met two, sometimes three evenings a week. I was totally infatuated with her."

"Did she ever ask you for money?"

"Never. She would not accept things from me; she said it would only cheapen our relationship. All she ever asked was to know me. We would lie in bed and talk. She asked questions about the people I knew, about my business transactions, about everything I did. Gwen said I was the first industrialist she had ever known, that she found my life fascinating. I suppose that I told her my innermost secrets, business and personal."

"Did she ever mention Ted Meyers?"

"We talked about him, I'm sure. He is not one of my favorite people."

Lipscomb returned to his chair, emotionally exhausted.

"Why weren't you at your cottage last night?"

He rubbed his face with his hand. "Because Gwen called me about 2:00 to tell me that she had something to do. She asked if we could meet at the Sheraton in Sandusky instead."

"What else did she say?"

"That was it. I didn't actually speak with her. She left a message on my voice mail."

"Are you certain it was Gwen?"

"Yes. It was her voice."

"Did she leave a number where she could be reached.?

"No. Excuse me for a moment."

Lipscomb left the room, returning a few minutes later with a manila folder. He handed me a sheet of paper from a yellow legal pad that contained a handwritten note. "Harry," I read, "it's Gwen. Something has come up at the last minute. I have to be in Sandusky this afternoon. Can we meet at the Sandusky Sheraton instead; just like the last time? Darling, I have something important to tell you that can't wait. Please, please, please be there." I raised an eyebrow.

"I copied the message off of my voice mail."

"Did she sound emotional or different from normal?"

"I think so. She sounded as though she was stressed. Also, she has never called me Harry. No one does. I was curious about "just like the last time," since we had never been to Sandusky together."

"Mr. Lipscomb, none of this makes sense to me. Gwen was working for Ted Meyers to gain leverage on you. Apparently, she was milking you for information that she was passing on to Meyers. For whatever reason, they decided that yesterday was the day that they were going to capture you on film entering and leaving the cottage with Gwen. About five hours before you were to meet with her, she called you to change the location of your tryst. Let's say for the sake of argument that she was under duress when she left her message, that she tried to give you a hint that something was wrong. Who wanted her dead?"

"Ted Meyers?" Lipscomb ventured.

"I doubt it. If he had wanted to kill her, why do it in a way that would obviously involve him and expose the fact that he was out to blackmail you? If you didn't kill her and Meyers didn't kill her, that leaves a third party who knew about your rendezvous, and who had a reason to kill her. Is there any chance your wife found out about the two of you, that she decided to eliminate her rival?"

Lipscomb shook his head. "No, never. I assure you, Julie did not know; even if she did, she would never murder anyone."

"Love causes people to do strange things, Mr. Lipscomb."

"Not Julie. Besides, she was with Toni Hines and Loretta Laston until 6:00 yesterday evening. It was their day to volunteer at the hospital. Julie and her friends work two days each week in the pediatric unit. Julie likes to be around children."

"If that's the case, you should do some serious thinking about who knew about you and Gwen and who had a motive to kill her."

"That's what I've been doing all day. I'm at a loss. That's why I want to hire you to find out who did it. Everything I know about Gwen is in this file." He handed it to me.

I didn't open it. "Mr. Lipscomb, how much of this have you shared with the D.A. and the Sheriff?"

Frank C. Dupuy

"None of it."

"You do know that your affair with Gwen Hiltie is going to have to come out, eventually?"

"Maybe. If it does, I will deal with it. Your job is to find out who killed Gwen."

"Why do you want to know? It's obvious she was using you."

"Mr. LeBlanc, I am not a stupid man. Yes, I have determined I was being used; nevertheless, I still have feelings for Gwen. Whatever she did, she did not deserve to die in that horrible fashion. My other reason for hiring you is selfish. I want to know if I am in danger."

I opened the file. The first thing I saw was an envelope with my name on it. I opened it. The check it contained was made out to me for $20,000. The other items included several photographs of Gwen Hiltie, her job application and two keys.

"Mr. LeBlanc, I know you charge $1,000 a day. The check is a retainer for five days. There's more if you need it. I included her job application and the keys to her apartment. Do whatever you have to do. All I ask is that you keep me informed."

Against my better judgment, I had accepted the folder and the check. After all, $20,000 is $20,000.

Gwen Hiltie's apartment was on the upper floor of an older house that had been converted into a fourplex. It was located in Rocky River, a pleasant community just west of Cleveland and an easy commute from Bay Village. Lipscomb had told me that he and Gwen Hiltie had often used her apartment for their intimate encounters.

I parked my car about a block from the house in case any neighbors were observant. One of the keys opened an outer door that led to a flight of stairs. The door at the top of the stairs was locked. I knocked. No one responded. Cautiously, I unlocked and opened the door. One look was all I needed to convince me that I was not the first person to have been in Gwen Hiltie's apartment recently. The place had been thoroughly ransacked. The contents of drawers and closets had been dumped in the middle of the floor. Even the cushions on the furniture had been cut open. Carefully, I relocked the door, before quietly making my way down the stairs. I wasn't worried about fingerprints; I had been wearing gloves.

Ohio Salt

By the time I had finished cogitating about my meeting with Lipscomb, my wine glass was empty. I considered having another one, but decided against it, since I wanted to be in good shape for my polygraph exam in the morning.

As I climbed the stairs to my bedroom, I thought about my marriage. It wasn't perfect; no relationship is, yet I was content. Jeannie's ominous comment about discussing "a few other things" caused me to reflect that it had been almost six months since we had had a meaningful talk about anything. I had chalked this up to both of us having been extremely busy the last few months, though, if I were honest, I had noticed a slight, but definite change in Jeannie. She had started going to lectures and attending classes that she was evasive about. I hadn't pried because I figured it was her business. Well, we would simply have to talk things out when she and Jules got back.

Jeannie was already in bed with the lights off. When I tried to snuggle next to her after crawling under the covers, she was as rigid and responsive as a frozen I-beam. Even the densest private investigator can figure out when he's in trouble, even if he isn't sure why.

Frank C. Dupuy

14

Thursday

Collin Yates surveyed the restaurant, spotted me and made his way to my booth.

"Sorry, I'm late. The rain had traffic backed up on 90."

I nodded. The weatherman had correctly predicted rain.

"Guess who called me yesterday?"

Yates shrugged.

"Harold Lipscomb and Ted Meyers. Lipscomb wants to hire me to find out who killed his mistress, and Meyers threatened me and my family if I dig into to his affairs. Both of them claimed that they didn't kill the woman, who, by the by, was one Gwen Hiltie."

Yates's somber demeanor conveyed the idea that he was not happy with his client. "Why don't you tell me what happened; all of it."

I did, except that I left out how much Lipscomb had given me as a retainer. Yates is a good guy, yet even the best of guys has been known to raise his rates.

"What is Harold Lipscomb's involvement?" Collin asked when I had finished.

"On the face of it, he wants to find out who killed Gwen Hiltie and if the same people are after him. He would also like to keep his affair with the deceased from his wife, if at all possible."

"What are you going to tell the detectives?"

"Well, that depends on the advice of my attorney. Certainly, I will pass on my conversation with Ted Meyers. For the moment, I prefer not to mention that Harold Lipscomb is now my client."

Yates's frown was almost audible.

"Look Collin, a lot of pieces are missing. For the sake of argument, let's say that neither Meyers nor Lipscomb killed Hiltie. That means that there is a third player who may or may not be after Lipscomb."

"Or you or Ted Meyers, for that matter."

"Or me or Ted Meyers," I agreed. "It's almost certain that Hiltie was passing on everything Lipscomb told her to Meyers. It took several months for Meyers to find out everything he wanted to know about Lipscomb's business operations. Once he decided he had all he could get, it was time to take pictures to use as leverage. Besides committing adultery after being set up, Lipscomb hasn't done anything wrong. The cops will figure out the relationship in a day or two; with Lipscomb's clout, it will probably never make the news. Right now, Yuhas and Kules don't need their noses pushed out of joint about my working for Lipscomb."

"Um hmm. You are still a suspect yourself, you know."

"I know, but after the polygraph I won't be."

Collin Yates sighed, "Adrian, you do know that the Sheriff's Department will not welcome your interfering with a homicide investigation?"

"I know. So, what?"

Yates shook his head.

"Come on, Collin. Look who's working this thing, a psycho named Yuhas who is out to hang me, and her partner, Kules, who has made a career of not making waves. Somebody tried to kill me and that jackass Meyers has threatened my family. I'm not going to simply walk away from this one. Besides, if you were in my position, you'd be doing the same thing."

"Hmph. Maybe. For the moment, we won't mention that Harold Lipscomb is your client. Now, let's go over the questions for the polygraph."

15

The gray, moist clouds producing the drizzle hitting my windshield must have been a portent of things to come. My office telephone was answered by a man.

"The Agincourt Company, may I help you?" he inquired professionally.

"This is Adrian LeBlanc, who are you?"

"It's me, Louie. What's up?"

"Nothing's up. Where's Karen?"

"She had to go to the little girls' room. Say, we may be on to something. We've been digging up a lot of good dirt on your pal Ted Meyers."

I choked back an urge to yell into the telephone. Damn Karen, anyway. She had no business involving Louie Kolakowski in my investigation.

"I can't talk now. Have Karen call me as soon as she gets back."

My mood was influenced by my run-in with detectives Fred Kules and Sally Yuhas after the polygraph exam, which, by the by, I passed with flying colors. The examiner, Bob Hodas, is a retired cop who is used by many of the local departments on important cases. The questions he asked me were variations of "Did you murder or cause to be murdered the woman whose body was found at the Lipscomb cottage?", "Do you know who killed the woman whose body was found at the Lipscomb cottage?", "Did you participate in the murder or torture of the woman whose body was found at the Lipscomb cottage?"

The detectives were waiting for Yates and me at Hodas's office which is located in Mentor. Everyone was cordial enough as we reviewed the questions prior to my taking the exam, though Sally

Frank C. Dupuy

Yuhas was rather subdued and avoided eye contact. I assumed that her suspension had only lasted until the Sheriff could personally chastise Yuhas for letting her hormones overload her mouth. When the exam, which lasted almost two hours, was over, Hodas showed the charts to Collin Yates and the detectives.

"These are the control questions. LeBlanc shows a definite response when he answers dishonestly. On the relevant questions, his charts show no signs of deception. I'll have to study these before I submit my report, but I believe he is telling the truth."

Yuhas was disappointed. She was wearing navy slacks, a white blouse and a gray tweed blazer this morning. I saw her hand go to her jacket pocket several times as she fingered a pack of cigarettes. She smelled of cigarette smoke whenever I got within a few feet of her. I wondered if her nicotine intake had increased after the sheriff had reamed her for crossing J.C. Jensen.

Fred Kules was wearing the same coat and slacks he had been wearing on Tuesday night. They didn't look any more or less wrinkled than they had then. To his credit, he had changed his shirt and tie.

Yates cleared his throat. "My client has some information he wishes to share with you."

Bob Hodas glanced at Kules who motioned with his head. Hodas left the room.

"Ted Meyers called me at my house last night. He said the woman he sent to my office was Gwen Hiltie."

Kules's face clouded. "Why did he call you?"

"He wanted me to know that he had nothing to do with the murder of the woman or the attempt to murder me."

"Uh huh. How did he know someone tried to kill you?"

"I told his general hatchet man, Lester Fazio, when I went looking for Meyers yesterday morning. Oh, I forgot to mention that he threatened me and my family if I went poking into his business."

"LeBlanc, you are interfering with a homicide investigation." Kules informed me. "You shouldn't have gone looking for Meyers, and you should have called me as soon as you had talked to him." His voice was louder than it needed to be.

"OK, I apologize. Here's the number he called me from. It's a pay phone. He called my answering service and left that number

Ohio Salt

for me to call him."

"What did he tell you about the woman?" Yuhas asked.

"Not much. He admitted he was using her to get dirt on Lipscomb. He didn't tell me directly, but I got the impression Gwen Hiltie worked for Harold Lipscomb."

The two detectives exchanged frowns.

"LeBlanc, you're supposed to be a hotshot investigator. That's fine. But, this is my case; I don't need you messing around behind my back," Kules snapped.

"Super. When do you plan to interview Meyers?"

Collin Yates kicked me in the ankle hard enough to make me wince.

"You have your attorney here; ask him what the law is regarding interfering with an investigation, smart ass."

"Detective Kules, the last time I saw you, your partner was being called on the carpet because she was convinced I was a murderer. All I was trying to do was clear myself. The best source of information, for my money, was Ted Meyers, the guy who started everything in the first place."

"You may have passed the polygraph, but as far as I'm concerned, you're still in this up to your neck," grated a less than cordial Sally Yuhas.

"Swell. My fate is in the hands of a touchy detective whose idea of finding the chief suspect is to make a few phone calls, plus he has a partner who won't rest until I'm convicted of something. Come on, Collin, let's get the hell out of here so the Bobbsey Twins can go solve a murder."

I won't bore you with what Collin Yates told me in the parking lot. Suffice to say that he read me the riot act, then cautioned me not to be too obvious when I started digging into the Meyers Group, Ltd.. He also promised to have some information on Ted Meyers later that day.

My cell phone buzzed. It was Karen Koenig.

"Hi, boss. Louie said you wanted me to call you."

"Yes, I did. Will you please tell me why you chose to involve Louie in this investigation without asking me?"

"Are you upset, Adrian?" Ms. Koenig is so perceptive sometimes.

Frank C. Dupuy

"Yes. You should ask me before you ever, ever bring in anyone on one of my investigations."

"Well, I think part of your investigation and what happened to Louie are linked."

"What?"

"I said I think that your investigation and the attack on Louie are linked. Guess who owns the land where Louie was harassed by the security guards?"

"Who?"

"Well, one of the buildings is owned by T.M. Development Corporation, a subsidiary of the Meyers Group, Ltd.; the other is owned by Ontario Enterprises, on Detroit Avenue."

"Wonderful. I'll be at the office in thirty minutes. Oh. Make damn sure you keep Louie out of my files."

My thought processes were not at their best. No matter how hard I tried, I simply could not connect a dead woman, Ted Meyers, a mystery company and Louie Kolakowski's quest for gold that had been squirreled away by a one-legged Polish count.

16

When I entered Karen's office, she and Louie were finishing the last of a pair of submarine sandwiches. I gaped at a totally transformed Louie Kolakowski. His hair, what was left of it, was dishwater blond, as were his eyebrows. The wire framed glasses perched on his nose gave him a studious, almost scholarly aspect. I wondered if Karen had provided him with a pocket protector as well.

"Nice flattop." I commented.

He ran his hand over his head. "Easy for you to say. That woman butchered me."

"Oh, she did not. You look very handsome, like an athlete," Karen chirped brightly.

"Gee, you really think so?" Louie endeavored to puff out what little chest he possessed.

"Are you wearing makeup?" I inquired. His normally pale complexion was almost ruddy.

"No way! Karen took me to a tanning salon. Not bad, huh?"

"No, not bad at all," I conceded, "You'd be hard to recognize, now."

He beamed. Evidently, Louie had gotten into his role playing.

"Karen, tell me what you found out."

"Well, I ran a D&B on the Meyers Group, Ltd. Ted Meyers has over a dozen companies under that umbrella, including T.M. Development Corporation. The only officers mentioned are Ted, Lester Fazio and a Donald Meyers, who, it turns out, is a brother. Ted Meyers owns eighty percent of the Meyers group, Fazio has ten percent and Donald has ten percent. There are almost two pages of UCC filings, most of which were filed in 1992 and '93. It appears Meyers purchased a lot of equipment in a short period of time. The

Frank C. Dupuy

Meyers Group has been involved in about a dozen lawsuits over the last ten years that have all been settled out of court. In 1990, the Meyers Group filed a law suit against Northern States Development, which is owned by Harold Lipscomb; Northern States Development filed a counter suit. D&B didn't provide details. Early last year, the Meyers Group took out some fairly hefty loans with OmniBank Corp., supposedly for business expansion. Let's see. Oh, Meyers is a bit slow in paying his suppliers although he hasn't stretched anything out over 120 days. The Meyers Group declined to give any financial details about their operation.

"When I did the title search on the sites where Louie ran into the security guards, I found that one of them was owned by T.M. Development and the other by Ontario Enterprises. Oh, D&B doesn't have a file on Ontario Enterprises."

"What do you think, Adrian?" Louie asked. "That's a pretty neat coincidence, those two buildings being owned by the guys who tried to frame you."

I blasted Karen with my most withering glare. "What else have you found out?"

"Harold Lipscomb owns 100 per cent of Newport Industries which has five manufacturing operations, three in Ohio, one in North Carolina and one in Tennessee. He is the Chairman of the Board. The president is listed as Samuel Silverstein; there are four vice-presidents, including Harold Lipscomb, Jr.. Harold Lipscomb, Sr. is shown as the president of four other companies which are real estate development and/or investment operations. It's my impression that only one of the four is active, Northern States Investments, Inc.. Lipscomb must have the Midas touch because everything he is involved in is pure gold."

I checked my watch. It was almost 12:30. If I sent Karen and Louie to Cleveland, they could get in at least three good hours of research. I thought about Karen's revelations before deciding that there was a lot Louie hadn't told me. The coffee in the glass pot of the automatic coffee maker didn't appear too old, so I poured a cup and gestured for Louie and Karen to follow me into my office.

"Louie," I announced as I settled in my chair and propped my feet on my desk, "we have to talk."

"Sure thing, Adrian. What are we going to talk about?"

Ohio Salt

"Oh, let's try talking about exactly where you were poking around Tuesday and why you picked those particular locations."

"I was looking for the gold that Count Petrowski and my dad had hidden after the Cuban deal."

"Cuban deal?"

"You know, the Bay of Pigs invasion."

"What has any of this got to do with the Bay of Pigs?"

"Well, uh, I think we need to meet with my source."

"What source?"

Louie squirmed in his chair, then blushed. "I can't give you all of the details without talking to my mom."

"Your mom?" I was beginning to sound like a bad Greek chorus.

"Yeah, my mom. She's the one who gave me the stuff I asked you to keep. I'm doing this for her."

"Doing what for her?"

"Trying to find the gold and trying to find out what happened to my father and Count Petrowski. Adrian, this is real complicated. We gotta talk things over with my mom. OK?" He stood up. "Can I make a call from the spare office?"

"Be my guest."

Louie walked out of the room. Karen was trying to avoid my eyes.

"Well, what do you know about this?"

"Not a lot. Evidently, Louie's mother has only recently told him that his father was doing work for the CIA in the 50's and 60's. She's dying of cancer. He says she kept a lot of secrets about his father until last month. That's about all I know."

"Karen."

"Yes?"

"Talk to me."

"It, um, would probably be better if she told you herself."

Yesterday, I had made arrangements for Louie to spend the night at Carl Branner's house. Carl is a retired librarian who occasionally does research for me. He lives by himself in a roomy turn-of-the-century house in Akron, which was left to him by his parents. He enjoys company and permits me to use his home to house clients who need to keep low profiles for short periods of time. I had a nagging hunch that Louie hadn't made it to Carl's last night.

"How did Louie get along with Carl?"

Silence. Karen was concentrating on her hands which she was clasping together in her lap. Suddenly, she raised her head. "Oh, alright. Louie stayed at my house. He was so lonely and everything, I thought it would cheer him up if I fixed dinner for him. He's such a nice young man – so appreciative. Well, after dinner I didn't have the heart to take him over to that old recluse's place."

"Carl is not an old recluse."

"Ha!" she snorted.

Normally, Karen is a very efficient, level headed secretary. I had the feeling that I had better wrap up Louie's case as soon as possible, or he would have her as totally goofy as he is.

Louie poked his head into the room. "Mom says we can meet with her at 7:00 tonight."

"Super. In the meantime, you and Karen can go into Cleveland to pull the real estate listings for Ontario Enterprises and the Meyers Group. If you have time, check the civil record index for all of the above. Oh, Karen, drop Louie off at the Bob Evan's on Rockside and I-77." I inclined my head towards Louie. "I'll meet you in the lobby at 6:00 sharp."

I had been scouring the Dun and Bradstreet reports for about fifteen minutes when the telephone rang. It was Collin Yates.

"Adrian, I have some news for you about Ted Meyers."

"Shoot."

"In 1992, Meyers was a contender for a fat Department of Defense subcontractor deal involving a retrofit of several thousand Abrahms tanks. His political guru was Donald Poje."

"Donald Poje, as in the congressman who resigned after he was caught taking bribes a few years ago?"

"The very one. He actually resigned in February of 1993, but he had been dead in the water politically for at least six months prior to his resignation. Based on promises from Poje, Meyers invested heavily in new, specialized equipment. When the Poje scandal broke, Meyers barely escaped being implicated in it. The bad news was that with Poje gone, the Abrahms retrofit program was canceled, leaving Ted Meyers in a precarious financial position."

"Meaning he had expensive equipment to fix army tanks and

Ohio Salt

no customers."

"Exactly. After the tank deal fell apart, the Meyers Group was so heavily leveraged that no one would lend him another penny. Meyers was facing financial ruin when, suddenly, he managed to establish a several million dollar line of credit with OmniBank."

I rocked back and forth in my chair as I listened to Yates.

"So who bailed him out? The last time I checked, OmniBank was considered a rather conservative financial institution."

"It still is. Apparently, the bank made a collateralized loan on some of Meyers' companies."

"Maybe the Meyers Group was healthier than people thought."

"Maybe." Yates rustled some papers. "About a year prior to the tank deal, Meyers had been one of the principals in the Sealake development project."

Vaguely, I recalled that a group of investors had purchased some land near downtown Cleveland that was supposed to be turned into a hotel/luxury apartment/shopping complex. There was a lot of hoopla until the negotiations with a major hotel chain had fallen through. The last I had heard was that the project was on hold.

"That project was put on hold wasn't it?"

"That is the polite term. When Century Hotels nixed the deal, the investors were left holding the bag. Rumor has it that Meyers had borrowed a lot of money on speculation; he took a bath when the deal soured."

"Collin, who did Meyers borrow the money from for the Sealake project? Those loans weren't listed in the Dun and Bradstreet reports I pulled."

"The same rumor has it that the loans were from private sources."

"How private?"

"The Calistro brothers."

"As in THE Calistro brothers?"

"Indeed."

"Wow. Since Ted Meyers is still alive, I assume he repaid the money?"

"My source was not aware that anyone has taken out a contract out on Meyers."

Frank C. Dupuy

The Calistro brothers, Benny, Joey and Donny were the sons of old Salvatore Calistro, one of the premier players in Cleveland's supposedly defunct crime syndicate. Salvatore's body had been found in the Cuyahoga River in 1977 minus its hands and private parts. His sons had allegedly "gone straight" by becoming respected business men. They had several contracting companies as well as real estate holdings. They also had been investigated numerous times for bid rigging and income tax evasion, but so far had managed to dodge the bullet. The Calistros were rumored to lend money at above bank rates to anyone desperate enough to borrow from them. Very few people failed to repay a Calistro loan. I filed the Calistro connection away for future contemplation.

"While you were tweaking your anonymous sources, did you happen to find out anything about Harold Lipscomb?" I queried, changing the subject.

"Only that he is a pillar in the community and respected for his abilities to consistently generate profits. It isn't public yet, but he will be named to OmniBank's Board of Directors in June."

My gray matter sluggishly churned as it tried to sort through what I had just been told.

"Hey, are you still there?" Yates inquired.

"Sorry, I was trying to gather wool without any sheep. You have any other hot information?"

"That's about it," he hesitated then added, "Are you on to something, Adrian?"

"Not yet, I'm still in the information gathering stage."

I thanked Collin and hung up. On the bottom of the stack of papers Karen had handed me was Gwen Hiltie's job application that Harold Lipscomb had given to me. Karen had run Hiltie's Social Security number through several data bases which corroborated that Gwen Hiltie had departed Cleveland in February, 1991 to go to Los Angeles. She listed her occupation as a freelance model and actress while on the West Coast. Maybe, I thought. She had the looks, although she would have been a little on the old side by L.A. standards.

Karen had typed a chronological list of everything she had developed on Gwen Hiltie, including the information from the job app. Gwendoline Lois Hiltie had been born on September 21, 1961,

Ohio Salt

in Mentor, Ohio. She graduated from Mentor Senior High School in 1979; she received an associates degree in accounting three years later from Cuyahoga Community College. From June 1982 until December 1990, she had worked for the Cleveland Yacht Club rising to the position of assistant manager. She listed her reason for leaving as "a desire to pursue other career opportunities." Evidently, this meant being a model/actress in Los Angeles. Hiltie had returned to Ohio in June 1994, landing a job as a marketing representative for T.M. Development Corporation. Her reason for leaving was "career advancement."

Karen's database search had produced several former addresses, including four in L.A.. I noted that Hiltie had lived at three addresses in Mentor while she had worked for the Cleveland Yacht Club. I tapped my nose a couple of times with my finger before deciding that I needed someone in Lake County to do a quick record search. Mentor is in Lake County which is just up the lakeshore from Cleveland. I called Patty Stone, a reliable private investigator whose office is in Painesville, the Lake County seat. Besides being reliable, Patty Stone knows how to keep a secret.

"My goodness, I didn't expect to receive a call from a local celebrity."

"What's that supposed to mean?"

"Only that Bob Hodas had you on the lie box this morning and that you were the person who discovered a dead woman at Harold Lipscomb's summer house."

"Cottage, not summer house."

"Whatever. The Ashtabula Sheriff's Department is really keeping the investigation hush-hush."

"Not hush-hush enough, evidently."

"A woman has to have her sources."

"Yeah, well, I have some work for you, if you can do it without attracting too much attention."

"I'm listening."

"I want a complete records check on a Gwendoline Hiltie, white female, born 9/21/61."

"Social Security number?"

I gave it to her.

"Anything else I should know?" Patty asked.

"Yes, the woman is recently deceased, and I do not want your inquiries to be associated with me in any manner, shape or form. Also, I want the information yesterday."

"Gotcha. When are you going to tell me the whole story?"

"Depends on weather conditions."

"Such as?"

"When hell freezes over."

"Bum. I'll get on it right away."

"Thanks."

I stared into space over the tops of my shoes. Since starting my own agency, I have worked with police all across the country. I was trying to think of someone on the West Coast who owed me a favor, or would at least do one for me. Finally, the old memory banks produced a name – Mark Wilson, San Bernadino County Sheriff's Department. We had worked an embezzlement case together a few years ago, becoming, if not friends, at least good acquaintances. I went into to Karen's office where I looked up Mark's number on her Rolodex. This was my lucky day; he was in his office. We exchanged pleasantries for a few minutes before settling down to business.

"Mark, I need a favor."

"Oh," he pronounced warily.

"It's a long story. Suffice to say someone tried to kill me Tuesday and pin a murder on me. It didn't work on both counts. The murdered woman spent a few years in the Los Angeles area, listing her employment as a free lance model/actress. I'd appreciate it if you would run her through your system to see what you come up with."

I could hear Wilson breathing, so I knew he was there. "Why aren't the locals making this inquiry?"

"They may contact L.A. directly, but it will be in a week or two. We don't exactly see eye to eye on the investigation."

"What the hell. It's only my career if I get caught. Give me your phone number. I'll call you back in about five minutes."

"I appreciate it."

I slowly counted the holes in my ceiling tiles while I waited for Wilson's call. I reached 452 before the phone rang.

"You owe me."

Ohio Salt

"I just placed your marker in the active file."

"Your girl has five arrests and two convictions, one misdemeanor and one felony. She was arrested twice for prostitution, no convictions. She was picked up three times for possession of cocaine; got off on one. Her first conviction was in 1991. The charge was reduced to possession of marijuana. She paid a fine and received probation. The last time was in January 1993. That time the judge wasn't so kind. He gave her a fine and sixty days to serve in the L.A. County jail. Oh, she also has a DUI conviction in August 1992. Her license was suspended for six months. You need any more detail?"

"No Mark, that's fine. I simply wanted to know what kind of a citizen she'd been out in the land of fruits and nuts."

"Not a really bad girl, but not one you would want to bring home to mother."

"You don't know my mother."

Frank C. Dupuy

17

The rain had stopped by the time I reached the intersection of Kinsman and 80th Street. This once thriving manufacturing and middle class area of Cleveland is now a high crime district with numerous abandoned and poorly maintained, aging buildings. I read the address Louie had given me. 805 80th Street. Slowly, I cruised the street searching for anything that resembled a street number. After several passes, I finally decided that a several story, dingy-brown brick building was in fact the one I was looking for. A rusted, sagging, eight foot high chain link fence surrounded the building while several battered signs proclaimed "No Trespassing."

I parked near the front gate which was loosely secured by a chain and a padlock. There was sufficient play in the gate to enable me to squeeze through it. If a security guard was on the property, I was unable to spot him. According to Karen Koenig, this building was owned by Ontario Enterprises.

Taking my time, I walked around the building. Most of the widows had been covered with sheets of green, corrugated fiberglass. The ones that hadn't been covered had been taken out by rocks. What had been the main entrance to the building was boarded over with weathered, rotting plywood. Evidently, the facility had been abandoned for a number of years. When I rounded the corner of the building, I observed a covered loading dock. A battered Chevrolet sedan was parked next to a flight of metal stairs that led to a truckers' entry door. I climbed the stairs and tried the door. It was unlocked.

As I opened the door, I could make out the murky interior which was dimly lit by dirty skylights and by light filtering through the green fiberglass window coverings. The building had been gutted years ago. Dangling wires showed where equipment, fixtures

Frank C. Dupuy

and electrical panels had been removed. Slowly, I scanned the building. I could hear a radio playing off to my left from what must have been the administrative offices. My footsteps echoed as I headed toward the source of the music, an easy listening station that was probably broadcast on elevators.

A central corridor led to a large open room containing a beat-up green metal desk and an old, wooden swivel desk chair. A security guard with his feet propped up on an overturned trash can was tilted back in the chair with his chin on his chest. The snoring indicated that he was alive. I kicked the side of the desk.

In his attempt to return to the world of the living, the guard knocked over the trash can and his chair as he fought his way to his feet. He required several seconds to realize that I was standing a few feet behind him. When he did, he jumped again.

"I uh, didn't hear you when you walked up," he stammered as he took in the fact that I was wearing a gray tweed sport coat, wool slacks and a conservative tie.

"I know."

"Who are you?" He hadn't made up his mind if I was someone in his company's management or someone he should inform about the no trespassing signs.

"Richard Rogers. Mr. Johnson told me that the security officer on duty would let me into the building." I graced him with a coldly disapproving frown. The guard, a white male in his thirties, whose uniform needed a trip to the cleaners, tried desperately to think of something to say. He was overweight, pale and needed a shave. If he had worked for me, I would have fired him on the spot.

"I wasn't expecting nobody."

"Obviously."

"I mean nobody told me you was coming." My stare was beginning to disconcert him.

"What is your name?"

"Bob, er, Robert Crannik, uh, sir."

"Well. Bob, Mr. Johnson, the gentleman whose company owns this building, told me that there would be a security guard here when I arrived and that you would be able to show me around."

"Around?"

"That's right, around. I am thinking of leasing the building."

Ohio Salt

"Gee, I wish I'd of known you was coming, I'd of met you at the gate."

"I see."

Bob's eyes swept the room desperately seeking divine intervention to bail him out of his current predicament. He was out of luck.

"I guess I could show you around Mr. uhh..."

"Rogers. That would be nice. The first thing you should do is unlock the front gate so I can bring my car in. This street isn't a good place to leave a car."

"No, sir, it sure isn't. I'll do that gate for you right away."

I followed Bob who was in a hurry to lead me out of the building and to open the gate for me. A couple of teenagers who should have been in school were surveying my rented Ford as we approached. With supreme indifference, they sauntered away. I started the car, then parked it next to the old Chevrolet.

"Lucky for you we came out when we did," Bob informed me after huffing and puffing himself back to the loading dock. "Another few minutes and those punks would have smashed out your windows, hot wired your car and been gone."

I nodded. "Is that why Mr. Johnson has a guard on duty?"

"I don't think so. We was told that all we had to do was to keep people outta here. The guy who owns this place is real particular about that."

"Do many people try to get into the building?"

"Not really. There's nothing to take. I've been here about nine months, and only one guy came messing around."

"Really?"

"Yeah, a skinny, funny lookin' guy who was dressed up like a priest or an undertaker. He said he was on some secret investigation. I ran him out and haven't seen him since."

"It takes all kinds. Did you call the police to arrest him?"

"Naw, our orders is to chase people away and write an incident report."

"Did you write one on the skinny guy?"

"I sure did," Bob nodded virtuously. "I wrote down every word he told me and even put in the cards he gave me. We don't have a telephone here, so I called the office from a pay phone. When

I asked them what they wanted me to do, they told me that a supervisor would pick up my report. Captain Morris came by before my shift was over and got it."

"Has Mr. Johnson ever been out here?"

"I don't think so."

"Well, Bob let's go inspect the building."

During the tour, Bob informed me that there was a security guard on duty only from 7:00 in the morning until 6:00 in the evening. He admitted that he was supposed to be stationed in the parking lot at all times, but since no one had ever come out, he protected the building from the inside. The patch on his uniform was from a fly by night guard company that specialized in supplying uniformed bodies for cheap.

"How much are they paying you, Bob?" I inquired solicitously.

"Below minimum," he mumbled, "and I have to buy my own uniforms. They don't pay time and a half neither."

I figured that Mr. Johnson was paying the guard company about $7.00 an hour for a body or about $2,400 a month to have someone keep trespassers out of the building. It didn't make any sense. There was nothing to steal, and any vandalism would probably take place at night.

"Bob do you know who owned this building before Mr. Johnson purchased it?"

"Yeah, I do. I grew up in this neighborhood. My old man used to work right down the street from here. That's when white guys could still get good payin' union jobs. It sure ain't like that today."

"Who owned the building?"

"The Catholic Church."

"What?"

"The Catholic Church. It was kind of a peculiar deal. Some Polish guy owned this place when it was a machine shop. They was doing pretty good until he disappeared or something. Anyway, he left everything to the Church. The Church didn't have much luck running the factory, so they sold all the machines. Then they leased the building as a warehouse. About a year ago, they put the place up for auction. I guess that's when Mr. Johnson bought it."

Ohio Salt

As Bob led me to my car he tugged my sleeve. "Uh, you ain't gonna mention that I was, uh, restin' to anybody, are you?"

I found myself confronting a down at the heels guy who was worried about hanging onto a job that paid $4.00 an hour. I felt sorry for him.

"As far as I'm concerned, I was never here. This building won't work for me. If you don't write a report, then it will be just as though nothing ever happened."

The man was visibly relieved. "If you ain't gonna say nuthin', then I'm sure not gonna say nuthin'." He waved at me as I drove away.

My next stop was 956 90th Street, which was conveniently near Kinsman as well. This building was in better shape than the one on 80th Street. A metal sign attached to the building proclaimed that I was looking at the T.M. Manufacturing Company. It was housed in a two-story brick structure that had been painted light green. The chain link fence surrounding the property appeared to have been recently repaired. On the side of the building, I perused two semi trailers backed up to loading dock bays. Only one vehicle, a mature Buick, was in the parking lot. Near the entrance gate, which was shut, rested an aging guard booth. I could see a head inside the booth. I parked the car in front of the gate and got out. An elderly security guard in a faded, but neat, uniform limped out to the gate and pushed it open a few feet.

"We're closed," he informed me.

"That's what Mr. Meyers told me."

The guard's brow wrinkled perplexedly.

"Ted Meyers owns this building," I explained helpfully.

"I wouldn't know. Besides the truck drivers, the only person I ever talk to is Mr. Fazio."

"Les Fazio works for Ted Meyers."

"Oh."

I noticed the way the guard wore his uniform. The shirt front was exactly lined up with his trouser fly while his belt buckle precisely touched the edge of the seam. Although faded, the uniform was clean and neatly pressed. It was a good bet he had been in the military.

"You get that limp in the Army?"

Frank C. Dupuy

"Nah, that was from a forklift accident. I was in Korea, though."

"Infantry?"

"Yes, sir. I was there with General MacArthur." The old man stood a little straighter. "You in the service?" he asked.

"Yep. Americal Division in Vietnam, 1969. 11th Light Infantry Brigade."

We regarded each other for a moment, then he extended his hand. "Henry Jirousek."

"Richard Rogers." We shook hands. I felt bad about lying to a fellow veteran.

"Henry, Ted Meyers mentioned that he might be interested in leasing some storage space to me. He told me to drop by and inspect the building when I was in the area. Well, I'm in the area."

Jirousek studied me for another moment before making up his mind. "You'd better bring your car inside. This is kind of a rough neighborhood."

Henry locked the gate behind me. In spite of his limp, he could move along at a respectable pace.

"There's not much to see, really. They don't do any manufacturing here. About two or three times a week they bring a trailer over to load or unload a few pallets of parts. Other than that, this place is dead."

The interior of the building was in fair shape. The paint on the walls was almost new; there were no dangling or loose wires where the machines had been removed. Henry conveyed me to the second floor on a huge, ancient freight elevator that creaked and groaned alarmingly. He didn't seem to notice. The second floor was totally empty. Feathers and pigeon droppings in the corners announced that the building was not totally unoccupied.

"Plenty of space," I commented.

"Yes, there is. It's a shame that all the jobs that used to be in these old buildings are gone."

"Henry, do you know how long Ted Meyers has owned this building?"

"Well, it would be about a year, I guess. That's when the Catholic Church sold all those buildings."

"Buildings?"

Ohio Salt

"Yeah, it was some deal where a guy left some property to the church. He must of died over thirty years ago. Anyway, this building was purchased from the church."

"Did the diocese own the buildings?"

"No, Saint Theresa's owned them. It's over on Broadway. I go to church there."

"It's funny that the Church waited so long to sell them."

"There was some odd clause in the will. The Church received the proceeds from renting the buildings, but if they sold them before 1993, everything went to some charity. Go figure."

We talked some more about the building as we walked through it. I never saw any likely hiding places for gold while I was there.

"You ever have any break-ins here?" I asked.

"No, I don't think so. I'm on duty from eight to five. After that, the building's on a burglar alarm." Henry pulled on his ear. "Now that you mention it, I did catch an oddball in here on Monday. I was making a round when I thought I heard a noise in the basement. As I was going down to look, this skinny guy all in black comes flying up the stairs. I hollered at him to stop, but he was running like a spotted ape." Henry chuckled. "My supervisor had come by to check on me. When he saw I wasn't in the guard shack, he came looking for me; this clown ran right into him."

"No kidding? Did you call the police"

"Nah, he hadn't hurt anything. He told us some cockamamie story about him being a private investigator. He gave us a card and I let him go." Henry paused. "I probably shouldn't have done that. When I called Mr. Fazio to report the incident, he was really steamed. He wanted to know all about the guy. I tried to tell him he was a nut case, but he was all upset that the guy was a P.I.. Between you and me, I think I know the guy's mother. She goes to Saint Theresa's. Maria Kolakowski. Nice lady." He shrugged. "Whatcha gonna do?"

Frank C. Dupuy

18

I pulled into the Bob Evan's parking lot at 5:59, parked, then walked into the restaurant. Louie Kolakowski was waiting for me in the outer vestibule, nervously pacing back and forth.

"How'd your research go?" I asked.

"We did pretty good. Karen kept the copies of the records we pulled, but I made notes for you," he replied, holding out a legal pad.

"Let's go over everything while we eat." I had missed lunch; suddenly I realized that I was hungry. I took it for granted Louie was too. He always is. The obliging hostess who seated us dispatched a waitress to our table immediately after I had explained we were on a tight schedule. As soon as we had ordered, Louie spoke.

"Ontario Enterprises was the easy one; they only own two pieces of property. The building on 80th street and a place over in Rocky River. I think it's a residence."

I felt my scalp prickle. "Where exactly in Rocky River?"

"2209 Lake Trail."

2209 Lake Trail was Gwen Hiltie's address.

"When was it purchased?"

"Let's see. November 3, 1992. I guess they paid cash because there aren't any liens on it. No liens on the 80th Street property either."

I had no idea what the relationship between Gwen Hiltie and the mysterious J.B. Johnson had been; however, I was willing to bet it had been more than spiritual. A Lexus and an apartment were fairly sizeable tokens of affection.

"What did you find out about Ted Meyers's empire?"

"That was more complicated, 'cause the guy has a zillion companies. Anyway, we found out that his companies own about three dozen pieces of property in Cuyahoga County. Every one of them has multiple liens on it except for the one on 80th Street. It only has one."

"Oh? Who has that lien?"

"OmniBank. The property was purchased in January 1993, and the lien was filed in March 1993."

"How much did Meyers pay for the building?"

"$176,000. Saint Theresa let all those buildings go cheap."

"Which buildings?"

"The ones Count Petrowski left to the Church in his will – four of them, counting his house."

The evening was starting to evoke a certain surreal atmosphere.

"Louie," I entreated with more patience than I felt, "Why didn't you tell me about this earlier?"

" 'Cause you never asked. Anyway when we see my mom, she'll give you the lowdown on everything."

I stifled a groan.

The Immaculate Heart of Mary nursing home was housed in a modest, single-story brick building in Maple Heights. The drizzle, and the fact that I was seeing the place in the dark, did not enhance its appeal. The first thing I noticed when I walked in was how clean and bright everything appeared. The second thing was the faint, but unmistakable smell of urine. About a dozen old people were gathered in front of a large screen television. Some were seated in wheelchairs; those who were ambulatory had canes or walkers next to their chairs. A pleasant woman at a desk near the entrance smiled as we passed her.

"That's Mrs. Welsnik," Louie confided in a stage whisper, "I don't think she recognizes me."

I nodded as I tried to overcome my claustrophobia. Nursing homes bother me more than hospitals. Louie Kolakowski was apparently familiar with the layout as he strode confidently down the corridor. The door marked 16-C was slightly ajar. Louie gently pushed it open and approached an elderly woman who was reclining in a hospital bed. At first, I thought she was asleep, then realized that her lips were moving. A moment later I realized that she was holding an old-fashioned rosary, the kind with dark wooden beads the size of marbles. Louie bent down and kissed her cheek.

"Hi, mom."

The woman turned her head, squinting questioningly at Louie. Then her face crinkled into a happy smile.

"Oh, Louie, your disguise is wonderful. Your father would have been proud of you."

I took a good look at Mrs. Kolakowski, observing a thin, dark-eyed woman in her seventies wearing a pink bathrobe with ornate embroidering. Her iron gray hair was pulled back in a pony tail. She was as pale as Louie, though I was not certain if it was from her illness or if it was a trait she had passed on to her son. The lines around her eyes and mouth had been produced by smiling. It took her a moment to realize her son had brought company.

"You must be Mr. LeBlanc. Louie has told me so much about you. I can't tell you how much it means to me to have a famous man like you helping my son." She held out a slender hand which I gently pressed with mine.

"It is a pleasure to meet you, Mrs. Kolakowski."

Louie placed his hand on his mother's shoulder. "Mom, it's time to tell Adrian what's going on."

Maria Kolakowski peered at me as though she could divine my innermost thoughts. For all I knew, maybe she could. Finally she nodded at Louie who carried a chair over to the bed.

"Please sit down, Mr. LeBlanc. I have a story to tell you that involves honor, deceit, a fortune in gold, and treason."

Maria Kolakowski motioned to her son. "Help me sit up, Louie."

Louie slipped an arm under his mother and slid her further up in the bed. A spasm of pain crossed her face.

"I am dying, Mr. LeBlanc." she stated matter-of-factly. "I rather think that my heart will give out before the cancer gets me. I have had a heart malady for many years, though I have managed to surprise my doctor by living this long."

I couldn't think of anything to say, so remained silent. I decided that Louie's mother had learned her English in Great Britain. Besides her British inflections, she had a slight European accent.

"I am an old woman," she continued, "if I live another month, I shall be seventy-five." She glanced sadly at Louie. "I had

Frank C. Dupuy

hoped to live long enough to see my son's children. Well, I mustn't complain. I have had a rich life.

"Mr. LeBlanc, I was born in Lithuania in 1919. My father, a French diplomat, married my mother while he was stationed there. We traveled extensively, my parents making certain that I learned the language of each country we lived in. I spoke six languages by the time I was eighteen. My parents insisted that I attend an English university. Unlike many Frenchmen, my father had the utmost respect for the English. I was at Oxford when the Germans invaded Poland. When they occupied France, my father, who was a senior diplomat, would not collaborate with the Vichy government; he was arrested along with my mother. I did not find out until the end of the war that my parents had died in a concentration camp run by the French." Her expression indicated what she thought of the French.

"In December 1939, a few weeks after the Germans had defeated Poland, one of my professors invited me to dine at his house. When I asked why, he told me he wanted to introduce me to some people who might be interested in my language skills. The people he introduced me to were a mixed bag of military men and Oxford dons who were forming what would become the nucleus of the British espionage effort.

"The meeting ended my academic career. I was recruited that night and spent the entire war decoding and translating enemy transmissions, including messages our Russian 'allies' did not want us to know about. It was all very exciting for a young woman. Very hush-hush. I was even taken to a range where they trained me to use a pistol to protect myself from enemy agents. My superiors were worried I knew too many secrets.

"When the war ended, I learned that my parents had died. I couldn't return to Lithuania, and post-war France had no appeal. For my efforts during the war, I was given a commendation and British citizenship. I decided that I would immigrate to Canada. It was a young country where I could make a new start. While I was in Montreal, I met Louie's father. He was a magnificent man, a war hero and so handsome. We fell in love and were married." She paused, smiling. "Louie's father was proud of being Polish, but he insisted on changing his first name, Casimir, to 'something pronounceable'. He chose John because it was acceptable to most

Ohio Salt

Canadians and Americans.

"In 1948, John and I immigrated to the United States where, through contacts, he was given a job as an assistant to Count Petrowski.

"Do you love your country, Mr. LeBlanc?"

The unexpected question left me momentarily speechless. It is not something I am frequently asked. Images of the IRS, dishonest politicians and a society that seems to have lost its way flashed through my mind. Finally, I answered.

"Yes, I suppose I do. Flaws and all."

Maria Kolakowski nodded. "That is a reasoned answer. With Count Petrowski, it was unreasoned love. He was totally committed to Poland. His every effort was to ensure that one day the Communists would be overthrown so that he could return home.

"Many historians will tell you that World War II was actually a continuation of World War I. I agree with that. Between the wars, Europe was leaderless. The economy was in ruins and no one wanted to risk another war. The few people who comprehended what was happening in Germany knew that if something was not done, total conflict was inevitable. Count Petrowski understood better than most how vulnerable his country was. Besides being a nobleman, he was a career soldier. He urged his countrymen to arm themselves with modern weapons, but only a few people listened. As Hitler's armies grew, Count Petrowski organized a group of businessmen, soldiers, politicians and diplomats to create a contingency fund in case the unthinkable happened. The money was to be used to finance a resistance movement. The men he recruited were sworn to secrecy, pledging to devote their lives to freeing Poland if it was invaded.

"Although events moved faster than even the Count anticipated, he was able to move over two tons of gold to the United States before the invasion. Even at $35 an ounce, that was over $2,000,000, a sizeable fortune in the late 1930s. Through his connections, including the Polish ambassador to the United States, he was appointed military attaché to the embassy in Washington. Count Petrowski used diplomatic couriers to bring the gold to the U.S."

"Wait a minute, why gold? Why not simply use bank drafts?"

Louie's mother conferred a pitying look upon me. "Bank

drafts leave trails; they are not secret. The funds could have been traced, perhaps confiscated. Gold is universally accepted, and it can be hidden. 4,000 pounds of gold is fairly compact"

Louie's mother, I decided, was as squirrelly as he was. "Mrs. Kolakowski, this is an interesting story, but I'd like to know what it is based on. Where did you get your facts?"

"Why from Count Petrowski. John had served under him before the war. When he came to work for him in 1948, it was John's responsibility to move the gold to Cuba."

"What?"

"Please. Let me tell the story in my own fashion. The gold was hidden in the United States before the invasion. Believing that war was inevitable, Count Petrowski returned to Poland to be given command of an armored unit as a colonel. Compared to what the Germans possessed, the Poles were pitifully equipped. My husband was a lieutenant in the count's unit. When the Blitzkrieg came, many of the Polish armored vehicles were destroyed by dive bombers before they even had a chance to fight. John's unit fought as infantry after their tanks were demolished. It was no use. In less than a month, the Germans had conquered Poland.

In the first weeks of the fighting, the count was horribly wounded, eventually losing a leg. He ordered John to help him escape. When Count Petrowski realized that all was lost, his only hope was to survive to organize a resistance. John told me that it was a miracle that the count lived. Through a series of narrow escapes, my husband and the Count reached the coast, where John commandeered a tiny fishing boat he sailed to Denmark. John left the count in Denmark, before making his way to England where he immediately joined the British army, even though he did not speak a word of English. He went through their commando training, participating in many raids before the D-Day invasion. When the British organized army units made up of Polish refugees, John transferred to a Polish paratrooper brigade and was made an officer. By the end of the war he was a major.

"Count Petrowski eventually recovered from his injuries. After being turned down by the British when he tried to enlist, he contacted some of the American officers he had met when he was the military attaché in Washington. He was given a commission in Army intelligence, ending up working for William Donovan. Do you know who Mr. Donovan was?"

"Yes, Wild Bill Donovan. He was the head of the OSS and, I believe, the first CIA director."

"Exactly. This turned out to be an extremely crucial contact. During the war Winston Churchill was totally dedicated to eradicating the Nazis. Though he was a great leader, he was a shortsighted fool. He gave away eastern Europe to Josef Stalin to encourage Stalin to fight a war he was already committed to." She sighed. "In many ways, the Communists under Stalin were worse that the Nazis. When Count Petrowski realized that his homeland had been betrayed by Great Britain, the very country that had gone to war over the invasion of Poland, he was devastated. He decided that the West could not be trusted any more than the Communists, yet he allied himself with the Americans after the war because they had finally realized that communism was a global threat."

Something was nagging at me. Then it clicked. "Did you meet Count Petrowski during the war?"

"See, mom? I told you Adrian was good." Louie beamed at me. I don't think he noticed his mother's sharp glance.

"Yes, I did. I was transferred to work with the OSS in 1944. I met Count Petrowski then."

"Who landed your husband a job with the count after the war?"

"I did, Mr. LeBlanc. Times were hard for us in Canada. John had been a professional soldier all of his life; he was having difficulty finding a job that suited him. I contacted Stan, er, Count Petrowski and arranged for him and John to meet."

"Stan?" I inquired, arching an eyebrow.

"Stanislas." She sighed again. "He preferred that his friends call him Stan. He never used his title unless he thought it aided him in business affairs."

"Mrs. Kolakowski, are you trying to con me?"

"A little," she smiled, "I need your help. Count sounds so much more impressive than Stan, don't you think?"

It was my turn to smile. I had never been conned by a dying woman before. "Yes, Count is more impressive. As long as we are dropping titles, why don't you call me Adrian?"

Frank C. Dupuy

"Thank you. I shall. Now, where were we?"

"Your husband was going to work for Stan."

"Oh, yes. The late 40s and all of the 50s were great years for the anti-Communists. While America was engaged in the Cold War, the CIA under Mr. Donovan could do pretty much as it liked. One of the things it liked to do was hire part-timers to perform its dirty work. Stan used this to his advantage. He was a brilliant man.

"A few of the members of his pre-war group had survived. Stan set about building his own network of Polish patriots. The first thing he required was funding. Although he had two tons of gold, he needed a way to convert it into cash. In those years, Cuba was controlled by Batista, a brutal, corrupt dictator who catered to wealthy land owners and foreign business interests.

Obtaining a charter for a bank in Cuba was as simple as paying a few bribes. John's first assignment was to establish a bank in Cuba, then smuggle the gold from Florida to Havana. It took a month to secure the charter, two weeks to purchase a bank building with a vault, and less than 24 hours to smuggle the gold, once everything was in place.

"Stan began making loans to the surviving members of his pre-war group to build businesses in Latin America and Europe. The companies served dual functions. They made money for the cause and served as fronts for the CIA. The CIA used its influence to channel legitimate business to the new companies. They flourished.

"At the same time, Stan wanted to do something for Polish refugees. He had decided, for a number of reasons, that Cleveland was an ideal base for his operations. Part of its appeal was its sizeable Polish community. Stan founded three manufacturing companies. Almost all of his contracts were supplied through CIA influence. He hired only Polish immigrants who had resisted the Nazis and the Communists. The people he employed were good workers, not to mention excellent sources of information about Poles who had collaborated with the Nazis.

"Stan compiled a list of collaborators. Many who had helped the Nazis prospered under the Communists. Adrian, you must understand how many Poles were killed and tortured under the Nazis. It was monstrous. Hitler believed that the Polish people were

Ohio Salt

sub-human, that they should be bred like cattle to serve the master race. Much of what the Nazis accomplished was due to traitors who collaborated against their own people. After the war, many of these same vermin ingratiated themselves to the Communists, rising within the government. My husband trained retribution teams."

"Retribution teams?" I asked.

"Hit squads, if you will. Their duty was to target collaborators and kill them. The easiest way was to wait until they traveled outside of Poland to a western country. The problem was that the Communists restricted travel and, after a dozen or so collaborators were killed outside of Poland, the rest were reluctant to leave the country. A few teams were infiltrated into Poland; they managed to assassinate another sixteen traitors. Unfortunately, several of the teams were captured. You can imagine their fate. Anyway, by 1953, it had become too difficult to continue the retribution program; besides, most of the worst collaborators had been eliminated.

"Stan was pragmatic; he initiated a long range program to unseat the Communists. He was very influential in working with Voice of America and Radio Free Europe, not to mention spending thousands of dollars of his own money printing and smuggling propaganda into Poland. As the cold war progressed, Stan and his resistance group prospered. To tell the truth, most of the group had lost their desire to fight communism by the mid fifties. They were more intent on amassing wealth."

Maria Kolakowski stopped talking and licked her lips. "Louie, be a dear and hand me that glass." Louie handed his mother a glass of water with a drinking straw in it. She gingerly sipped the water before handing the glass back. Then she closed her eyes and sagged against her mattress. I looked at Louie.

"It's alright. She's just resting," he assured me, although his expression registered concern. After a few minutes, his mother opened her eyes.

"Forgive me. Sometimes, I tire easily."

"Mrs. Kolakowski, we can let you rest and come back another time," I said.

"No," she responded fiercely, "You must hear me out."

"Please continue."

"Fidel Castro was thought to be a hero of democracy when he

Frank C. Dupuy

started his revolution against the Batista regime. Once again, Stan correctly predicted the events that followed. He transferred most of the bank's assets out of Cuba months before Castro's forces captured Havana. His warnings to the CIA and the State Department that Castro was a Communist went unheeded.

"When John Kennedy became President, he was committed to ridding Cuba of its Communist regime. The ill-fated Bay of Pigs invasion was orchestrated by the CIA, though Mr. Hoover's FBI had a finger in that pie. Before the CIA, Cuba had been the FBI's jurisdiction, and Mr. Hoover never gave up anything gracefully.

Stan and my husband were instrumental in establishing commando-type training for the Cuban refugees. John hired several former members of his old unit to function as drill instructors. The CIA paid well and was delighted to have refugees from a communist country training other anti-Communists. Some of John's former comrades actually landed in Cuba with the invasion force." Maria Kolakowski's gaze dropped to her hands.

"There are men who were in the United States government who have much to answer for. In contradiction to President Kennedy's orders, many of the soldiers in the invasion force were Batista supporters, corrupt men who had caused the revolution. Factions within the CIA and the FBI were at cross purposes with their president. As a result, the U.S. government organized and trained an invasion force of splintered Cuban factions to overthrow an inconvenient Communist government. As the invasion forces prepared for the landing, they were promised air support. At the last moment, after the invasion was under way, the air support was canceled. Because of infighting in the U.S. government, 1,200 brave men were either slaughtered or captured. My husband lost many friends on April 17, 1961. The worst thing was that someone in the intelligence community made certain that the invasion would fail. In addition to canceling the air support, someone provided Castro detailed plans of the invasion several weeks before it was launched.

"It was almost a year after the invasion that Stan and John realized the extent of the betrayal. They began to put bits and pieces of information together, reaching the conclusion that they had been double-crossed by some of the very men who had recruited them to train the Cubans."

Ohio Salt

"What did they do?" I was intrigued in spite of myself.

"What they did, was to quietly amass details of the invasion to determine exactly who had circumvented the President's orders and who was directly responsible for canceling the air support. Stan and John became obsessed with this. They were determined to ferret out the betrayers and expose them.

"Late in the summer of 1963, John and Stan traveled to Mexico to interview a defector from the Castro government. If you remember your history, Castro eliminated most of his early group of revolutionary comrades. A few were astute enough to escape before they fell out of favor. The man they spoke with confirmed that Castro had been given the invasion plans several weeks before the invasion. He evidently furnished them enough information to identify the man who had supplied the plans. The Cuban was paid for his information. At the end of the interview, he told Stan that for an additional $20,000, he would give them information that was vital to the United States. They dickered on price before agreeing that Stan would pay half when he heard the story. If he felt the information was valid, he would provide the other half. The man told Stan and John that there was a plot to assassinate the President. The Cuban promised to meet with them the next day to provide details when he received his money. The Cuban never made it to the second meeting. His throat was cut that night.

"When John returned home, he was extremely agitated. He revealed that he believed there was a plot to assassinate President Kennedy and that for my sake he would not tell me any more. It was the first time since we had been married that John would not confide in me. After that, Stan and John began leaving town for days at a time. When I asked John what he was doing, he refused to tell me; he said I would be in danger if I knew the details.

"Early in the morning on November 21, 1963, John left the house stating that he was going to meet Stan, that they might be gone for a few days. He did something he almost never did. He took a pistol with him. I never heard from my husband again."

Maria Kolakowski stopped talking and motioned to Louie, who handed her the glass of water.

"Do you have any idea what happened to him?"

"I didn't, but I always suspected it was connected to the Kennedy assassination. JFK was murdered on November 22, 1963."

I hoped that my skepticism did not show.

"What did you do after your husband disappeared?"

"When the horrible news that the President had been assassinated was broadcast, I instinctively knew that Stan and John had been involved somehow in trying to prevent it."

"You didn't think that maybe they had something to do with it? Maybe they were sore over being sold out at the Bay of Pigs."

"Never, never, never. You would have to know my husband. John was a loyal American. He would never have done such a thing. Besides, he and Stan had tried to warn the government about a plot. John never told me directly, but he hinted that there were men within the government who wanted Kennedy dead."

"OK, so what did you do after your husband disappeared?"

"You have to remember that the entire nation was in shock. The disappearance of two immigrants was not a priority with the police. When I told the police that John and Stan had worked for the CIA, they refused to believe me. They said they had made some calls and were told that neither the CIA nor the FBI had ever heard of them. I would not give up. I wrote letters to the FBI, the CIA, my congressman and the newspapers. They considered me to be a crazy woman. I was beginning to think so too, until my daughter was kidnaped."

"Oh?"

"I got two older sisters," Louie informed me.

"My eldest daughter, Katherine, was in the sixth grade at that time. In February, 1964, she was on her way home from St. Theresa's school when she was abducted by two men. They put her in a car, blindfolded her, and took her to an abandoned house. When Katherine didn't show up after school, I was frantic. I had the police, my neighbors and everybody looking for her. Then, I received a telephone call at 5:00 that afternoon. When I answered the telephone a man with a muffled voice told me where I could find Katherine. He told me to come alone. I did. When I arrived at the house, the front door was unlocked. I found Katherine in the kitchen tied to a chair. Thank God, she had not been harmed. As soon as I reached home, the telephone rang. It was the same man. He informed me that this was a friendly warning. That the next time something awful would happen to all of my children if I caused trouble. I asked what he meant. He told me to accept the fact that my husband would not be coming back, that if I caused anymore inquiries to be made, my children would join their father."

"What did you do?"

"I quit making inquiries. I gave up trying to discover what had happened to my husband until two months ago."

"That's when she found the papers," Louie interrupted.

His mother shot him another glance. "Yes, I found several boxes of documents in the basement. One of the walls was cracking, so I called a contractor to fix it. When he was examining the wall, he found a hollow spot behind the bricks. Three steel boxes were in the hollow."

"Actually, they were three old ammo cans," said Louie. "You know, the green ones with the rubber liner in the lid. These were big 'cause they were for 20mm shells."

Maria Kolakowski ignored her son. "The boxes contained John's diaries. He had documented all of his activities with Stan. The last entry was on November 16, 1963. I read everything John had written. I was tempted to do nothing with the information. Then, a few weeks ago, I went to my doctor. I had been feeling ill, thinking maybe my heart was getting worse. He ran tests and discovered the evil news. I have cancer that has metastasized. It is untreatable. Even if I took chemo treatments, it would only prolong my suffering for a short time; besides, the chemicals are hard on the system. With my heart, the treatments would probably shorten my life.

"Well, my daughters are grown and living in other states with their families. Louie is the only one who is single, the only one who might be able to do something with this information."

"What information is that?"

"The location of a fortune in gold and the identity of the men who were responsible for the assassination of John F. Kennedy."

Frank C. Dupuy

19

The mug that I had just washed and dried stared tiredly back at me from the mirror, reflecting each one of my forty-five years. Making a face, I decided that even if I wouldn't win any beauty contests, I at least wouldn't scare too many babies. For the record, my hair is still in place even if the brown is starting to be invaded by white, although the frosting has not reached my moustache. If crowns are counted, I still have all of my teeth. Having reached that stage in life where I have to watch what I eat, I work out four times a week in a futile effort to hold back the effects of aging and gravity. I have managed to hold my weight to 160 pounds, in spite of my build, which was inherited from a short, broad shouldered French ancestor who eventually settled in Louisiana. Sighing, I went into the kitchen and poured myself a glass of wine from the bottle I had opened last night.

The telephone rang.

"Will you accept a collect call from Jules LeBlanc?"

"Yes."

"Go ahead, sir."

"Dad?"

"Hi, son. Where are you?"

"A really weird place called Lily Dale."

"Where?"

"Lily Dale. It's in New York, near Lake Chautauqua."

"What's going on?"

"Well, we're staying at this old hotel – it's the only one here, in a psychic community."

"Huh?"

"This was Mom's idea. Lily Dale is a place where a bunch of psychics live. They give readings. They tell you who you used to be."

"Huh?"

"It's like reincarnation stuff. Anyway, Mom says we're here to find out things. She's starting to weird out, like she says that I used to be her father and you were her brother and we still have to work things out from past lives."

"Jules, has your mother been drinking?"

"Just fruit juice. She says she's fasting to purify her system."

"Has anyone tried to do anything to you?"

"Not really. I'm supposed to go for a reading tomorrow. This place is real quiet and peaceful. People come here to be healed spiritually with crystals and things."

I groaned. "Is your mother there?"

"No, I snuck out to find a pay phone. Mom's at a meditation seminar or something. They have lots of talks and stuff. Anyway, she didn't tell me not to call you."

"Do you want me to come get you?"

"Not really. This place is kind of cool and I've met some interesting people. I just wanted to let you know where we were so you wouldn't worry."

"Thanks son. I appreciate that. Anything else?"

"No, I guess that's it. I love you, Dad."

"I love you, too, son. Kiss your mother for me."

"OK."

We hung up. Psychics? What in the hell had possessed Jeannie? She had never in her life mentioned an interest in psychics or reincarnation. A lukewarm relationship with the Episcopal church was the known extent of her spirituality. I shook my head, then decided that my wife would never do anything to harm Jules. Oh well, the experience would probably expand his horizons.

I glanced at my watch. 8:40. I had promised to call Harold Lipscomb before 9:00. He answered on the second ring. I told him what I had found out about Gwen Hiltie's past. He listened without comment. Then I asked my questions.

"When you first met Gwen, was she living at the apartment in Rocky River?"

"No, she was living in Mentor with her parents. She moved to her apartment about a month after she came to work for us."

"What kind of a car did she drive?"

Ohio Salt

"She had a Ford Tempo. It was a few years old."

"You ever seen her in a white Lexus?"

"No, although there was one parked in the driveway by her apartment house. I assumed it belonged to a neighbor."

"Can you have your accountant print a list of all of your vendors and customers?"

"I suppose so. You do understand that is highly sensitive information. Do you mind telling me why you want it?"

"It's just a hunch. I promise I'll take care of the information."

"Very well. Come by my office in the morning. I'll have a printout for you."

We said good night and hung up.

Without Jeannie and Jules, the house was unnaturally quiet. I drifted off into a fitful sleep, dreaming about demented psychics chasing me with flaming crystals.

Frank C. Dupuy

20

Friday

I awoke to another drizzly Ohio day. A cold front had moved in and the temperature was only supposed to creep into the upper forties. I shivered, vowing that one day I would move back to the Gulf South where spring acted like spring. I was headed into Cleveland to Newport Industries when my pager went off. It was my office.

My office telephone was answered by an all too familiar male voice.

"The Agincourt Company. May I help you?"

"Louie, where's Karen?"

"She ran out to the bakery."

"The bakery?"

"Yeah, to get us some muffins."

I tried not to curse. "Who paged me?"

"I did. A man named Collin Yates wants you to call him."

I punched in Collin's number. I was too preoccupied to bother with a pay phone.

"Hello, Adrian. As we speak, the Ashtabula County Sheriff's department is releasing the identity of the woman you found."

"They're saying it was Gwen Hiltie?"

"Yes. They ID-ed her from medical records and a tattoo. Evidently she had a butterfly tattoo at the base of her spine. Also, Hiltie had broken her clavicle while she was in high school. The coroner took X-rays and compared them to her old ones. They matched. Oh, Hiltie was an unwed mother the year she graduated from high school. The coroner confirmed that the corpse had given birth in the past.

Frank C. Dupuy

"Nice. She have any relatives?"

"Yes, her parents live in Mentor. They were told last night."

"Anything else?"

"As a matter of fact, yes. The cause of death was multiple gunshot wounds to the head. Additionally, the coroner stated that the body showed signs of sexual penetration. The kicker is, whoever she had sex with used a condom."

"How could the coroner tell that?"

"It seems that it was a condom lubricated with a spermicide. He found traces of the lubricant in the vagina. He can't be sure until the lab results are in, but he is fairly certain."

"Collin, how do you know all of this?"

"I was told unofficially by a man who uses his initials. I think he wants your unofficial assistance."

I thought that one over. J.C. Jensen must not have too much faith in the detectives assigned to the case. I couldn't blame him. It took me less than two minutes to brief Collin on what I had found out and what I planned to do. He gave me a non-committal "Do as you think best," and hung up.

The corporate offices for Newport Industries are located in a three-story office building on Cleveland's west side. I guessed that the building, which was immaculately maintained, had been built in the 60s. When I entered the lobby, it was evident that the interior decorator had been instructed to be practical, not creative. The effect was to enlighten visitors that they were in a building where business was conducted. I gave my name to a courteous receptionist who asked me if I wanted a cup of coffee while I waited. I declined. In less than a minute, an efficient woman in her early forties introduced herself, then escorted me to Harold Lipscomb's office.

Lipscomb stood up as I walked in, extending his hand.

"Good morning, LeBlanc. Please, have a seat." With that, he punched a button on his telephone.

"Harry, will you bring me those reports?"

A few moments later, a tall man in his early thirties sauntered into the office carrying a stack of computer paper. The resemblance to his father was noticeable; however, the younger man had the build of a football player who was going to seed, with shoulders only slightly wider than his waist. His face was heavier than his father's,

Ohio Salt

and it was scowling.

"Mr. LeBlanc, I would like you to meet my son, Harry. Mr. LeBlanc is doing some work for me," Lipscomb stated, confirming that I was in the presence of Harold Lipscomb, Jr., one of Newport Industries' vice presidents. I proffered my hand which was reluctantly accepted by Harry. He had not made vice president on his charm.

"What kind of work are you doing?" he demanded.

"Consulting."

"Harry, it is a private matter," his father informed him. "Did you pull the reports I asked you to?"

"Yeah, I have them right here," Junior answered, making no move to hand them to anyone.

"Good. Please give them to Mr. LeBlanc."

Harry's eyes shifted from me to his father. "Dad, these printouts contain the names and addresses of all of our vendors and customers. We can't give these to an outsider."

"Harry, hand me the reports." The glint in Dad's eye must have done the trick. Junior relinquished them with poor grace.

"Thank you. Now, Mr. LeBlanc and I have things to discuss." With that, Harry grimaced in my direction and stalked out. I rose and shut the office door.

"I apologize for my son. He is sometimes overly protective of the business." Lipscomb handed me the reports which I tucked into my briefcase "Will you tell me why you want these?"

"Gwen Hiltie was driving a car that was registered to a corporation the day she came to my office. I wanted to see if it was anyone you do business with."

"What was the name of the corporation?"

Lipscomb did not need to know everything I knew, at least not yet.

"I prefer not to say."

He glared, started to say something, then thought better of it.

"Very well. Call me this evening."

I was dismissed. As I exited the building, I was confronted by Harold Lipscomb, Jr..

"LeBlanc, I want to know what you're doing here."

"It's none of your business."

"It is if it involves this company. I'm a vice president, and I have a right to know."

"You are a vice president because your daddy made you one. If you want to know, go ask Daddy."

Harry's complexion metamorphosed into an interesting shade of vermilion. His big hands clenched.

"You little shit. I can take you apart."

I'd like to think that I controlled my complexion better than Harry, although I did feel the back of my neck warming up.

"You're welcome to try, sonny, or can you do anything without a note from Daddy?"

"You son of a bitch!" Junior bellowed as he charged me with outstretched hands reaching for my throat. Just as his fingers grazed my necktie, I brought my briefcase up in a short, vicious arc that caught him squarely in the crotch. There was a moment of stunned silence before the nerve endings conveyed the entire story to his brain. When the neurons connected, Harry emitted an agonized oof before clutching his crotch as he toppled over. I stepped around him as I strode to my car. A muffled "mother fucker" drifted past my ears as I drove away.

21

OmniBank was everything a modern financial institution should be, an impersonal conglomerate built on dozens of smaller banks that had been merged out of existence. The gleaming tower housing its corporate offices was impressive. I wondered if the stockholders were pleased with it. I found the bank of elevators that serviced the 18th floor, entered an elegant car and punched the appropriate button before being swiftly conveyed to said floor, which happens to house the office of Daniel D. Dutton, Vice President of Bank Protective Services. For those of you who don't speak bankese, that means security. Also, being a vice president in a bank is about as exclusive as a lifeboat in a shipwreck. If Danny and I hadn't been drinking acquaintances, I might have been more impressed.

Molly, his secretary, smiled when she spotted me. "Adrian, how are you? You shouldn't stay away so long."

"If I weren't married, I'd be here every day."

"Ha! Are you looking for Dan?"

"Alas, yes. Is his nibs in?"

"Yes, I'll tell him you're here."

She spoke into her receiver. A moment later, the office door behind her desk opened to reveal a man of medium height, weight, coloring and build, dressed in a dark gray Brook Brothers suit and black Johnson & Murphy wingtips. When he had been a detective, Dan Dutton possessed the knack of blending in anywhere. Today, he was in his Mr. Bank Executive mode. He grinned when he saw me.

"My goodness, I hadn't realized that the parole board had met. When did they let you out?"

"Yesterday. My mother sent them a note. They released me in spite of her objections."

Frank C. Dupuy

Molly interrupted. "You take your coffee black, right?"

"I certainly do. Marry me."

Dan and I traded banter for a few minutes while we waited for Molly to bring coffee. We had known each other for over a dozen years, ever since I had been the Corporate Director of Loss Prevention (security) for Erie Bank and Trust. We still get together for a drink every few months. Molly brought in coffee, appropriately served in black and gold OmniBank mugs, then she closed the door behind her.

"I hear you've been finding dead people in Ashtabula."

"Gee, a fella can't keep any secrets." I proceeded to furnish Dan the condensed version of what had happened, including the fact that Ted Meyers had set me up and, later, threatened my family. Dan took everything in without changing his expression. When I had finished, he arched an eyebrow.

"Your visit here wouldn't have anything to do with your recent adventures?"

"Possibly."

"How possibly?"

"I want to look at Meyers's loan file, especially the documentation."

"Oh, is that all? Just an itty bitty favor that could get me fired, sued and/or prosecuted?"

"You could end up a hero."

"Yeah, a dead one."

"Look, if I'm right, your bank may be the victim of a massive fraud. Not only that, you probably have a crooked loan officer."

Dutton leaned back in his chair, expressing his unhappiness by nibbling on his bottom lip. Finally, he sat up propping his elbows on his desk. "Tell me what I'm looking for; I'll let you know if I find anything."

"Nope."

"What do you mean, nope?"

"I mean I need to look at the file. Look, you big shot bankers hire consultants all the time. Why not let me be a fraud consultant?"

"In your dreams, LeBlanc." He frowned into his coffee mug as if searching for inspiration. "How certain are you that it's bogus?"

"Ninety percent." I can lie with a straight face.

"And you can tell simply by looking at the file if it's bad?"

"I'll have to see the documentation."

"Jeez, the things I do for people. When do you want to see the file?

"Now would be good."

"C'mon, this is a bank, remember? I'll have Molly locate the file, then send one of my investigators to get it. If I'm lucky, I may have it on my desk first thing in the morning."

"Thanks, Danny, I appreciate it."

"Thanks, Danny, my ass. If I let you look at this file, the deal is that you level with me. Capisce? You give me your word you'll tell me everything?"

"I give you my word."

"OK, I'll see you in the morning."

"Oops, I almost forgot. While you're at it, see if Ontario Enterprises has an account with you."

"Get out of here!"

"You'll check?"

"Yes, now scram while I still have a job."

Frank C. Dupuy

22

It was almost 10:30 when I parked in front of 2209 Lake Trail in Rocky River, the abode of the deceased Gwen Hiltie. The entrances to the first floor apartments were sheltered by a large front porch. I knocked on the door of apartment A. No one answered. I tried B. The door was opened by a gray-haired woman wearing a pink cardigan over an old-fashioned blue dress. Faded blue eyes scrutinized me, registering that I was wearing a coat and tie.

"May I help you?"

"Yes, ma'am. My name is Adrian LeBlanc. I'm a private investigator. I'd like to ask you a few questions about one of your neighbors." I handed her my card.

"You mean that poor Hiltie woman? It was on the news this morning."

"Yes, ma'am."

"Are you working with the police? I talked to a detective yesterday. He didn't tell me she had died."

"Did you speak with Detective Kules?"

"Yes, I believe that was his name. He was from Ashtabula."

"I've been hired by a friend of the family, Mrs....?"

"Glicksman, Cynthia Glicksman."

"Do you mind answering some questions? It might help us find out who did this."

"Certainly." Mrs. Glicksman appraised me again before making up her mind. "Come in. We can talk in the front room."

She ushered me into a neatly furnished room that contained a couch and two upholstered chairs. She seated me on the couch.

"Now, ask your questions; I'll tell you what I know."

"How long have you lived here?"

"About six months. I sold my home after my husband died.

Frank C. Dupuy

The house was simply too much for me to take care of."

"I see. How well did you know Gwen Hiltie?"

"Oh, not very well. We spoke in passing. She only lived here a few months, you know. She was such a pretty girl. Once she came by to ask if she could park her car in my parking spot. I told her that was fine because I don't have a car."

"What kind of car did she have?"

"She had two, actually. When she first moved here, she had a little red car, a Ford, I believe. Then, about a month ago, she bought a fancy white car. That's when she asked me if she could use my parking spot."

"Did she ever have any friends visit her?"

Mrs. Glicksman's eyes narrowed, then she sighed. "I don't suppose it matters now, but, yes, she had a gentleman friend who came over two or three evenings a week. He never spent the night, if you know what I mean. I assumed he was a married man."

"Did you ever get a good look at him?"

"Oh, I saw him often enough. He was a tall man, older than her. He drove a big, dark car. It wasn't a Cadillac. Maybe a Lincoln."

"Did you ever see any other people visit her?"

"A couple of times. I remember that about a week before she disappeared, she had a fight with a man."

"You mean the man she was seeing?"

"No, it was somebody else. I heard them shouting. The man got really loud and used vulgar language. I had her telephone number, so I called her. When she answered, I asked if she needed help. I told her I would call the police if she did. She told me no, the man was leaving. A few minutes later, I heard a door slam, then this man stormed out. When he got into that little sports car, he squealed the tires when he left."

"Did you get a good look at the man?"

"No, it was dark and he was wearing a winter coat. I had the impression that he was a big man."

"Could you identify his car?"

"It was a sports car, the kind with only two seats. I couldn't see the color clearly, but it was dark. It might have been black or dark blue."

Ohio Salt

"Was that the only time you saw this man?"

"It's the only time I actually saw him. I saw his sports car parked on the street a couple of times, but I never saw him."

"Were there any other visitors?"

"A few times a woman came to see her in the evenings. Because it was dark, I couldn't see her too well. She was kind of tall for a woman, kind of like Gwen Hiltie."

"Within the last week did you hear any unusual noises coming from her apartment, like somebody was looking for something?"

"Not that I can recall. I was staying with my sister in Toledo on Monday and Tuesday. My nephew drove me there. Milly twisted her ankle, so I went to keep her company."

"Who is your landlord?"

"Walters Realty. They manage the apartments. I don't know who owns them. That's how I found this apartment. Walters sold my house for me."

I cursed silently. J.B. Johnson, the elusive owner of Ontario enterprises, was always a step ahead of me.

"Did the detective go into Gwen's apartment?"

"I believe he did. I could hear him moving around for almost an hour."

Mrs. Glicksman and I spoke for another ten minutes. She didn't impart any additional information. When I left her apartment, I walked around to the back of the house. I still had the key to Hiltie's apartment Lipscomb had given me. It took me all of thirty seconds to decide that I wanted to have a look. Now that the police had searched it, I figured a quick peek wouldn't hurt anything.

When I turned the key in the lock, the door opened noiselessly. It was a safe bet that Mrs. Glicksman could tell the police to the minute how long I had been in the apartment if they ever bothered to ask. The interior of the apartment was exactly like I had seen it on Wednesday – a total mess. Whoever had gone through it had been thorough. I wondered if they had found whatever it was they were looking for. I spotted a telephone on the floor, next to the desk. It had been disconnected. I moved the desk so that I could examine the telephone jack. A brown box was connected to the jack with two wires coming out of it. Next to the phone jack was an electrical outlet with a Radio Shack transformer plugged into it, the type

Frank C. Dupuy

used to provide DC power for battery operated devices. I consumed several fruitless minutes trying to locate the tape recorder that had been connected to her phone.

Next to the far wall, a hefty, oak antique bookcase had been overturned. Various books and knickknacks were strewn beside it. You can learn a lot about a person by her reading habits. With a heave that Mrs. Glicksman was certain to have heard, I set the bookcase on its base. Glass shards from smashed picture frames made kneeling hazardous as I gingerly sorted through the books on the floor. Hiltie's tastes ran to Harlequin romances, New Age spiritual awareness and a half dozen paperbacks from the Amazon Press. It took me a moment to realize I was looking at works from a publisher that catered to lesbians.

The photos inside the broken frames were snapshots of what I assumed were family gatherings. A large, hard cover book was partially obscured by fallen mementos. It was the 1979 Mentor High School yearbook. After shaking off the glass splinters, I turned to the seniors where I located a picture of a young, but attractive, Gwen Hiltie. Setting the yearbook on the desk, I thumbed through it casually until I came to a photo of the girls' basketball team. Hiltie was one of the players. I scanned the other girls in the picture, then froze. I flipped back to the senior pictures to make certain. There staring back at me was the smiling face of Sally Yuhas, Ashtabula County Sheriff's Detective Sally Yuhas.

23

My pager buzzed, informing me that I was wanted at the office. This time Karen answered.

"How were the muffins?"

"Oh, they were fine. Uh, how did you know about that?"

"Louie answered the phone while you were out."

"Oh. Well, I paged you because you have a phone call from Patty Stone. She says she has some information for you."

"Anything else?"

"Yes. You and Louie have an appointment with Mike Ungar tonight."

"He agreed to see us?"

"Yes, he was very pleasant."

"What time?"

"8:00. He wants you to meet him at Hunter's Tavern in Chagrin Falls."

"Why there?"

"He says he lives in Chagrin Falls."

"Good reason. Karen, I want you to take Louie to a mall and buy him a few more things to wear. His clothes are probably getting a little ripe."

"I washed and ironed everything last night."

"Wonderful. Well, buy him a few shirts and another pair of Dockers. I want him to have some clothes in case we have to travel for a few days. And remember, this is my money you're spending."

"I know. That's what makes it fun."

I called Patty Stone.

"High there, handsome. I have news for you."

"Shoot."

"Gwendoline Lois Hiltie was a woman of many parts."

Frank C. Dupuy

"How many?"

"In high school, she was a good student and a better athlete. She ran track, played basketball, volleyball, and baseball. Nobody knew it, but she was three months pregnant when she graduated. She had an affair with one of her teachers, had a baby and gave it up for adoption. The teacher was fired; he did about a year for statutory rape. No one knows what happened to him. Before she got pregnant, she was involved in a bit of a scandal. It seems she was caught in a compromising position with another student on a field trip."

"Well, at least he was her own age."

"Not he. She, dearie."

"How did you find this out?"

"Sources. My cousin graduated from Mentor High in 1979."

"Did your cousin give you the name of the other student, perchance?"

"Certainly. It was Sally Yuhas. Detective Yuhas to you. It seems they were an item for a while. My cousin says Gwendoline also liked boys. Go figure."

"What else?"

"Gwen Hiltie attended Cuyahoga Community College part time while she was pregnant. After she had the baby, she went full time earning an associates degree. Graduated with honors. Apparently, she got her act together because she landed a job at the Cleveland Yacht Club where she was a rising star – until she acquired a taste for cocaine. Seems she was having an affair with a high roller who hooked her on nose-candy. Anyway, there was an accusation that she stole money from the club, probably to support her habit. She resigned, or was fired, depending on who you talk to. She left town. I heard she went to California."

"That's it?"

"What do you mean, "that's it?" I moved heaven and hell to get you this information, buster."

"And a damn fine moving job it was. You didn't happen to catch the name of the man she had the affair with at the yacht club did you?"

"No, I didn't. My source couldn't remember."

"You did your usual excellent job, Patty. Thank you. Fax me

Ohio Salt

a bill and I'll have Karen cut you a check."

"Thank you, Mr. LeBlanc. Fast pay makes fast friends."

I called Collin Yates. He was out so I left a message with his secretary. I asked Collin to find out who at the yacht club had introduced Gwen Hiltie to cocaine. I was fairly certain I knew the culprit's identity.

Instead of returning to my office, I turned down E. 93 in Cleveland and proceeded to 721 Reno Street, the residence of one Joseph Jablonski, retired custodian from St. Theresa's Catholic School and former member of John Kolakowski's paratrooper unit. Louie's mother had told me that Jablonski had been with her husband and Stan Petrowski in south Florida in 1961, helping them train Cubans for the Bay of Pigs invasion. I thought back to my conversation with a dying, determined woman.

"Some of the men my husband and Stan would have confided in are dead," Maria Kolakowski told me, "and others I would not trust. One of the men my husband trusted was Joseph Jablonski. He functioned as Stan's valet and orderly; he was utterly devoted to him. John told me that Joseph had been a sergeant in the paratroopers and was with him when they dropped into Normandy. He said Joseph was an excellent NCO, brave, reliable and totally lacking in imagination. Joseph contacted my husband in the early 50s to see if he could help him find work. One thing led to another; Joseph became Stan's shadow. He took care of Stan's house, clothes, car or whatever else Stan needed. John and Stan sometimes took Joseph with them on their 'business' trips. John once told me that 'if you ever need someone to watch your back, Joseph is the man to have.'

"After Stan and my husband disappeared, Joseph was distraught. He was like a lost soul."

"Did you ever ask him what happened to your husband?"

"I did before my daughter was kidnaped. He claimed he couldn't tell me anything, though I always believed he knew much more than he ever admitted. After the kidnaping, I never asked him again, at least not until I found John's diaries.

"When Stan and John disappeared, I was contacted by Stan's attorney, Milo Frankiewicz. He told me Stan had left provisions on how his businesses were to be handled in the event of his death or absence for more than two months. I believe Stan had a premonition that something would happen to him. He never took much money for himself, even though he was a wealthy man. Stan left instructions that his assets were to be given to the Catholic Church. In his will, St. Theresa's Church was given the revenues from the factories and his house for twenty-nine years. The income was to go to the school. At the end of twenty-nine years, the property could be sold with the parish keeping the proceeds. If the school closed, or if the property was sold before twenty-nine years, the proceeds went to the Salvation Army." She smiled. "You can be assured that the Church would never allow that to happen.

"Milo Frankiewicz informed me that Stan wanted to insure that St. Theresa continued to support its school. Stan was a strong advocate of church run schools. Unfortunately, when he died, most of the contracts the CIA had directed to his factories were canceled. Within two years of Stan and John's disappearance, the factories closed and the Church sold of all of the equipment. Over the years, St. Theresa's had managed to earn an income by renting the properties. Last year, the Church finally sold the old factory sites and Stan's house."

Maria Kolakowski gave a small shrug. "It was as though Stan knew what would happen. The diocese announced last month that they will close St. Theresa's school after this semester. Stan's endowment was the only reason it lasted this long. It is such a shame that the beautiful grotto that he built at the school will probably be torn down."

"What grotto?" I asked.

"Stan believed that he owed his life to the intercession of the Virgin Mary. He said he had a vision when he was wounded. The doctors thought he would die; instead he recovered, claiming that he had seen the Virgin and that she had prayed for him. In 1951, Stan built a magnificent grotto to her on the grounds of St. Theresa's school."

"He sounds like he was very religious."

"In some ways, when it was convenient."

"I'm curious. Were Stan and John ever declared legally dead?"

"Eventually. It required seven years before the court would

Ohio Salt

issue a death certificate."

"I take it you didn't receive any insurance when your husband died?"

"My children and I were provided with a small annuity that Stan had purchased for us in the event of John's death or disappearance. In addition, the mortgage on the house was paid. I had to go to work, but we managed fairly well, didn't we, Louie?"

"We did, Mom. You always took care of us." Louie appeared as though he were about to cry. I changed the subject.

"Joseph Jablonski tried to call me Tuesday night. On Wednesday morning, he told my secretary that he was coming to my office, then never showed up. Do you have any idea why he called me?"

"Yes. I told him to."

My sense of reality was diminishing by the minute. It seemed that I was being masterfully manipulated by a seriously ill, little old lady.

"Any particular reason why you told him to call me?"

"Mr. LeBlanc, Louie and I had already talked this over. We needed help; you were the only person we could trust who has the skills to pursue this. You are my son's friend. I know this is an imposition, but we are desperate."

She had me and she knew it. With the best grace I could muster, I said, "I will do what I can. Tell me why you asked Mr. Jablonski to call me."

"After Stan's disappearance, Joseph went to work for St. Theresa's as the custodian. He looked after the school as though it were his duty to Stan. Joseph must be eighty years old, yet he didn't retire until last year. Anyway, when I read the last few weeks of John's diaries, it was apparent that Joseph must have known all of the people that Stan and John had spoken to. I called Joseph to ask him to visit me. He did. I told him I had found John's diaries. I demanded that he tell me what he knew about my husband's disappearance.

"Joseph adamantly denied knowing anything until I told him I was dying. I told him it would be a sin to let me die without telling me what had happened to my husband. At last he agreed to tell me a few things. He stated that Stan and John had learned of a plot to assassinate Kennedy; that the men behind it were in the U.S. government. He claimed that they were ruthless and powerful. I reminded Joseph that it had been thirty years since the assassination, that by now most of the men involved were retired or dead. He told me he would have to think about what to do. When I asked what he had to think about, Joseph confided that he had a dilemma. He asked me for advice."

"What was his dilemma?"

"Stan had entrusted Joseph with a secret. He had confided the location of 'emergency funds' to Joseph. In the event of Stan's death, he was to contact whoever from the old group of Polish patriots was working to overthrow the Communists. Joseph was to make the money available to that person. The problem was, that after Stan disappeared, no one from the old group was doing anything to liberate Poland from the Communists. So, Joseph, like a good soldier, kept his mouth shut and waited. While he was waiting, Poland became a democracy. For thirty years he has known the location of a hidden fortune."

"Excuse me, but how much are we talking about?"

"Over $5,000,000. I finally persuaded Joseph to tell me the entire story. Shortly before Castro overthrew Batista, Stan converted some of the bank's money to gold, then smuggled it back into this country. Joseph believes that it was roughly half a ton. At today's prices, 16,000 ounces of gold is conservatively $5,600,000."

"Are you trying to tell me that some old janitor has sat on a fortune for thirty years because he couldn't figure out who to give it to?"

"Yes. You would have to know Joseph to understand. He was, and is, totally loyal to Stan's orders."

"Yeah? Then why didn't he say something when Stan and your husband disappeared? Why didn't he blow the whistle on the bad guys?"

"He didn't have any proof. He kept waiting for Stan to come back. He didn't want to believe that he was dead. After Katherine was kidnaped, Joseph decided that he couldn't fight the government. I told him what had happened and what the man who called had said. Without Stan, Joseph didn't know what to do, so he kept silent."

Ohio Salt

    I shook my head. "Mrs. Kolakowski, forgive me, but I am having a hard time believing this story. For the sake of argument, let's say I do believe you, why would Joseph Jablonski talk to me after thirty years of silence?"

    "He will talk to you because I told him you are the man who will bring justice to the men who murdered Stan and John. He will talk to you because I told him you would finish what Stan and my husband started." Maria Kolakowski was sitting straight up in her bed, her eyes blazing. "You must help me! I have set the wheels in motion. The assassins and the traitors will surface, I promise you. I have dangled a bait they cannot resist." She coughed twice, then collapsed against the mattress. "Please," she whispered, "do not let my sacrifice be in vain."

    "What sacrifice?"

    "Me. I am the bait. The assassins will come to kill me."

Frank C. Dupuy

24

The 700 block of Reno Street was trying desperately to hang onto its Eastern European ethnicity. The row houses probably had been built in the late 20s or early 30s by people who thought that one set of blueprints would be sufficient for an entire neighborhood. The homes were all two story frame buildings with large, covered front porches. The tiny front yards were neatly maintained; judging by the occasional bicycle or tricycle on the porches, younger families were staying in the old neighborhood. The only thing distinctive about 721 was that the front door had been painted a bright blue.

I stood on the front porch, listening for a moment before I pushed the door bell. The house was quiet. The sound of the door bell ringing in the interior of the house was clearly audible from where I was standing. I waited, then rang again. Nothing. I checked my watch. 12:14. I wondered if Mr. Jablonski had gone out to lunch. Walking around to the side of the house, I located another entrance. I opened the screen door and rapped a heavy wooden door with my knuckles. It swung slowly open at my touch. An unpleasant odor wafted out of the house. You don't have to be an expert to know what death smells like.

After stepping through the door, I had the choice of walking up a short flight of steps to the first floor or down a long flight to the basement. I opted for up. At the top of the steps, I poked my head through a doorway and found myself peering into a kitchen. A bowl of soup and two bread rolls were on the table. The soup and the bread appeared to have been sitting out for a few days. Slowly, I explored the first floor. Mr. Joseph Jablonski's home was furnished with old, but well maintained, furniture. The house was in perfect order except that every drawer, cupboard and closet had been opened, with the contents neatly laid on the floor. Whoever had searched the house had taken their time. I found a large blood stain on the threadbare carpet by the front door. It had turned black, but was not totally dry. Reluctantly, I climbed the stairs to the second floor. The same neat, methodical search had been conducted in both bedrooms. I didn't spot any blood stains; however, the same putrid odor I had smelled when I first opened the door permeated the house.

I returned to the kitchen, debating whether I should call the police or descend the steps into the basement. I lost the debate. Peering down the steps into the darkness did not cheer me up. Fortunately, I located a light switch. The glow at the bottom of the steps was reassuring. As my foot touched the basement floor, the stench intensified. An old-fashioned furnace was located in the center of the basement. Behind it was a smaller room that had been the coal cellar. I removed my handkerchief from my pocket and pressed it tightly over my nose. I located another light switch on the wall and flipped it. A light came on in the small room.

Finding Gwen Hiltie's mutilated body was horrible. What I found in Joseph Jablonski's coal cellar was depravity. I stepped through the door – and gagged. It required all my concentration not to add the contents of my stomach to the vileness in that little room. A heavy, old fashioned work bench covered most of the far wall. What had been a gaunt, raw boned old man was tied to it. His arms were spread eagle, fastened with nylon rope to the rear legs of the bench. He was face up with the small of his back pressed against the front edge of the work surface. The wood had cut deeply into it. He was wearing an old pair of faded blue work pants. His upper torso was bare. A large pool of thick, blackened blood had formed on both sides of the work bench; misshapen objects protruded from the mess. It took a moment before I realized what I was seeing. When I did, I gagged again. The man's fingers had been cut off; they were lying in the puddles beneath his hands. A pair of long-handled pruning shears lay on the floor near the work bench. Its blades were smeared with clotted blood.

At some point the old man's sphincter and bladder had given way, adding their contents to the fluids on the floor. A knotted shop rag was in his mouth. I could imagine his muffled screams as his fingers were lopped off, one by one. Whatever the monster who had

Ohio Salt

done this had wanted, the old man had not given it to him. He had died in agony rather than betray his long dead boss. I hoped Stan Petrowski appreciated Joseph Jablonski's sacrifice.

Frank C. Dupuy

25

It was almost 4:00 by the time the cops let me go. I had given them a detailed statement as to what I knew about Joseph Jablonski, and why he had contacted me. I basically told the truth, stating that I had been retained by the Kolakowski family to research the disappearance of John Kolakowski and Stanislas Petrowski. The cops corroborated that Mr. Jablonski had placed several calls with my answering service on Tuesday night. Two Cleveland detectives from the 4th District were handling the investigation. The younger one, Mullins, was a thin man in his mid-thirties with curly red hair, whose facial features fluctuated between mournful and resigned. His partner, Green, a thick-bodied black man in his early fifties, seemed to be counting the days to his retirement. I found out I was mistaken about Green.

"Tell me the name of your client again," prompted Mullins.

"Mrs. Maria Kolakowski. She is in the Immaculate Heart of Mary nursing home in Maple Heights."

"Kolakowski, Kolakowski," mused Green. "I wonder if she's any relation to that bird who claimed people were shooting at him over lost gold?"

"Her son's name is Louie, and, yes, he told me somebody tried to shoot him on Tuesday afternoon."

The two detectives exchanged glances. "You think that this murder was related to the shooting?"

"It's a good possibility."

"And I thought he was just a harmless nut," muttered Mullins. "Now we gotta take him seriously. You know where we can find him?"

"No, I don't. He calls my office once a day, though. It's my impression that he's hiding out in the southern part of the state."

"Yeah, well the next time he calls, have him call us."

"OK."

Mullins and Green were not too enthusiastic about putting down anything in their report pertaining to mythical lost gold from WWII; I couldn't blame them. They accepted my story that I was trying to bring closure to an old case for a dying woman. While we were talking, a technician from SIU (Scientific Investigation Unit) tapped Green on the shoulder.

"Judging by the blood on the floor, I'd say the old man's been dead for at least two days."

"Yeah, well my nose told me that much," Green stated. "Has the coroner made any guesses about the cause of death? Did the old man bleed to death?"

"All he told me was that it was amazing a man that old could take so much abuse before dying. Jablonski would have been eighty-one in July."

Green laid a heavy hand on my shoulder. "Why don't you and I step out into the back yard for some fresh air?"

"Fine."

We walked out of the kitchen to the back of the house where I saw a six foot high grotto made out of fist-sized rocks that had been cemented together. A small statue of the Virgin Mary was inside of it. Green examined it for a moment.

"That looks like a miniature of the one at St. Theresa's school."

"That's where Mr. Jablonski used to work."

"Yeah, I know." Green reached into his sport coat pocket, then produced a cheap cigar with a wooden mouth piece. He lit it with a green Bic lighter and exhaled two large clouds of smoke before speaking.

"You know how long I've been a cop?"

"No."

"Twenty-nine years. In that time I thought I had seen just about everything, but I gotta tell you what I saw in that basement was the worst. Now, the druggies do bad things to each other – it's part of the culture. But even the slimiest don't take the time to do what was done to that old man." He eyed me speculatively. "You ever seen anything like that before?"

"Not that bad."

"I guess a woman with her face blown off by a shotgun doesn't compare, does it?"

"It wasn't very pleasant."

"It wasn't very pleasant," he mimicked me. "You make it a habit of finding corpses of people who've been mutilated?" He was still puffing lazily on his cigar, but his eyes had taken on a glittering hardness.

"No."

"You passed a polygraph in Ashtabula. That don't mean shit to me. The lie box can be beat."

I didn't say anything.

"I recognized your name from the news. While Mullins was taking your statement I called the Ashtabula S.O., talked to a Detective Yuhas. She doesn't like you very much."

"Considering the source, I'll take that as a compliment."

"Yeah, well, I'm trying to figure out how a professional, such as yourself, manages to find two people who were tortured to death in one week."

"The woman wasn't tortured to death. She was beaten and burned. I'm guessing they used cigarettes on her. She was killed when she was shot in the face by a shotgun. The people who hurt her weren't in the same league as the ones who cut off the old man's fingers."

"You know or you just guessing?"

"Guessing. I don't think the murders are related."

Green knocked the ash off of his cigar.

"You know what pisses me off?"

"No."

"Smart-ass P.I.s who don't tell the whole story."

Neither one of us spoke for several minutes.

"The people who tortured the old man took their time," Green informed me. "Dopers would have ransacked the house. I've never seen a house so neatly or thoroughly searched before. Have you?"

"No."

"For someone to take that much time tells me three things. One, the guy, or guys, were professionals. Amateurs aren't that methodical. Two, for them to take that much time, and to do what they did to Jablonski, they must have wanted something real bad. And, three, the old man must have thought his secret was important enough to die for. Now, suppose you tell me what an eighty year old, retired custodian had that was important enough for someone to torture him to death."

I now harbored no doubts that Green was anything other than a hard-working, hard-nosed cop. I wondered how he would react to what I was about to tell him.

"He may have known the location of over $5,000,000 in gold."

"Wait a minute; you tryin' to tell me that Kolakowski kid was on the level? That he was shot at because he was looking for $5,000,000 in gold?"

"It's possible."

"Alright, LeBlanc, it is time for you to quit bullshitting. Tell me what's going on here."

I sighed. "I'll tell you, but I'm not putting it in writing, and I want your word that you won't have me locked up as a loony."

Green grunted. "Hmph. Talk."

So I did. I told him almost everything Maria Kolakowski had told me, including the part about the conspiracy to assassinate Kennedy. He was on his second cigar when I finished. His expression indicated that he had encountered a new species of nut.

"How long did it take you to make up that story?"

"Look, Green, you asked and I told. I didn't say I believed it. I told you everything I know."

"Sure you did. So how does this tie in with the murdered broad in Ashtabula?"

"I don't know that they are connected."

"Yeah, well for my money they're connected, and you're the connection. Now, Ashtabula can take care of its own problems, but I gotta take care of mine. I don't buy your story; if I thought it would help, I'd haul your ass in."

"It wouldn't help."

"Yeah, Yuhas told me you got a high price lawyer."

"Look, Green, I don't like this any more than you. I was pushed into taking this case by Mrs. Kolakowski. All I did was come by to talk to Mr. Jablonski. When I knocked on the side door, it

Ohio Salt

opened and I smelled a terrible odor. I went in to see if anyone needed help, found the body, then called the cops. That's all I did; I've told you what I was told. Can I go now?"

He chucked his cigar butt on the ground. "Yeah, get the fuck outta here."

Frank C. Dupuy

26

I called my office. Karen Koenig answered.

"Karen, is Louie there?"

"Yes, would you like to speak with him?"

"No. Now listen carefully. I want you and Louie to go to the nursing home and spring his mother. Then I want the three of you to go to Carl Branner's house and stay there. Don't go to your house and make certain that you aren't followed. I want you and Louie to go now."

"Adrian, what's wrong?"

"Mrs. Kolakowski is what's wrong. She concocted a scheme to smoke out the people who killed her husband. Well, she succeeded better than she expected to. I'm just now leaving Joseph Jablonski's house. He's been dead for two days. He died after somebody cut off all of his fingers."

"How awful!"

"Karen, you know where I keep the revolver in my office?"

"Yes."

"Take it with you. Be careful. It's loaded."

"I'll be careful. What about you? Are you still meeting with Mike Ungar?"

"Yep."

"Do you want Louie to meet you there?"

"No. You and Louie take care of his mother. And Karen,"

"Yes?"

"For God's sake be careful. Whoever killed Jablonski won't hesitate to kill again."

I hung up, then called Carl Branner.

"Branner residence."

"Carl, it's Adrian, how are you?"

"Fine, or as fine as an old man can be."

"I need a favor; I'm warning you in advance that it may be dangerous."

"Thank God! I've been so bored lately."

I briefly explained my problem. Then I gave him some names to research.

It was a little after five before I reached my house. The dogs barked their appreciation at my return. They would have come out to greet me in the driveway, but were prevented by the limits of their Invisible Fence, the only device I have ever installed that they cannot dig under or chew through. With as much speed as I could muster, I fed them and changed their water. After that, I went into my basement where I unlocked my gun safe. Unlike Hollywood private eyes, I seldom carry a pistol. The State of Ohio has laws against carrying concealed weapons, and does not grant exemptions to private investigators.

I removed a Smith and Wesson .38 Chiefs Special from a shelf and loaded it. The Chiefs Special is a five shot revolver with a two inch barrel that has the advantage of being reliable, yet concealable. Carefully, I threaded a holster onto my belt and slipped five extra bullets into my pocket. I stared into the safe for a moment before deciding to humor my paranoia. Opening a small wooden box, I extracted a vintage Browning .25 automatic, a tiny, powerless popgun that fits nicely between my belt and the small of my back. Thus armed, Two-Gun LeBlanc donned his sports coat and returned upstairs to admire himself in the mirror. The weaponry did not show.

I telephoned Collin Yates. His secretary put me through immediately.

"Hello, Adrian, how are you?"

"Fine, Collin. I have a few things to discuss with you, but first, did you find out who introduced Gwen Hiltie to cocaine at the yacht club?"

"Rumor has it that it was Ted Meyers. Evidently, Meyers is one of those characters who can take or leave cocaine. From what I can determine, he is a recreational user, his idea of recreation being to get his partners high while having sex."

"Collin, I'm surprised. Is that a hint of disapproval I detect in your voice?"

"More than a hint."

"Good for you. Now, I need you to contact J.C. Jensen. Find out if Gwen Hiltie had cocaine in her system. Also, Hiltie was wearing a large diamond ring on her right hand when she came to my office. Ask J.C. if they found the ring in the mess that had been her hands."

"All right."

"I'm going to share something with you that you are not to tell J.C., at least not yet."

"Oh?"

"Detective Sally Yuhas and Gwen Hiltie went to high school together. In fact, they were lovers in high school."

"What?"

"Yeah, evidently Hiltie went both ways."

"You never fail to amaze me."

"There's more. I talked to Hiltie's neighbor, Cynthia Glicksman. She's a sharp-eyed widow who doesn't miss much. She told me she had been interviewed by Fred Kules sans his partner. She also told me that Hiltie had a female visitor on several occasions. I have a base, low mind, so I'm willing to bet it was my favorite detective, Sally Yuhas."

"Interesting. Have you drawn any conclusions?"

"Not yet. By the by, I had a small adventure today."

"How small?" I hate it when my own attorney is apprehensive.

"I found the body of an old man in the basement of his house. He had been tied to a work bench; his fingers had been cut off with pruning shears. I gave a statement to the police who are not happy with my story; however there's not much they can say because it's true."

"Adrian, what are you talking about? Does this have anything to do with the Gwen Hiltie murder?"

"Not directly, although that's only a guess. Collin, I need a favor. I want you to interview a woman tonight, then I want you to give me your opinion as to whether or not she should be committed or," I paused, "if she has stumbled onto one of the best kept secrets of the century."

Frank C. Dupuy

"What are you talking about?"

"Humor me. With a little luck, she and her son and Karen Koenig will be at Carl Branner's house in Akron in about an hour."

I gave Collin directions after extracting a promise that he would talk to Maria Kolakowski. With that, I left my house to meet with Mike Ungar, retired FBI agent and former confidant of one Count Stanislas Petrowski.

27

Chagrin Falls, located about fifteen miles east of Cleveland, is a picturesque town of prosperous citizens who do their best to preserve its New England atmosphere. Mike Ungar had asked me to meet him at Hunter's Tavern, a cozy establishment popular with the L.L. Bean crowd. Under normal circumstances, I would have considered two pistols to be overdressed for most Chagrin Falls restaurants.

I parked at the far end of the large parking lot Hunter's Tavern shares with a number of other trendy shops and eateries. The clock in my rented Ford informed me that it was 6:55. After scanning the area and not spotting anything obvious, I decided to meander through the shops while keeping an eye on the parking lot. I took my briefcase with me. The earlier drizzle had given way to a dull, overcast sky which harmonized with my mood.

Michael Ungar, whose name had originally been Ungarski, was the son of a Polish industrialist who had contributed money to Count Petrowski's contingency fund. The elder Ungarski had sent his wife and children to the U.S. about a month before the Germans invaded Poland. He had been executed by the Gestapo shortly after the Blitzkrieg. Michael was eight years old when his father died. On his eighteenth birthday, Michael became a U.S. citizen and changed his name to Ungar. He attended Notre Dame on a scholarship, graduating with a degree in Romance languages in only three years. At twenty-one, he joined the Army, received a commission and arrived in Korea in time to see some serious combat. He was wounded, receiving several citations for valor. As soon as his enlistment was up, Ungar applied to the FBI and was accepted. Because of his fluency in French, Italian, Spanish, Portuguese and Romanian, not to mention Polish, he was assigned to counter-intelligence.

Maria Kolakowski had been introduced to Mike's mother in

Frank C. Dupuy

1948. Evidently, Stan Petrowski had made it a point to look after the families of his old group. According to Mrs. Kolakowski, Stan provided part of the scholarship money for Ungar and had pulled strings to help him into the FBI. Stan Petrowski had assisted several sons of his friends land FBI and CIA appointments, partly from altruism, but mostly to insure he maintained reliable sources within those agencies.

In the late 1950s, Mike Ungar was stationed in the FBI field office in Havana where he collaborated, unofficially, with Petrowski's network. Ungar was a rising star within the Bureau. With his war record and solid work in counter-intelligence, he was the youngest agent ever assigned to one of J. Edgar's "special projects" teams. The existence and purpose of these teams were never made known to Congress, although the director considered the team members to be his handpicked warriors in the fight against communism.

All of this was told to me by Maria Kolakowski. She asserted that her husband and Ungar had worked together closely when John Kolakowski was training Cuban refugees for the Bay of Pigs invasion.

"John and Stan were so proud of Mike. They viewed him as their protégé, doing their best to provide him with information that would enhance his career. Of course, Stan wanted to insure his continued access to government agencies by cultivating a new generation of agents."

"Where is he now?"

"In the Cleveland area. Michael left the FBI about 1968, when Congress began probing the activities of Hoover's "special teams." He went to work for the State Department training counter-insurgency units in Latin America where he developed close ties to the Somoza regime in Nicaragua, eventually becoming their head of security. After Somoza was ousted, Michael formed his own company to consult with countries having problems with terrorists and insurgency. He often had the blessing of our government. Nowadays, Michael's clients are mostly multi-national companies. Not many Communist groups are real threats anymore."

I asked Mrs. Kolakowski how many people Stan and John had confided in regarding the assassination plot.

"I don't know, exactly. John's diary sometimes referred to

people by a code name or only by a first name. Two of the men he mentioned are dead. I have been able to identify three who are still alive: Milo Frankiewicz, Stan's attorney; Michael Ungar; and Stephen Wlosowicz."

She went on to provide concise accounts of all three men, although she was better acquainted with Ungar and Frankiewicz than Wlosowicz. Milo Frankiewicz had been a twenty-one year old student in Poland when he led a protest against the Communists in 1946. He managed to escape and immigrated to the U.S. where he eventually obtained his law degree in 1953. Frankiewicz devoted part of his practice to aiding immigrants and working with groups that assisted dissidents in escaping from Communist countries. His and Stan Petrowski's paths crossed in 1954. Petrowski was sufficiently impressed with Frankiewicz's sincerity to place him on a retainer. From that time on, Frankiewicz handled all of Petrowski's legal affairs, ultimately serving as the treasurer of Petrowski's Cleveland companies.

"He was more than simply Stan's attorney. He was his confidant. Stan trusted Milo's judgment, conferring with him on many matters, including some of the 'dark' business Stan was engaged in." Maria Kolakowski focused on the foot of her bed. "Milo and I have never discussed it, but I believe that he was silenced by threats to his family at the time my daughter was kidnaped. He hinted to me that someone had brought pressure to bear on him through his family.

"When John and Stan disappeared, Milo was having personal problems. He is a sensitive man; I believe that he took to heart the problems of the people he was trying to help. He became an alcoholic, and it affected his work. A few months before John and Stan disappeared, Milo's wife left him. I know that he, John and Stan had words shortly before they disappeared. Milo always regretted never having a chance to make amends."

"What happened to him?"

"The shock of John and Stan's disappearance brought Milo back from the edge. He was in charge of disposing of Stan's assets. Evidently, the companies' financial condition had not been the best when Stan vanished. When the CIA-sponsored contracts ran out, the companies foundered and had to be liquidated. As you know, the money went to the Church.

Frank C. Dupuy

"Milo and his wife never divorced, but they remained separated. He was devoted to his children, always maintaining close ties. In fact, his oldest son has taken over his practice."

"Milo is retired?"

"Partially. He still goes to his office for a few hours during the week and on Saturdays to take care of his older clients, especially the ones who have never mastered English. Milo was never good at making money, though his son is doing better."

"What about Stephen Wlosowicz?"

"A complicated man, he was a university professor before the Blitzkrieg. His wife and child were killed when the Lutwaffe bombed and strafed a road that was packed with refugees fleeing the German advance. Stephen survived and escaped to enlist in England to fight the Nazis. After being wounded early in the war, he was transferred to intelligence where he became involved in analyzing aerial photographs. Someone recognized he had a gift for analysis that went beyond photo interpretation. Stephen became what would later be known as an intelligence analyst.

"Although many Polish expatriates were fighting under the British, relatively few were in military intelligence, and they sought each other out. Stan made it a point to meet Poles involved in intelligence and cultivate their friendship. Then, as now, success depended almost as much on informal contacts as on departmental chain of command. Stan and Stephen became fast friends. They were very much alike in that they could deduce future events from relatively little hard data. After the war, Stephen continued to work as an analyst, first for U.S. military intelligence and finally for the CIA."

"What was Wlosowicz a professor of?"

"Theology. In fact, his code name was 'The Priest,' although I think it had to do more with his aesthetic life style than with his theology."

"What happened to him?"

"After suffering a nervous breakdown in 1965, he left the CIA and went into teaching. Stephen retired a few years ago from Loyola; the last I heard, he is living in Florida."

"He sounds like the absent-minded professor."

Mrs. Kolakowski shook her head. "Not at all. Stephen was an

ambitious, calculating man before his breakdown. He had advanced rapidly within the CIA; it was his unit that discovered the Russians intended to install missiles in Cuba. He had extremely hardline views about the Communists, being adamantly opposed to anything that furthered their cause."

"How did Wlosowicz react to the news that someone had slipped Castro the Bay of Pigs invasion plans?"

"I don't know. John's diaries never mentioned how Stephen or any of the others reacted."

I regarded the frail woman in the pink dressing gown, trying to figure out what was going through her mind. For all of her guileless demeanor, she was not telling me everything she knew, not by a long shot.

"Mrs. Kolakowski, what makes you think one of these men had anything to do with your husband's disappearance?"

"Process of elimination. They are the only ones Stan and John told about the assassination plot."

"How about the two men who died?"

"I don't think they were the ones."

"Why not?"

"My intuition, more than anything."

Intuition, my ass. "So, what do you want me to do?"

"I want you to talk to them. Watch them, evaluate their reactions. One of them will believe that I have evidence of what he did," she paused, "and he will believe that I know where the gold is hidden. It will bring the guilty party out."

"Just like that?"

"I sent each man a letter, telling him that I had found John's diaries and that I wanted to speak with him after I had finished reading the diaries. I mentioned that I might know where Stan had hidden what I referred to as his gold reserve. The letter will be enough."

"Uh huh. When did you did you send the letters?"

"On Friday. They should have received them by now."

Standing at the edge of the parking lot, my jaw clenched as I reflected on my conversation with Louie's mother. Jablonski's murder had transformed my attitude from polite skepticism to frustrated apprehension. Maria Kolakowski was playing a dangerous game;

Frank C. Dupuy

and she was holding out on me. I wondered if Louie had told her about Jablonski. There was no doubt in my mind that her letter had caused the old man's murder.

A maroon Mercedes Benz cruised into the parking lot, slowed, then parked near Hunter's Tavern. I checked the time. 7:44. Two men, one tall and one short, were illuminated by a parking lot light as they emerged from the car. The tall man was bald with a close-cropped, gray fringe surrounding his shiny pate. The short man had wavy silver hair, reminding me of the late Cesar Romero. Both of them were wearing dark suits and white shirts. The men scanned the parking lot before entering the restaurant.

Removing the cellular telephone from my overcoat pocket, I dialed the number of a service I use, giving the operator the license number from the Mercedes. It was registered to Global Protective Services, Ltd., Michael Ungar's company. Once more, I carefully surveyed the parking lot before concluding that no nefarious killers were lurking behind the parked cars.

Five minutes later, I entered the restaurant.

28

A smiling woman greeted me as I stepped into the restaurant. "Will anyone else be joining you?" she inquired.

"No, actually, I'm supposed to meet a Mr. Ungar here."

"Oh, you must be Mr. LeBlanc. Mr. Ungar is waiting for you in the bar."

I followed her into the dimly lighted bar where she led me to a table. The two men in dark suits watched as we approached. Each had a drink in front of him. The tall man stood, offering his hand.

"Mr. LeBlanc, I'm Mike Ungar. This is my associate, Claudio Mondragón," he said, indicating the short man with the Cesar Romero hair. Claudio did not stand nor did he extend his hand. We merely nodded at each other. As I sat down, Ungar motioned to a waitress who arrived promptly and accepted my order for a Bushmills and water.

From what I had been told by Maria Kolakowski, Ungar would be about sixty-two, a fit, tanned sixty-two, apparently. If I hadn't known better, I would have guessed him to be in his early fifties. His suit, which had not been purchased off the rack, accentuated his lean build. The corner of his left eye was pulled slightly down by an old scar that ran from his eye to his ear lobe. If he had shaved the fringe of gray hair that circled his skull, he could have given Yul Brynner a run for his money.

His companion, Claudio, was an olive-skinned, round-faced, chunky individual, in his fifties. His broad shoulders and thick neck made him appear shorter than he was. His suit, also expensive, didn't fit him as well as Ungar's. Claudio's eyes exuded the warmth of a boa constrictor.

"I believe we have a mutual acquaintance, Mr. LeBlanc, Maria Kolakowski. How is she?" Ungar inquired in a deep, well-modulated voice. I wondered if he ever did commercials.

"Barely alive. She has untreatable cancer and a weak heart. She doesn't know if she has weeks or hours."

"That is a pity. Maria is a remarkable woman."

I didn't comment. The silence stretched out for almost a minute.

"Mr. LeBlanc, how well do you know her?" His tone and manner were relaxed, but his eyes never left my face.

"Not well at all. I only met her once."

"I see. May I ask when you met her and what you discussed?"

"We met at the nursing home day before yesterday. She told me her life history, all about her husband and Stan Petrowski. She also mentioned you and some other people. Mrs. Kolakowski wanted me to find out what had happened to John and Stan. I guess she's looking for some kind of closure before she dies."

Ungar nodded. "She wrote to me, you know."

"She said she had, but didn't give me the details. She asked me to talk to you and some of her husband's other acquaintances to see if I could piece together the events just prior to his disappearance."

Ungar sighed. "This is so sad. May I guess, Mr. LeBlanc, that Maria told you what heroes John and Stan were? How they bravely kept alive the flame of Polish freedom, how instrumental they were in fighting communism?.

I nodded.

"And was her son there? Louie, isn't it?"

"Yes."

"It is a shame that he grew up to be just like his father."

"Oh?"

"I'm going to level with you. Maria Kolakowski is now a delusional old woman whose illness has affected her mind. Her son lives in a fantasy world, always chasing imaginary conspiracies, or what have you. His father was much the same. As for Stan Petrowski, he was a world class con-artist who milked the CIA for hundreds of thousands of dollars by supplying information from a bogus spy network."

I sipped my drink. To my right, Claudio Mondragón sat like a tight-lipped, silver-haired statue. "If that's the case, it confirms

Ohio Salt

some of my worst fears about the CIA."

"Let me tell you a story. In World War II, Stanislas Petrowski was a staff colonel in the Polish army. Rumor has it that what he lacked in military expertise he made up in political skills. When the Germans attacked, he was injured when his car ran off the road trying to avoid a dive bomber. Petrowski managed to bribe his way out of the country. When he tried to obtain a commission in British intelligence, they weren't impressed. The Americans were more gullible; not only was he commissioned, he was assigned to the OSS. While Petrowski may not have been too skilled at the spy game, he was a master politician. William Donovan was totally taken in.

"After the war, Petrowski convinced Donovan to provide funds so he could establish a series of companies that the CIA could use as fronts. Petrowski gathered some of his cronies, bankrolling them with CIA money. To his credit, the CIA did use the companies as fronts for a few years. Petrowski made a name for himself by making broadcasts for Voice of America and Radio Free Europe. He also peddled a lot of bullshit information at outrageous prices to various government agencies. What kept him going was that every now and again he contrived to come up with something credible.

"When the Bay of Pigs invasion was in the planning stages, Petrowski wangled a fat fee to provide training. This was totally unnecessary because the Army had provided a cadre of Special Forces personnel to handle that end of it. I was the FBI liaison agent. Mr. Hoover insisted on being kept in the loop because the training was taking place in the United States and because Cuba had been under the Bureau's jurisdiction before Castro.

"I had known Stan and John for years. Stan did help Polish refugees, and he had provided some money for my education. He told me that he had pulled strings to help me when I applied to the Bureau. Later, I learned that wasn't true. Stan never had any influence with the FBI. Anyway, I spent a number of evenings with Stan and John in Florida. Stan thought it was funny that the U.S. Government had spent so much money on training Cuban expatriates when the entire effort was likely to be a fiasco. That was the first time I realized that Stan had been using the Government. Up until then, he had been one of my heroes. To make a long story short, the invasion was mismanaged and failed. It was symptomatic of the Kennedy

Frank C. Dupuy

Administration." Ungar motioned to the waitress to bring us another round.

"I met Claudio in Florida while the Cubans were training for the invasion. He was only twenty-one, yet had already made several reconnaissance missions into Cuba to scout the invasion beaches. He and his team were dropped off by submarine. They would spend several days concealed in the jungle observing military traffic in the area and photographing the beaches. If all went well, the team would be retrieved at night by another submarine. Claudio can tell you that there was nothing wrong in the planning. A week before the invasion, he broke his ankle in a training exercise. He and I were in a command center when the invasion was launched; there we listened to the entire, horrible outcome.

"After the invasion, rumors were flying that Castro had known for weeks exactly when and where it would take place. At first I thought it was a lot of smoke from Kennedy Administration officials trying to cover their incompetent butts. When Hoover heard the same rumors, he assigned us to find out if there had been a leak. It took time, but we kept at it, finally gathering enough evidence to confirm that Castro had been tipped off. We just weren't sure who had done it.

"In 1963, one of Castro's lieutenants, Mario Guzman, fell out of favor; he managed to escape to Mexico before the Cuban secret police could arrest him. Guzman contacted the U.S. embassy in Mexico City to determine if anyone was interested in purchasing information he had to sell. He claimed he could name U.S. government agents who had betrayed the Bay of Pigs invasion to Castro. A meeting was arranged in Mexico City, but Guzman failed to show up. Someone had cut his throat the night before." Ungar's sincere gaze settle upon me as he attempted to gauge how his revelation about the unfortunate Guzman had affected me.

"Bummer. I guess Castro's boys caught up with him."

"We considered that possibility. That was before we were informed that Guzman had been visited by Petrowski and Kolakowski on the day he was murdered. Once we had that information, things began to fall into place. Although we couldn't prove it, there was considerable circumstantial evidence pointing to Petrowski and Kolakowski as having played a double game.

Ohio Salt

"At some point we screwed up. Stan and John learned that they were under investigation in October or November of 1963. I discovered later that they spent about six weeks scurrying around liquidating property and conning money out of associates. We were closing in on them when Kennedy was assassinated. Every available agent was pulled in to assist in the investigation. During the uproar, they vanished."

"What do you mean vanished?"

"I mean vanished as in disappeared. They booked."

"You mean they left without telling their families or anyone? That's pretty incredible."

"It is on the face of it. You have to realize that they were on the verge of being arrested for treason, not to mention what would happen to them if they had met up with one of the thousands of Cubans who had relatives killed or captured at the Bay of Pigs." He paused, weighing his words carefully. "Stan did not have a family and John Kolakowski was totally under his sway. I might have believed that they had been killed out of revenge if we hadn't received word that they had surfaced briefly in Bolivia in 1975 in connection with some kind of mining fraud. They disappeared again and that's the last I ever heard of them."

The three of us sat in silence as I tried to assimilate a totally disparate version of the Petrowski/Kolakowski saga. At least Ungar and Maria Kolakowski agreed that Stan and John had actually existed at one time.

"Tell me about John Kolakowski. Did he serve in World War II?"

Ungar nodded. "He certainly did. He was in a Polish airborne unit, or paratrooper, as they used to call it. That's about all I know for certain. When you talked to John, his facts changed each time he told a story. He was the type of individual who could put a spin on a minor incident to make it seem like a major feat, usually with him as the hero. The trouble was he would tell a tale and end up believing it. He was the perfect underling for a man like Petrowski. Stan could pump him up to do anything."

"Any truth to the rumor that Petrowski was a Polish count?"

"No, that was another of Stan's fabrications. He used the bogus title to impress gullible Americans he came in contact with.

He felt that Count gave him an aura of European mystery."

More silence. Ungar motioned to the waitress to bring another round, even though I had barely touched my second drink.

"Maria Kolakowski did a marvelous job of raising her three children after John abandoned her," Ungar stated. "She was a hard worker and a decent woman who provided a good home for her children. I was sorry to hear about her illness."

"Yeah, the only thing that was keeping her going was her hope that I could find out what had happened to her husband."

"Are you going to tell her the truth?" Ungar asked, eyeing me intently.

"I don't know. I may stall by having John's diaries translated. That would take time; maybe she will have passed on by then."

"She really does have John's diaries?"

"Oh, yes. They're quite extensive. She didn't have time to read all of them and now she's too weak to finish. Since they were written in Polish, Louie and I will have to have them translated before we can read them."

"Where are they now?"

"Louie has them."

"I see. If you would like, I could help you with the project."

"I'll have to check with Louie. I think he lined up a couple of retirees from the Polish American Club."

"Where is Maria being treated? I would at least like to send her flowers."

"That's very kind of you. She's in the Immaculate Heart of Mary nursing home in Maple Heights."

It was my turn to gaze earnestly at Mike Ungar.

"I appreciate your telling me the truth about Petrowski and Kolakowski before I waste any more of my time. I suppose there is no truth in the story about Stan's gold?"

"What gold?"

"I was afraid of that. Damn. The ingot Louie showed me certainly looked real. It just goes to show that you can never tell."

"Louie showed you an ingot?"

"Yeah, it must have weighed twenty pounds. Mrs. Kolakowski said she found it with John's diaries. Supposedly, Stan had a thousand pounds of gold as a contingency fund hidden away somewhere.

Ohio Salt

Well, if he and John absconded to Bolivia or wherever, they certainly didn't leave a fortune in gold behind. Just my luck. Of course, now that I think about it, the entire story must have been a pure fabrication."

Ungar nodded. "As you said, it is unfortunate. I hope you didn't invest too much time in this, ah, gold hunt."

"Not too much." I looked at my watch. "I have to run. I really appreciate your candor, and taking the time to meet with me." I pulled out my billfold to leave some money on the table. Ungar stopped me with a wave of his hand.

"No, I insist. This is my treat."

"Well, thanks very much. It was nice meeting you."

Ungar and I stood up and shook hands.

"It was a pleasure," he assured me.

"Nice meeting you, too," I said to Claudio, as I headed for the exit.

Frank C. Dupuy

29

On my way home, I called Carl Branner from my car. He answered on my second ring.

"Good evening, Carl. Did your guests arrive?"

"Yes, they did. I put Mrs. Kolakowski in the downstairs bedroom. There's a hospital bed in that room."

I remembered that Carl had cared for his mother for several years before she died.

"Any problems?"

"None at all. Mrs. Kolakowski is sleeping. Her conversation with Collin Yates tired her."

"Did you talk to Collin?"

"We exchanged a few pleasantries. He appeared preoccupied when he departed."

"Anything else?"

"Louie and Karen have been helping me with your research project."

"How's it going?"

"Quite well, actually. I should have enough data to present to you by tomorrow afternoon."

"Super. Why don't we plan on my coming over at about 6:00 tomorrow evening."

"That would be fine. I will expect you to have dinner with us."

I thanked Carl and hung up.

It was almost 10:00 when I arrived home. I filled the kettle with water, then set it on the stove to boil. While I was waiting, I placed the computer printout Harold Lipscomb, Jr. had so grudgingly provided on the counter. The vendors had been sorted by vendor number rather than alphabetically, and there were hundreds of them. Muttering to myself, I began to scan each page. The kettle started to whistle insistently. I marked my place. Taking a coffee packet out of a foil envelope, I let it soak in a cup of hot water about a minute longer than the directions recommended. At least the finished product looked and smelled like coffee.

I was on the next to the last page when I spotted Ontario Enterprises. It was listed under two addresses, 10124 Detroit Ave., Ste. 210., Cleveland, OH., and 805 80th Street, Cleveland, OH. Bingo.

I dialed Harold Lipscomb's home number. The telephone was answered by a pleasant-sounding woman who informed me that Harold would be with me in a minute.

"Hello."

"Mr. Lipscomb, this is Adrian LeBlanc."

"How are you?"

"Fine. I'd like to meet with you first thing Tuesday morning, if I could."

"Why Tuesday?"

"Because, by then, I believe I will have information that may shed some light on the Gwen Hiltie case."

"What have you got, LeBlanc?"

"I'd rather not say until I have all my facts."

Lipscomb let out a deep breath. "I suppose you know that you are an exasperating individual?"

"Only sometimes."

There was a moment of silence. "Do you mind telling me what in the world went on between you and Harry in the parking lot this morning?"

"Your son demanded to know what I was doing for you. I told him to ask you. Words were exchanged; he tried to grab me by the neck. I thumped him in the balls with my briefcase."

"Did he hurt you?"

"No."

"Well, I hope he learned a lesson. My son is something of a bully at times."

No shit. "No harm done. Is he all right?"

"Just a little swollen, according to the doctor." Lipscomb sighed. "I blame myself. After my wife died, I sent Harry to boarding schools because he needed more supervision than I could provide. In retrospect, it was probably a mistake."

I didn't comment. At least Lipscomb was honest enough to realize that his son was a horse's ass. We spoke for a few more minutes before confirming that we would meet at 8:00 Tuesday morning. I called Patty Stone.

"Christ, LeBlanc, can't you find anyone else to talk to you at this hour?" she crabbed.

"Patty, truly professional P.I.s never sleep."

"Sez you. What do you want?"

"I need an all day surveillance Saturday and possibly Monday. You can name your price."

"You romantic devil. You certainly know how to charm a woman. What's up?"

"You still have a surveillance van?"

"Sure."

"I want you to set up on 10124 Detroit Avenue in Cleveland at 8:00 tomorrow morning. An outfit called Reliable Office Services lives in that building. They provide an accommodation address for people who don't want customers to know they work out of their homes."

"Neat."

"You have something to write with?"

"Yes."

"I want you to address a package to J.B. Johnson, President, Ontario Enterprises, 10124 Detroit Avenue, Suite 210, Cleveland Ohio. Make certain that the package is big enough and distinctive enough to be recognized when someone carries it out. Have one of your people deliver it after you set up. I want a good face shot of the person who picks up the package, and his license number. If you can, follow him. However, don't get made. I don't want him spooked."

"Gotcha. What do you want me to put in the box?"

"Something heavy. Use your imagination. If no one picks up the box on Saturday, I want you back on station Monday morning."

"Can do. Anything else?"

"That's it. Thanks, Patty. Sorry about the short notice."

"You can apologize after you get my bill."

My next call was to Collin Yates. From the sound of his voice he hadn't been sleeping.

"You're keeping late hours, Adrian."

"The pure of heart need no sleep. Did you find out if there were traces of cocaine in Hiltie's body?"

"There was more than a trace. J.C. wants to know how you knew."

"Tell him to have his hot shot detectives conduct a basic background check."

Yates cleared his throat. "When are you going to tell him about Sally Yuhas and Hiltie?"

"Early next week. Tuesday, if I'm lucky. How about the diamond ring? Did they find it?"

"No. She wasn't wearing a ring. Jensen said the coroner and the crime scene techs were certain about that. They dug every pellet and shred of flesh out of the floor."

"You can tell J.C. that Hiltie was wearing at least a three carat rock on her left hand when she was in my office."

I could almost hear Yates pursing his lips. "J.C. wants to talk to you."

"Tell him we can talk Tuesday. I should have something solid for him by then."

"Very well. I will convey that to him. You wanted my opinion on Maria Kolakowski?"

"Yes."

"She is a very clever lady who is not telling everything she knows."

"Great minds think alike."

"I also believe that she is telling the truth, at least for the most part."

"Joseph Jablonski's murder have anything to do with your opinion?"

"Some. On the face of it, it is an incredible tale. If true, we are sitting on the story of the century. The implications are staggering."

"Agreed. I met with Michael Ungar and his stone-faced sidekick, Claudio Mondragón tonight. Ungar had an interesting spin on the story." I gave Yates a detailed account of my meeting.

"What do you think?" he asked.

Ohio Salt

"I'll have an informed opinion after I talk to Carl Branner tomorrow evening. Depending on what he comes up with, I may or may not strangle Louie's mother."

Frank C. Dupuy

30

Saturday

At 7:30 on a Saturday morning, downtown Cleveland is almost deserted. The weatherman claimed that the sun might poke through the clouds. I hoped it would. I was tired of drizzle.

The radio newscaster was titillating his audience with the story of the ghastly torture/ homicide of a retired custodian. The police had not released the fact that Joseph Jablonski's fingers had been cut off. The announcer stated that the body had been discovered by an acquaintance. I was thankful that my name had not been released.

A lone security officer in a blue blazer greeted me as I crossed the OmniBank lobby to the elevators. Daniel Dutton was a man who valued his weekends. For him to agree to meet me in his office on a Saturday morning was rare indeed. When I reached his office the door was open; I could smell coffee. I rapped on the door frame.

"Come in, LeBlanc. This had better be good." Dutton was seated at a table with the contents of what had been a thick file spread over the surface. Without asking if I wanted any, he poured a cup of coffee from an insulated carafe and handed it to me. Dan was wearing olive cotton slacks, an open-necked plaid shirt and vintage cordovan loafers. He had dropped his banking executive persona.

"It's all here, hotshot. From what I can see, everything is in order. The loan officer did a thorough job."

"I hope he did. But just in case he didn't, I'll take a quick peek."

"Be my guest." Dan sat down at his desk, leaving me alone at the table. Within twenty minutes I had determined that the loan officer was up to his eyeballs in a $2.5 million loan fraud. I had to admit that it was professionally done. When I pushed my chair away from the table, Dutton closed the magazine he was reading.

"Well, professor?" he inquired.

"You have a problem. Everything in this file is fiction. It was nicely compiled by Ted Meyers and his trusty CPA/attorney, Les Fazio, with the able assistance of your loan officer."

"How do you know?"

"The loan was made to one of Meyers's companies, T.M. Manufacturing Company located at 956 90th Street in Cleveland. According to the financials, T.M. Manufacturing has been at that location for four years and has turned a handsome profit each year. The building and equipment are shown as being owned free and clear, valued at $4.8 million. Accounts receivable is another $1,000,000. That's pretty good considering that Meyers purchased that building last year from the Catholic Church for $150,000. Not only that, the building is a shell. There's nothing in it."

"How do you know?"

"The security guard took me on a tour of the place the other day. Also, I pulled the real estate records. The Dun and Bradstreet report in your files is also bogus. The one I've got bears no resemblance to this one."

"The loan officer's documentation shows that he verified everything he submitted," Dutton rasped.

"Indeed, it do. Meyers corrupted him."

"Jesus Christ, Adrian, are you certain the information is cooked?"

"Yes. Ted Meyers's shenanigans have finally caught up with him. His sweetheart government contract deal with ex-congressman Poje fell through after Poje was caught with his hand in the till. Meyers was in hock to everyone because of all the specialized equipment he had invested in to retrofit tanks. He was also one of the principals in the Sealake development project. When that went bust, he had to scramble to repay the Carlucci brothers the money they had loaned him. That's one transaction that won't show up on any D&B.

"Meyers was desperate for capital, so he and Fazio concocted this scheme to fund his operations. All is well until it becomes known

Ohio Salt

that Harold Lipscomb is about to be appointed to the board of directors of OmniBank. Lipscomb and Meyers hate each other. You don't have to be a rocket scientist to figure out that Lipscomb would have gone over all of Meyers's loans with a microscope. So, what does Meyers do? He concocts a scheme to get something on Lipscomb to blackmail him. He sends Gwen Hiltie to my office, then strong-arms me into taking photographs of a romantic indiscretion. Something goes awry, Hiltie is murdered and here I am."

Dan Dutton lowered his head and massaged the bridge of his nose with his thumb and forefinger. Finally, he raised his head. "LeBlanc, you are a certifiable menace. You know that?"

"You say the sweetest things. By the by, who is the loan officer?"

"Herb Kramer, a solid citizen. He's been with the bank for over ten years."

"Can you do me a favor?"

"Now what?" Dan's eyes did not quite bulge.

"I would be grateful if you would call Mr. Kramer to inform him that you would like to speak with him on Monday regarding the loan to T.M. Manufacturing Company."

"Why ruin his weekend?"

"I want him to call Meyers. I want Meyers good and panicked for what I have planned."

Frank C. Dupuy

31

I like Slavic Village. Many of the old Cleveland neighborhoods have turned into slums, but the descendants of the hardheaded eastern Europeans who settled in Slavic Village in the early part of the century have stubbornly clung to their values and their neighborhood. Small family-owned businesses, bars and restaurants prosper because very few chains have encroached on their territory.

Milo Frankiewicz's office was situated in an aging brick building on Broadway, not far from the Third Federal Savings and Loan building. A battered building directory informed me that Frankiewicz and Frankiewicz, Attorneys at Law, was located on the second floor. I climbed a worn flight of stairs to the second floor where an old-fashioned wooden door with gold lettering on a frosted glass panel proclaimed I had found the offices of Frankiewicz and Frankiewicz. After turning the ancient iron doorknob, I entered a reception area decked out with office furniture that must have been pre-World War II. An elderly man and woman seated on a wooden bench were conversing, in what I assumed was Polish, with a secretary in her sixties who was seated behind a desk that was as old as she was.

"May I help you?" the secretary queried after meticulously evaluating me. She had deduced that I was a foreigner from the suburbs.

"Yes, ma'am. I'd like to see Mr. Milo Frankiewicz."

"Junior or Senior?"

"Senior."

"Do you have an appointment?"

"No ma'am. I'm a friend of Maria Kolakowski's." I handed her my card.

The secretary evidently knew Mrs. Kolakowski. "Have a seat,

Frank C. Dupuy

please." She conveyed my card through a doorway behind her desk. I inspected a collection of antediluvian, well-thumbed magazines on an end table, noting that almost half of them were from Poland. A few minutes later, the secretary returned.

"Mr. Frankiewicz has someone in his office. If you care to wait, he will see you when he is finished, Mr. LeBlanc."

I entertained myself with a nine month old edition of Time while the secretary and the couple on the bench resumed their conversation. About nine minutes later, an ancient, tiny woman leaning on a cane inched slowly out of the doorway from behind the secretary. The couple on the bench rose and went over to her. With glacial speed the trio made their way out of the reception area.

"Mr. Frankiewicz will see you now," the secretary announced.

She led me out of the lobby and down a short hallway before ushering me into a spacious, though sparsely furnished, corner office. A slender elderly man in a dark-blue three piece suit greeted me. A pair of intense blue eyes peered at me from behind wire framed bifocals. He approached me with shuffling steps.

"Mr. LeBlanc, I am Milo Frankiewicz. Forgive me for not shaking hands, but my arthritis is acting up." He motioned me to a chair. I noticed that his fingers were bent and misshapen.

"I understand you are a friend of Maria's?"

"A friend of her son's, actually. He introduced us. She asked for my assistance in trying to learn what had happened to her husband." I noted that Frankiewicz's accent was not quiet perfect.

"What is it that you do, Mr. LeBlanc?"

"I'm a private investigator."

"I see." Frankiewicz assessed me thoughtfully. "When did you speak with Maria?"

"Night before last at the nursing home."

Frankiewicz's features settled into an attorney's professional sad mode. "It is such a shame. Maria is a wonderful woman. This illness came upon her so suddenly. One day she was healthy, the next she is in a nursing home with only weeks to live. Ah, well. How may I help you?"

"I am trying to reconstruct John Kolakowski's and Stan Petrowski's activities before they disappeared. I understand that Stan frequently confided in you."

Ohio Salt

The old lawyer opened a desk drawer and extracted a pack of unfiltered Chesterfields. "Would it greatly bother you if I smoke?"

"No, sir."

With difficulty, he drew a cigarette from the pack, holding it between his thumb and forefinger in the European manner. He gestured toward a disposable butane lighter on his desk. "If you would be so kind."

I picked up the lighter, thumbed the striker and held it out to him. Frankiewicz lit his cigarette, inhaling deeply. His features relaxed.

"This is such a deplorable habit, but I do so adore it. Would you care to join me?"

"No, thank you."

"Did Maria tell you that she had written me a letter?"

I nodded.

"What do you want to know?"

"I'd like to know whether or not Mrs. Kolakowski is a mental case."

Frankiewicz snorted a cloud of smoke through his nose. "Maria is as sane as anyone I have ever met."

"I would appreciate it if you would tell me what John and Stan were up to before they disappeared."

"I do not think I will be able to help you," he informed me in a tone that he might have used to discuss the weather.

"Why not?"

"Because I have three children and seven grandchildren to think of. Maria and I were silenced by threats to our children thirty years ago. A few days after I received a letter from Maria, my old friend Joseph was tortured to death in his home. There is nothing I can help you with. I would appreciate it if you never contact me again."

I watched with anticipation as Milo Frankiewicz smoked his cigarette down to the point where I was certain that it would burn his fingers. He dropped the tiny butt into an ashtray.

"All right," I acquiesced as I stood up.

"I'm sorry. I am not afraid for myself, and these men know it. They would get at me through those I love."

"I understand."

Frank C. Dupuy

He pointed to an envelope on his desk. "Take that with you. It contains the address and telephone number of Stephen Wloso-wicz."

I made my way out of the building to the street. I walked about a half block, then turned to stare at Frankiewicz's corner office. He was standing with his back to the window holding a telephone receiver to his ear. I wondered whom he had called.

32

After several rounds with directory assistance, I was finally given the number for the hotel in Lily Dale, New York. The desk clerk promised to deliver a message to my wife to call me as soon as possible. I hadn't heard from Jeannie or Jules in a couple of days and was worried that they would return home without calling me first. The way things were going, I wanted them to stay out of town for a few more days. I hoped Jeannie would be reasonable.

I was en route to sign some papers at my insurance agent's office (the insurance company had decided to total my truck and cut me a check) when my pager buzzed. My answering service had a message for me to call Patty Stone on her cellular phone. I punched in a number.

"Stone here."

"What's up, Patty?"

"Your boy came by at 10:22 to pick up his package. He was driving a dark-green Mazda Miata, Ohio plate number 733 ALA. It comes back to a Harold Lipscomb, Jr., at 234 Royce Avenue, in Rocky River. I got some good shots of him, he's kind of a big guy. Anyway, he puts the package in his trunk, then drives away like a maniac. We tried to follow him, but he was too damn fast. We went by the address on Royce and, sure enough, the green Miata was in the drive."

I could feel my heart trying to thump its way out of my rib cage. Son of a bitch. Junior was fleecing his old man; he'd probably been tapping his mistress, too.

"Adrian, are you there?"

"Yeah, I'm here, Patty. Bear with me for a minute. I need to think. Oh, by the way, congratulations on a job well done. I'll tell you what. Hang loose for a few minutes and I'll call you back."

Frank C. Dupuy

"I'll be here.

"Thanks."

I pulled into a parking lot. Harold Lipscomb, Jr. was J.B. Johnson, president of Ontario Enterprises. He was also the man who had provided Gwen Hiltie with an apartment and a Lexus. I wondered if Harold, Jr. had loved her, or killed her, or both. I thumped my steering wheel in frustration. I was about out of bright ideas. Inhaling deeply, I forced myself to relax. Then it hit me. I called Patty Stone.

"Patty, when can you get me copies of the photos you took?"

"If I take them to a Fotomat, I can have them to you in an hour. I also have him on video tape."

"Super. I want you to call my attorney, Collin Yates." I gave her Collin's office and home numbers. "Tell him you are working for me. Make arrangements to deliver the photos and the tape to him. Tell him everything you saw today."

"Got it."

"By the by, are you certain that the box Lipscomb picked up was the one you sent him?"

"Yes, sir. I don't think that there were two boxes wrapped in red foil wrapping paper."

"Probably not. Uh, what did you put in the box?"

Patty chuckled. "A brand-new bowling ball."

"Say again?"

"A bowling ball. It was for a guy I was seeing last year. I bought it for him for Christmas, before I discovered that the two-timing schmuck had a thing going with a waitress at the bowling alley. It's been taking up space in a closet ever since. I figured receiving a new bowling ball in a box wrapped in red foil would drive J.B. Johnson crazy."

"No doubt. Are you somewhere you can write?"

"Yeah, I'm in a Burger King parking lot celebrating with a cup of coffee."

"I want you to call the Sandusky Sheraton on Monday; tell them you are in accounts payable for Newport Industries. Tell them that Harold Lipscomb, Jr. has lost his hotel receipts and needs them for his expense report. Tell them that he needs the receipts for January, February and March. Ask the hotel to fax them to you."

Ohio Salt

"That's it?"
"That's it. Page me as soon as you receive them."
"Will do."

Frank C. Dupuy

33

One of the greatest ways for a man to kill a Saturday afternoon is to shop for a new truck. My old pickup was three payments shy of being paid off on a thirty-six month note when it had been helped into the Grand River. The insurance company had been fair, though not extravagant, in their settlement; still, I had enough for a generous down payment.

At the third dealership I tried, I struck a deal for a brand-new, loaded Dodge Dakota 4x4 with a testosterone pleasing V-8. Oh, did I forget to mention it had an extended cab? I had all of the papers signed by 3:45. The sales manager promised to have the truck serviced and ready to roll by noon on Monday. Life can be sweet.

I went home to play with the dogs for a couple of hours. They hadn't received much attention lately with Jules and Jeannie out of town. I was about to leave for Carl Branner's when the telephone rang. It was Jeannie.

"Hi, Sweetheart, how are you?" I asked.

"Fine."

"And Jules?"

"He's fine, too.

"Jeannie, I called because there has been an unforeseen development." I told her about finding Jablonski, although I toned it down.

"Are you alright?"

"Yes, I'm fine. The reason I called is because I want you and Jules to stay where you are for a few more days. The bad guys seem to have a penchant for going after people's families."

Silence.

"Jeannie, I'll have this wrapped up by Wednesday, I promise,"

I told her with more conviction than I felt.

"Perhaps it's just as well."

"Huh?"

"It will take several more days for me to finish working with my psychic advisor and the hypnotist."

"Huh?"

"Really, Adrian, you should learn some more expressions than simply huh."

I stifled the next huh. "You mind telling me what you are doing?"

"I am learning, and I am improving myself. You still have a long way to go," my wife informed me pityingly.

"To go where?"

"I'm talking about spiritual perfection."

The effort not to say what I was thinking almost strangled me.

"Adrian, are you there?"

"Yes, oh perfect one. I are here."

"Hmph. My advisor certainly has you pegged."

"Huh?"

"There you go again. I have another lecture to attend in a few minutes. Jules and I will be home Wednesday evening."

"OK. I love you, Jeannie."

"Yes. I have to go. Bye."

I gaped at the telephone receiver for over a minute before it occurred to me to replace it in the cradle. I hoped that Carl Branner had a good supply of booze.

34

Sunday

7:05 AM is an ungodly hour to catch an airplane on a Sunday. At least the flight to Miami was direct. I leaned back in my seat and tried to sleep. My mind wouldn't cooperate; it kept straying back to my meeting with Carl Branner.

As I mentioned, Carl is a retired librarian who lives in a stylish older home in west Akron that had been purchased and extensively refurbished by his father. The elder Branner had been a well-to-do executive with one of the smaller rubber companies back when Akron was truly "Rubber City." Carl never married, but has a host of "widow women" who vie for his attention. He is a researcher's researcher who is online with university libraries, newspapers and private data bases. Being on a first name basis with numerous writers and historians makes him one of the best resources a private investigator can have. Carl and I have been friends for over ten years.

His house sits on an acre of ground surrounded by a low stone fence and high hedges that maintain the private environment he enjoys. I parked near the front entrance, then proceeded up the flagstone walk to the front porch. The door was opened before I reached the first step.

"Come in, Adrian, come in." Carl Branner beckoned to me with his free hand. He was clutching a brandy snifter in the other. Very few men can carry off wearing a red velvet smoking jacket; however, Carl is one of them. He is a slightly-built individual of medium height who is blessed with a head of thick white hair, which he wears slightly long, claiming that it gives him a literary quality women relish. His other affectation is a meticulously trimmed mustache, a la Douglas Fairbanks. Dapper is the term most people use to describe Carl.

He hustled me into his den which is equipped with a beautiful walnut bar, stocked with expensive booze and the ingredients for almost any cocktail you can name. Among his other attributes, Monsieur Branner is a superb bartender whose services are frequently sought after by socialites hosting charity events.

"The usual?" he inquired.

"Bless you."

Carl dropped several ice cubes into a glass, then added a generous dollop of single malt Bushmills, placed the glass and a small pitcher of water on a tray and carried it over to me. He observed critically as I added water. Satisfied that I had not overly diluted the product of Ireland's oldest distillery, Carl settled himself into a restored Morris chair across from me.

"The things you young people involve yourselves in," he declared admiringly.

"What things?"

"Why, a lost treasure, scurrilous villains, spies and the secret of the JFK assassination."

"You buy Mrs. Kolakowski's story?"

"Most of it."

"Yeah? Which parts?"

"Well, I have been in contact with several of my professional acquaintances who have written books on the periods you are interested in. One of them, Delbert Little, is an ex-CIA operative who is currently out of favor with his old employer for exposing some of their dirty linen to public scrutiny. Anyway, Delbert actually knew Stanislas Petrowski and Casimir, AKA: John, Kolakowski in the 1960s."

"Really? What did he think of them?"

"Delbert confided that Petrowski was the most astute, devious, and conniving man he had ever met. There was no doubt that Petrowski was fiercely anti-Communist and a Polish patriot. He established and ran a fairly effective, private espionage service network."

"Service network?"

"Apparently, he did create a number of front companies for

the CIA; almost all of them were run by Polish refugees. That said, Petrowski was a master of acquiring funding from the CIA and other U.S. intelligence agencies."

"You mean he was a con-artist?"

"No, he was a hard negotiator, and a sharp businessman."

"Did your source mention if Petrowski ever peddled bogus information?"

"He told me that Petrowski had a reputation for integrity, for getting the job done. The people who used his services knew in advance that they would pay handsomely for what they received."

"Was he really a count?

"Yes, although the title was simply a title; there was no estate, castle or serfs to go along with it. As the eldest son, he inherited the title from his father. The Petrowski family had been minor players in Polish affairs for centuries."

"How about the bank in Cuba?"

Carl pulled at his chin. "That is a trifle murky. There was a Banco Cubano del Carribe that was established in Havana in 1948. The principals evidently were Polish nationals. Delbert thinks that the bank story is probably true, although he hasn't a clue about how it might have been financed initially. I did verify that Colonel Stanislas Petrowski was the Polish military attaché in Washington from 1937 to 1938."

"How about John Kolakowski?"

"An interesting man. When World War II ended, he was a major in a Polish paratrooper brigade. He received a number of commendations, including the Distinguished Service Medal for bravery. He changed his name from Casimir to John when he immigrated to Canada after the war.

"Delbert told me that John Kolakowski was a perfect number two man for Petrowski. He was organized, efficient and hardly spoke unless it was business related. It was Delbert's opinion that Kolakowski was not a man you would want to cross swords with."

"Did Delbert give the impression that Kolakowski was a dreamer, the kind of man who would make up tales or chase fairy stories?"

Carl regarded me quizzically. "Nothing like that, why?"

"Idle curiosity."

Frank C. Dupuy

"Ha!"

"Was Delbert your only source of information?"

"Not by a long shot, sonny. You know better than that." He tapped a thick folder of computer printouts on a small table by his chair. "I ran their names through over a dozen different data bases and contacted seven of my associates. I only mentioned Delbert Little because he was personally acquainted with the men in question."

"What did you dig up on Michael Ungar, Claudio Mondragón, and Stephen Wlosowicz?"

"Some facts and some rumors. Michael Ungar, formerly Ungarski, was a 1st lieutenant in a rifle company in Korea. He received two Purple Hearts, a Bronze Star and a Silver Star. After his military service, he entered the F.B.I., becoming one of J. Edgar Hoover's fair-haired boys." Carl paused long enough to swirl the cognac in his snifter and take a sip.

"Hoover was a powerful man in Washington. He had dossiers on almost every politician, and they knew it. When they didn't, he would inform them. Because so many of our elected officials have indiscretions they would prefer to remain secret, he ran the Bureau pretty much as he pleased. Under Hoover, the F.B.I. was notorious for illegally wiretapping the telephones of political activists, or others, who were outrageous enough to exercise their rights under the Constitution.

"Fortunately, even a man like Hoover can go too far. He had several 'special units' that carried out his dirtiest deeds. Hoover burned his fingers badly when he assigned a special unit to probe an extramarital affair of one of Johnson's cabinet members. Even J. Edgar learned to steer clear of LBJ. When Lyndon Johnson discovered that the FBI was investigating a member of his cabinet over a love affair, he went ballistic. Johnson pushed the right buttons; suddenly, Congress convened a committee to investigate Mr. Hoover's special units. To make a long story short, Hoover disavowed all knowledge of what his teams had done. He fired all of the agents involved, then quietly placed them in jobs with other government agencies. Michael Ungar was one of the agents caught in the fallout.

"The State Department was supplying former police officers and FBI agents to friendly Latin American governments to train

Ohio Salt

their counter insurgency forces. Ungar was assigned to Nicaragua where he became friends with the Somoza family. After a year, he quit the State Department and went to work for Somoza as his Chief of Internal Security. Ungar was brutally successful, but even his Gestapo tactics could not hold back the insurgents forever. After Somoza was deposed, Ungar's name was brought up in congressional probes of human rights violations. In the end nothing was proven, probably because of the efforts of Reagan Administration officials. Ungar had, after all, worked for a regime supported by the United States."

"What about Claudio Mondragón?"

"He is a somewhat shadowy figure. His father, Dimitrio Mondragón, was a captain in Batista's secret police. By all accounts, he was a corrupt and brutal man. Dimitrio was assassinated in the closing days of the Cuban revolution. Claudio fled with thousands of other Cubans to the United States. His name is on the list of volunteers who participated in the Bay of Pigs invasion although it did not appear on the list of those captured.

"His name first showed up in newspaper files in 1965. He was arrested by the Miami police, charged with extorting 'protection' money from businesses owned by Cuban immigrants. The charges were dropped. After that, he was mentioned in several articles as being connected to organized crime. Evidently, nothing was ever proven.

"In 1969, he went to Nicaragua where he was employed by Ungar. Mondragón's name was mentioned in numerous articles that focused on the Somoza regime's human rights violations. His specialty was interrogation using torture." Carl extracted a thin packet of papers that had been stapled together. "These are reports from the few eye-witnesses who survived a Mondragón interrogation. They aren't pretty. A typical Mondragón session would start with him numbing a victim's hand or foot with Novocain, then letting him watch as Mondragón cut, mangled or shredded it. The victim couldn't feel a thing as he viewed a part of his body being destroyed. If, after all of that, the victim was still reluctant to talk, Mondragón would wait until the Novocain wore off before starting again."

"Jesus, Carl. Is that for real?" It takes a lot to revolt me; however, Carl had succeeded.

Frank C. Dupuy

"Yes, it is. He did worse things, too. You can read about them if you like."

"I'll pass. What else did you find out?"

"Not much more about Mondragón, and there wasn't a lot to learn about Stephen Wlosowicz, either. The man maintained an extremely low profile, although he was briefly mentioned in several books on World War II espionage. It seems he had an exceedingly analytical mind."

"Did Delbert Little know him?"

"He met Wlosowicz a few times. Little said he had a reputation for brilliance and for quote 'cutting the nuts off of anyone who crossed him.' His biggest coup was predicting that the Russians were going to install missiles in Cuba months before anyone else had a clue. Wlosowicz was a power within the agency and was believed to be headed for an assistant director's slot when he had his breakdown in 1965."

"What caused the breakdown?"

"Who knows? The man was probably too tightly wrapped. Delbert told me they shipped him to a CIA funny farm for almost a year before deciding he was not going to babble secrets to the enemy if he was released. Anyway, Wlosowicz was pensioned off; he was accepted at Loyola of the South as a theology instructor. He translated two of his pre-war books into English and published a new work in 1977. I found a review of it in the Catholic Press. The reviewer described it as brilliant, but predicted that very few people would understand it. He was probably correct on both counts."

"What else?"

"That's it. The man retired from Loyola in 1986. I located an address for him in Coral Gables, Florida. That's a suburb of Miami, you know."

Crossing my ankles, I leaned back in my chair and closed my eyes. The vision of Joseph Jablonski tied to his work bench flashed through my mind. No one should die that way. I opened my eyes to find Carl regarding me with concern.

"Are you alright?"

"Yeah, I'm fine."

"Well then, do you want to hear what else I found out?"

"Give."

Ohio Salt

"As you know, the Kennedy assassination has spawned an entire generation of conspiracy nuts. As more and more FBI agents retired and wrote books, they all seemed to agree that the Bureau had received warnings that there was a plot to assassinate the President in Dallas several weeks before it happened. One retired agent, Peter Collins, claims that the warnings came from the Cleveland field office and were referred directly to Hoover, who apparently ignored them. Collins asserts that following Kennedy's death, the existence of that warning was the focus of a massive cover-up orchestrated by J. Edgar himself."

"Did Collins say who told the FBI?"

"Not exactly. He claimed that all paperwork and notes relating to the tip were destroyed. He heard later that the information had come from a CIA source."

"Did any of your sources have a clue as to what happened to Petrowski and Kolakowski?"

"No. Their disappearance coincided with the Kennedy assassination. No one appeared to be too interested at the time."

The ice cubes in my glass tinkled as I drained the last drops of my drink. My host killed the amber liquid in his snifter about the same time.

"Another round?" Carl inquired hopefully.

"Sure. After your Novocain story, I need it."

I accompanied him to the bar while he did the honors.

"By the by, how is Mrs. Kolakowski?"

Carl set his glass down, then pursed his lips.

"How sick did you say she was?"

"She has a weak heart and terminal cancer."

"I see. One of the side effects of her illness must be a healthy appetite."

"Huh?"

"The dying woman eats like a horse."

"Are you certain?"

"Of course I'm certain. I prepared pancakes and sausage for breakfast yesterday for Karen, Louie and myself. When I asked Mrs. Kolakowski if she had any special dietary requirements, she told me that she could only hold down a small bowl of oatmeal. I served her first, before preparing our meal. Louie finished two healthy helpings of everything, then left with a huge pile of pancakes and sausages telling me that he would finish his breakfast with his mother. Karen volunteered to do the dishes, so I went outside to feed my birds and my squirrels.

"I was across the yard when I glanced in Mrs. Kolakowski's window. She was seated on the side of the bed devouring every last crumb of that huge plate of food Louie had carried into her room."

"Maybe she suddenly felt better."

"Right. Louie went through the same routine at lunch. Karen told me she would cook lunch; she sent me to the store for chicken breasts and vegetables, specifying the quantities. I told her she had enough for six people. She replied that Louie has a healthy appetite. I grant you that Louie eats enough for two ordinary people; nevertheless, after he had eaten, he took three chicken breasts, two rolls and a mound of vegetables into his mother's room. With the exception of some well-picked bones, the plate came back empty."

"Are you trying to tell me something?"

"I'm telling you that whatever illness that woman has, it isn't terminal cancer, and I'll wager her heart is as solid as oak."

"Maybe she's trying to indulge herself just before she cashes out."

"If that's the best you can do, you had better find another line of work."

I pondered Carl's revelation. Somebody was sure as hell up to something, and it wasn't me. I shrugged my shoulders.

"Keep an eye on things, Carl; keep me posted." It suddenly occurred to me that I had not seen Louie or Karen. "Where is everybody?"

"Everybody is in Mrs. Kolakowski's room watching the 'Godfather'. Louie asked me to rent the entire series. I think they are on 'Godfather II' at the moment. He says his mother adores Al Pacino."

"That's nice."

Carl swirled his cognac before lifting his snifter to admire the contents. He harumphed twice as he cleared his throat.

"How long have Karen and Louie been dating?"

"They're not. Louie inspires Karen's maternal instincts."

"You know, for a professional private investigator, you haven't a clue as to what's going on beneath your very nose."

"Oh?"

"They think they're being discreet, but those two have been making goo-goo eyes at each other ever since they arrived."

"Be reasonable, Carl. Karen is twenty years older than Louie."

"So? In case you haven't noticed, your secretary keeps herself in pretty good shape."

"Give me a break."

"My bedroom is between the rooms I put Karen and Louie in. I may have a few years on me, but I'm not deaf. About twenty minutes after we went to bed last night, Karen tiptoed past my room and into Louie's. The subsequent moans, groans and mattress thrashing did not cause me to think of maternal instincts. Those two animals kept at it all night. Stop bugging your eyes at me."

I blinked, then emptied the contents of my glass. Louie Kolakowski and Karen Koenig? I groaned. No way in hell. I thought about it, and groaned again.

My reverie was broken by the flight attendant inquiring if I wanted another cup of coffee. I declined, pushed my seat back and dozed fitfully as images of Karen and Louie making goo-goo eyes danced through my confused mind.

Frank C. Dupuy

35

The bright Florida sunshine was a welcome relief after the recent soggy Ohio weather. As I drove past houses with yards covered in lush vegetation, I could understand the state's attraction to retirees from Ohio. Using a map of Coral Gables purchased at a convenience store, I located Wlosowicz's street which was about fifteen blocks from the downtown area. His modest bungalow, a white stucco affair with a red tile roof, was in an older well-maintained neighborhood.

For several minutes, I inspected the house from inside my rented Buick. The door of the detached, single car garage on the side of the residence was shut. No newspapers or mail had accumulated on the porch or in the mailbox. After vigorously ringing the door bell and knocking on both the front and back doors, I concluded that if anyone was home, they were hiding under the bed.

I went back to my car where I used my cellular telephone to call Wlosowicz's residence. The phone was answered on the second ring by a man whose English had a moderate eastern European accent.

"Hello."
"Hello, may I speak with Stephen Wlosowicz?"
"May I say who is calling?"
"Adrian LeBlanc. I'm a friend of Maria Kolakowski."
"Go ahead, please."
"Is this Stephen Wlosowicz?"
"Yes."
"I would like to meet with you. I am calling from my car in front of your house."
"I am not home."
"Is there somewhere we can meet?"

Frank C. Dupuy

Silence.

"Mr. Wlosowicz?"

"Is your car phone capable of receiving a local call?"

"I've activated the roaming feature. You'll have to call my Cleveland number."

"What is it?"

I gave it to him.

"Are you by yourself?"

"Yes."

"Make certain that you are not followed. There is a municipal parking lot behind the First Florida Bank on Main Street. Park there, then proceed to the corner on foot. Take your phone with you."

"OK. What else?"

"What are you wearing?

"A navy blazer, tan slacks, and a light blue shirt."

"When you reach the corner wait for my call."

After consulting my map, I drove to Main Street where I located the parking lot behind the bank. Although I thought it ridiculous, I had made several meanders through side streets to check for a tail. No one had followed me. Ensuring that my telephone was on, I walked to the corner and waited. About three minutes later, my phone buzzed.

"LeBlanc."

"What is your secretary's name?"

"Karen Koenig."

"What is her birth date?"

"Hell, I don't know. She's fifty-three."

The voice on the phone chuckled.

"Cross the street and turn left. You will see a men's clothing store about half way down the block. Next to the store is a door that leads to offices above the store. Come up to the second floor. I will meet you."

I did as I was instructed. Sure enough, there was a glass door next to the clothing store that had The Caldwell Building painted on it. Through the door I could see a narrow flight of stairs ascending to a dimly lit landing. Shrugging, I opened the door to the Caldwell Building and climbed the stairs. At the top of the stairs, a voice

Ohio Salt

called to me. "This way, Mr. LeBlanc."

It emanated from an open door about halfway down the hall. With only a moment's hesitation, I proceeded along the corridor and stepped through the door into an office that was barely illuminated by light filtering through closed venetian blinds concealing a small window. The light was sufficient for me to notice that the muzzle of a Browning Hi-Power 9mm automatic was centered on my navel. The Browning is not a small pistol, yet it appeared tiny in the mitt of the behemoth holding it. The behemoth was seated behind a table. He spoke.

"Please remove your jacket, then turn around slowly."

Carefully, I slipped off my blazer; keeping my hands in plain view, I carefully rotated.

"Lift your billfold out, slowly, and set it on the table."

I complied, taking my time, concentrating on not upsetting the man with the pistol.

"Thank you. Now, take three steps backward and turn around. Keep your hands where I can see them."

Again, I did as instructed.

"You may face me, Mr. LeBlanc."

My eyes were becoming accustomed to the dim light. As I regarded the man at the table, I realized that for all of his size, he was ancient. Time had not been kind to his flabby face. The mottled skin was a mass of wrinkles; his features drooped as though they were starting to melt. Even his bald head was wrinkled. He peered at me through thick black-framed glasses.

"So, you are Maria's friend."

"Yes."

"Well, what can I do for you?"

"I would like to talk to you about Stan Petrowski and John Kolakowski."

"Indeed. It makes me uncomfortable when you stand. Please close the door and be seated."

I shut the door and sat down on the only thing available, a cheap metal-framed chair with torn vinyl upholstery.

"Why do you want to know about two men who died over thirty years ago?"

"Mrs. Kolakowski wants to know what happened to them."

"Perhaps Maria is a foolish woman."

"It's possible."

"Why did Maria send you here?"

"She found John's diaries. You were one of the last people he mentioned in them. I also tried to talk to Milo Frankiewicz. He declined to say anything. Instead he gave me your address and telephone number."

The big fleshy head nodded. "That was thoughtful of him."

Wlosowicz placed the pistol on the table, then steepled the fingers of his huge hands. I noted that they were puffy. He caught my stare.

"For some years I have suffered from circulatory problems. Now my kidneys are failing as well. I do not know how long I have to live, but I intend to hang on to every second with all of my ability. Death is not something I look forward to."

"Will you tell me what you know about Stan and John? About what happened to them?"

His eyes fixed on mine.

"Do you believe in the immortality of the soul?"

"Yes."

"Unfortunately, so do I. You see, I am afraid to die because I do not think that my soul will have an easy time of it once I am judged."

I said nothing.

"Do you know how old I am?"

"No."

"I am eighty-three. I have outlived most of my contemporaries and all of my family. The only thing I have to show for my long life is this corrupt body which is dying. You see, Mr. LeBlanc, I wasted all of God's gifts. He blessed me with intelligence and a magnificently strong body. Maybe it was because I had everything that I became self-centered and selfish. I am a genius, or at least I was. My genius lay in being able to unravel the mysteries of life. I was drawn to theology, not from a love of God, but from conceit. I was the mortal who was going to decipher the immortal secrets.

"My career at the university was a resounding success. I was the youngest man ever to hold a full professorship in theology. I married a beautiful, caring woman who loved me deeply. In my arrogance, I put my work, my career before her. We had a child, a healthy, happy boy I should have doted on. Instead, I took him for granted, for being no more than my due. When the news of the German invasion reached us, my wife begged me to leave immediately. She wanted me to take her to safety. Instead, I sent her and our child to her parents without me. I was working on my third book and couldn't be bothered. It would take me several days to pack my materials; besides, I believed I had plenty of time. I totally failed to appreciate how fast my country would be conquered.

"As the Germans advanced, they made war on the entire country. Whenever they encountered refugees on the roads, they slaughtered them in order to prevent our armies from using the roads. A squadron of Stukas attacked the road my wife and child were on. They died, and I wasn't even aware of it until a week later."

Wlosowicz seemed to forget I was in the room with him. I remained perfectly still.

"When I learned what had happened to my wife and child, I was consumed by rage, rage against the Germans and rage against God. I did not blame myself. I told you I was selfish. The news of the German advance was not believed by many of my countrymen. They could not comprehend the Blitzkrieg. I, on the other hand, finally realized that all was lost, that if I wanted to fight the Nazis, I would have to leave the country. Poland was finished.

"I was two months in reaching England. When I arrived, the entire country was in a state of confusion. So many Polish refugees were trying to enlist that, for a while, we were being turned away. I persisted. Do you know I was almost rejected because of my height? I was 6' 7" tall which caused problems in fitting me with uniforms, not to mention boots. My active military career was cut short after an artillery shell landed near my position in North Africa in 1941. I was sent to England to recover. The army was going to discharge me, but I insisted that they find a job for me. Because of my university credentials, I was assigned to intelligence, ultimately being placed in a unit that evaluated aerial photographs. My natural ambition asserted itself. I studied my new profession day and night. By examining photographs of the same area that had been taken over a period of time, I began to predict future enemy activities. I was correct often enough to be promoted to a section where I was provided data along with aerial reconnaissance photographs. My projections were so precise that generals began to ask for me by name. By the end of the war, I had developed into a gifted analyst. I met and cultivated American intelligence officers, realizing that after the war, the United States was going to be the world power; there was a very limited future for a man of my abilities in a washed-up colonial empire.

"I was employed by U.S. Army Intelligence until 1950, before being recruited into the CIA. Once I determined to rise to the top of that organization, my ambition knew no limits. Had things been different, I might have retired as an assistant director."

"What happened?"

"Stanislas Petrowski happened. We met in England during the war, becoming friends. After the war Stan pursued his own agenda which was to free Poland of Communist control. I told him he was chasing a fool's dream. For some years, he was a thorn in the side of the Polish Communists, but hardly a real threat to the regime's stability."

"Did Stan Petrowski start a bank in Cuba with funds he had smuggled into the U.S. before the war?"

"I don't know. Stan did control a bank in Cuba, though I never knew if it was funded by the CIA, or if Stan had used the legendary gold."

"Legendary?"

"Stan was a master of misinformation to mask his own purposes. Once, he related to me a story about his pre-war organization that had foreseen the German invasion, and about the gold it had stockpiled to fight the Nazis. When he established the front companies for the CIA, he spread the word they were funded by Polish gold. It made a good story; certainly it masked any CIA involvement."

"Did Stan ever come to you about a traitor who leaked the Bay of Pigs invasion plans to Castro?"

The old giant sighed. "You are asking me to reveal my sins against my friends and my country. How old were you when the Cuban expatriates launched the Bay of Pigs fiasco?"

"Twelve."

"Then you were too young to know about the politics sur-

Ohio Salt

rounding John F. Kennedy. He was a young, idealistic man with a vision. Youth and idealism sometimes threaten established interests. When Kennedy was elected, the Bay of Pigs invasion had been in the planning stages for several years under President Eisenhower. Kennedy was in favor of the invasion, however he insisted that the invasion force be free of Batista supporters. He wanted to replace Castro with enlightened, democratic leaders. Unfortunately, many of the American business interests that had lost property to Castro had secretly cut deals with the Batista faction in the event Castro was overthrown. The business interests had the ear of a number of politicians, many of whom were opposed to the President's strategies.

"Kennedy had plans to replace J. Edgar Hoover as the head of the FBI, correctly believing that Hoover had grown too powerful. Hoover was aware of his intentions. Before Castro, the FBI had a field office in Havana where the resident agents had nurtured ties with many of the leaders in the Batista government. As the invasion force was being assembled, Hoover, working behind the scenes, did his best to circumvent Kennedy's orders by maneuvering Batista supporters into key roles. By the time the invasion was ready, he had only partially succeeded, though it was enough to splinter the expatriate soldiers. Hoover correctly deduced that if the invasion succeeded, Kennedy would be a national hero with enough popular support to do whatever he wanted, including replacing the Director of the FBI. If the invasion failed, and that failure was attributed to Kennedy's bungling, things might be different.

"When it became apparent that the invasion forces were not controlled by the Batista faction, one of Hoover's trusted men delivered the invasion plans to Castro. This same man, through intermediaries, did what he could to insure that air support would be canceled."

"Wait a minute. Are you telling me that J. Edgar Hoover ordered someone to give Castro the Bay of Pigs invasion plans?"

"I am saying that one of his trusted men performed the deed. Whether or not he was ordered to do so is conjecture. However, Hoover remained in power after the invasion failed."

I focused my most penetrating stare on Stephen Wlosowicz. It didn't seem to bother him.

"How do you know this?"

Frank C. Dupuy

"I was an intelligence analyst. As I reviewed the data, it was apparent that Kennedy's orders had been flouted and the invasion deliberately undermined. Even the press was aware that Castro had the invasion plans in advance. It wasn't until later that I learned the identities of the people involved."

"How did you find out?"

"A few weeks after the invasion, Stan invited me to dinner. He asked me for my assessment of the invasion. I shared with him that I believed that the invasion had been sabotaged by people in our own government who were at odds with the Kennedy Administration."

"Did you tell him about Hoover?"

"No. Stan was a big boy. If he wanted to start a fight, all of the clues were there for him to follow." Wlosowicz sighed heavily. "You must understand that at the time, I still had career aspirations. My job was to analyze foreign intelligence data and make projections. Precipitating a battle with J. Edgar Hoover was an insanity I did not care to indulge."

"So what happened?"

"The world went on. My agency had been aware for some time of the potential for the Soviet Union to install nuclear missiles in Cuba. In May, 1962, Stan Petrowski brought me a Cuban military survey for a missile site and photographs of an intermediate-range Soviet missile at a Cuban Air Force base. He claimed he had purchased the survey and the photos from a Cuban defector. With the other data we had collected, I felt justified in alerting my superiors that there were now Soviet missiles in Cuba. I did not show them Stan's documents. I took credit for it as my own analysis. The skeptics wanted proof, yet it wasn't until July that the first U2 photos confirmed the construction of the missile sites. Events escalated. By October we almost went to war with Russia. Fortunately, Krushev backed down."

"Are you telling me that Stan Petrowski beat the CIA to the punch on the Cuban missile crisis?"

"Yes. Because of his information, my reputation was enhanced to the point that I was promoted over a number of senior analysts. Stan knew what he was doing. He wanted me to be promoted, to be indebted to him. That's why he brought the materials to me in the first place. It is the way the world works."

"Surely, there is more to this story?"

"Unfortunately, yes. Stan would not relinquish his search for the people who had betrayed the invasion. I know that he deduced that Mr. Hoover tacitly had a finger in the debacle. What Stan wanted was the bag man, the person who actually delivered the plan. If he could expose him, the rest of the plot would unravel, or so he thought.

"In the summer of 1963, Stan was contacted through his network by a Cuban intelligence officer, whose loyalty was being questioned by Castro. Mario Guzman was one of Fidel's original revolutionaries who had been rewarded with a position in intelligence. Stan never divulged his contacts, but I believe that Guzman was the source of the missile site survey and the photographs. Whether Guzman was motivated by sheer greed or a genuine disillusionment with the Castro government is open for speculation. I imagine it was a combination. At any rate, Guzman chose to leave Cuba after he had acquired what he considered to be a highly marketable commodity." Wlosowicz paused expectantly so, I obliged him.

"What was that?"

"It was the details of a plot to assassinate John Fitzgerald Kennedy."

Frank C. Dupuy

36

My plane landed at Cleveland Hopkins at 5:28 PM. By the time I had retrieved my car from airport parking, it was a little past 6:00. I called Carl Branner to make certain his guests were still safe. He assured me they were, and that he was charging extra for his food expenses.

I headed east on Interstate 480, mulling over what I was going to say to Les Fazio. I figured that by now, Herb Kramer, the corrupted OmniBank loan officer, had received his invitation from Dan Dutton to visit him in his office on Monday. That being the case, Kramer had probably burned up miles of telephone wires trying to relay the good news to Ted Meyers. If Ted was still hiding out, it was a good bet Kramer had called Les Fazio. I wasn't certain where to find Meyers, but thanks to the telephone directory, I knew where Fazio lived.

Solon is an upscale, newer suburb of Cleveland, popular with young, upwardly mobile professionals. Personally, I have nothing against Yuppies; I simply don't want my son to marry one. West Wood Estates is a planned community, or so the gilt-edged sign proclaimed. I followed a broad, winding avenue until I reached Bentwood Court, the street where Les Fazio resided. His house was a large, faux Tudor, two-story structure with an attached two car garage and two bicycles in the front yard. I parked in the driveway behind a maroon Chrysler mini-van.

I rang the door bell. A few moments later, the door was opened by a skinny, eight year old girl with bright eyes and a skinned knee.

"Hi, is Les home?" I inquired politely.

"D-A-D-D-Y!" she bellowed over her shoulder. "There's a man here to see you."

Frank C. Dupuy

"Heather, for goodness sakes, stop yelling," yelled a mature female voice.

More muffled noises emanated from the interior of the house. Finally Lester Fazio ambled up to the front door. It was the first time I had ever seen him without a starched white shirt and tie. He was wearing a long sleeved Cleveland Browns sweatshirt and a pair of old, checked golf pants. The outfit did nothing to conceal his obesity. When he recognized me, he scowled.

"Heather, go in the kitchen with your mother."

"Why? Who's he?"

"Heather, now."

Heather shot her father the "look" before running off down the hall.

"LeBlanc, what in the hell do you mean by coming to my home?"

"We need to talk, Les."

"Bullshit. You get your ass offa my property." His complexion was evolving into an unhealthy shade of pink.

"Suits me. I guess I'll just mosey on over to Herb Kramer's house for a little chitchat. Of course, I don't think he'll be as rude when he hears what I have to say."

Fazio's color faded from pink to parchment. His belligerent expression diminished.

"What do you want?" he finally asked.

"I want to talk. You are about to land in more trouble than you ever dreamed of. I can keep you out of some of it."

"What are you talking about?"

"I'm talking about a 2.5 million dollar loan fraud scheme that has just gone bust. Not to mention your being an accessory to murder."

Glossy sweat beads formed on his head and face. He really should have something done about his thermostat.

"Jesus, LeBlanc, what do you want?"

"I want to talk to you and Ted. Just the three of us. If Ted agrees to help me, I can get the murder charge dropped."

"Help you how?"

"Les, the three of us need to talk. Is Ted in there?" I gestured toward the house.

214

Ohio Salt

"How did you know?" Fazio inquired resignedly.

"When Ted paged me the other night to call him at a pay phone, it had a Solon extension. The cops would never think to look in your house."

"Wait here for a minute, will you?"

I waited. I heard a back door slam. A few minutes later, Fazio beckoned me to come in. I followed him down the hall to a spacious den. Seated on a couch, wearing khaki shorts and a polo shirt was Ted Meyers, holding a glass in his hand.

"Well, hell. Come join the party." He raised his glass.

"You want a drink?" Fazio inquired, "I'm gonna hit the Scotch."

"Sure, I'll join you."

He poured two stiff drinks and handed me one. I sat in a chair where I could peruse both of them.

"Cheers," I intoned.

Fazio and Meyers nodded a glum acknowledgment.

"What's up?" Ted inquired with a poor attempt at being casual.

"I want to tell you a story. Stop me at any point if I get it wrong. Let's go back to over a year ago, to the time your sweetheart government deal fell through. You barely managed to avoid being sucked into your pal Congressman Poje's mess. What you ended up with was a hell of a lot of debt and specialized equipment you couldn't unload. Then, when the Sealake project failed to materialize, you had to do something to prevent the Carlucci brothers from breaking off portions of your anatomy. So what did you do? You purchased an old factory building for cheap from St. Theresa's Church, then transformed it into T. M. Manufacturing. Your extremely competent right hand man, Lester Fazio, created a beautiful set of fictitious financials, plus spurious supporting documents. All that was needed was a sympathetic loan officer, say one like Herb Kramer. I won't ask you how you recruited him, but I can guess. A little wining, dining and a $500 a night hooker. You probably threw in a finder's fee.

"Through Kramer's connivance, you received two and a half million, which was enough to keep the Carluccis off your ass, and sufficient to maintain your solvency. All was well until it was announced that your bosom enemy, Harold Lipscomb, was about to be named to the OmniBank board of directors, the very financial institution where you have a spurious loan. What to do? Sometimes fate intervenes. Who should come along but Gwen Hiltie, your old girl friend from the Cleveland Yacht Club. You remember Gwen? She's the one you hooked on cocaine. You managed to have her hired by Lipscomb; before you knew it, she had him in bed divulging all sorts of useful information into her shell-like ear.

"Well, all good things come to an end. When you decided it was time to obtain the evidence you needed to blackmail Lipscomb, you sent your girl spy to hire good ole Adrian LeBlanc to take the pictures. Which he attempted to do in good faith, though he almost got killed in the process. Gwen wasn't so lucky; she died. How'm I doing so far?"

Meyers and Fazio were like two men who had just received invitations to spend some time in Auschwitz.

"How much of this do the cops know?" Meyers implored weakly.

"None of it, yet. Dan Dutton, the OmniBank head of security, knows about the loan."

"What do you want?"

"Information. Let me finish. On the morning I came in to see Les, he was nervous when I mentioned you were an accessory to murder, yet he was utterly dumbfounded when I told him about Gwen Hiltie, although I didn't know her name then. Later, it occurred to me to wonder – if not Hiltie, then who did Les think you murdered? The answer -- Louie Kolakowski, a relatively harmless P.I. who was chasing a fantasy on your T.M. Manufacturing property. When Les read the security officer's report, he spazzed out.

"Which one of you decided to kill Louie?"

Meyers and Fazio swivelled their heads towards each other.

"We both did," Meyers mumbled, "Only they weren't supposed to kill him. Just frighten him is all I wanted them to do."

"Them, as in a couple of charmers you met through your drug connections?"

"Something like that."

"The only reason Kolakowski is alive is because those two goons missed."

"Christ, LeBlanc, we were panicked," Fazio said. "We

Ohio Salt

thought Lipscomb or somebody had set him on us."

"Yeah, I suppose you were going to use those same two angels to scare me and my family?"

Meyers almost choked on his drink. "I swear to God, Adrian, I would never have done anything to you, or your family. I was petrified; I just wanted to say something to make you lay off me."

"Did you guys have someone break into my office?"

"No, never. You might have us on everything else, but not that." Meyers declared virtuously.

"How about Kolakowski's office?"

They both shook their heads. I watched them without expression.

"Look, we're telling you the truth." Fazio pleaded, "You're right about everything else, but we didn't break in to your offices."

"OK. Ted, did you know Gwen Hiltie had a girl friend?"

He gawked at me open mouthed. "Jesus Christ, Adrian, is there anything you don't know?"

"Tell me about Hiltie."

"Ah, Jeez, where to begin? Gwen Hiltie had a body that wouldn't quit, and knew how to use it. I've slept with a lot of women, but she was the most sensuous, provocative woman I ever screwed. She was incredible. I only learned that Gwen went both ways after she came back, the day she told me she was seeing her high school lover. When I asked what his name was, she laughed and said "Her name is Sally." I found out later, this Sally is a cop somewhere."

"Did Gwen ask you to supply her habit?"

"Habit? Do you mean did I buy her coke?"

"Yes, that's what I mean. It's an expensive hobby."

"I know. I only got her an ounce, one time. After that, she didn't ask me any more. She told me Sally could get her all she wanted."

"What?"

"It's true, I swear. She told me Sally could supply her with all the coke she needed."

I tried not to register the shock I felt. I didn't notice that the conversation had stopped as I tried to assimilate that last bit of information. Eventually, my silence started to upset Fazio.

"Say something, will you?"

"Whose idea was it to take the pictures of Lipscomb at his cottage?"

"Mine," said Meyers. "I told her I wanted photos of them going into and leaving some place. She suggested the cottage and told me how it could be done."

"Did she tell you she already had her own evidence?"

"What evidence?"

"I think she recorded all of her telephone conversations."

"Damn. You think she was recording me?"

"I think she recorded everyone."

"Why?"

"Insurance, or maybe she decided to go into business for herself. You might have even ended up paying a little hush money. Now that I think about it, that's an excellent motive for you to have murdered her."

The last drop of blood drained from Ted Meyers's already pallid features. "I swear I had nothing to do with killing her. I didn't even know the bitch was planning to do anything to me."

"I believe you." I leaned back in my chair, leisurely examining the dynamic duo. "Les, how about another round? I think it's time to negotiate."

37

It was a little after 9:00 when I reached Carl's house. My meeting with Ted Meyers and Les Fazio had gone as well as I could have hoped. They would do their part when I asked them to. I wondered how my meeting with Maria Kolakowski would end.

Carl Branner greeted me at the door. "How goes it, Hawkshaw?" Carl reads vintage detective novels.

"It goes. How are your guests?"

Carl made a face. "Well, they are pleasant and entertaining company. Karen and Louie insist on taking care of most of the chores. As for me, I have made another discovery."

"Oh?"

"There is absolutely nothing wrong with Mrs. Kolakowski."

"How do you know?"

"Most mornings I sleep until 8:00. I arose a trifle early this morning to confirm my nasty suspicions. A truly ill and weak person has to stay in bed. On the other hand, a healthy person cannot abide spending days in bed. When my alarm went off at 6:00, I quietly let myself out of the house by the back stairway. I selected a spot by the rear hedge where I could observe Mrs. Kolakowski's window. The lights were already on in her room. At 6:15, Louie and Karen entered her room dressed in sweat clothes. Mrs. Kolakowski already had hers on. They pushed the bed against one wall, then turned on the television set. For the next thirty minutes the three of them engaged in vigorous aerobic exercise. That woman really has some moves," Carl remarked admiringly.

"Karen?"

"No, Mrs. Kolakowski."

"You're kidding."

"Cross my heart. That woman is in better physical condition

than most twenty year olds."

"Well, hell. I think it's time I had a little chat with Mrs. Kolakowski."

Carl led the way past a formal dining room and a spacious living room to Maria Kolakowski's sick room. She was propped up in her bed watching an old John Wayne flick on one of the cable channels. Karen and Louie were seated in chairs next to her holding hands, blissfully observing John Wayne setting explosive charges at an oil well fire. I cleared my throat. The two love birds let go of each other's hands.

"Adrian, you're back," exclaimed Louie. His grasp of the obvious is amazing.

"Yes, I am. Now, I want you, Karen and Carl to leave the room. I have some information that is for Mrs. Kolakowski only."

Four sets of eyes followed me as I turned off the television set.

"Out." I gestured toward the door. As soon as everyone had trooped out of the room, I closed the door, then sat in a chair next to the bed.

"What is it, Mr. LeBlanc?" Maria Kolakowski queried in a faint voice.

I sighed heavily as I dropped my gaze to the floor. "I'm afraid I have some bad news."

She gazed at me, her eyes large with concern.

"What is it? You can tell me."

"It's from the Surgeon General," I confided, using the tone favored by funeral directors.

"The Surgeon General?"

"Yes. He says that there is nothing wrong with you, you brass-bound old fraud."

Maria Kolakowski gaped at me in shock. Then, so help me, she giggled twice, before convulsing with laughter.

"You're amused?"

"Oh, it was.... oh, it was your face – the look on your face," she managed to gasp as she failed to control her mirth.

I waited. It took her almost a minute before she could meet my eyes without cracking up.

"I am so sorry. You must think I am a horrible person. It was a reaction to the tension and the strain. I am not used to this."

Ohio Salt

"Used to what?"

"This lying and play acting and danger. I am out of my depth."

I forbore telling her that I thought she was out of her frigging mind. Instead, I stood up and headed for the door.

"Mrs. Kolakowski, I would appreciate it if you would get dressed and come into the den. We need to have a serious discussion."

I located Carl in the kitchen and asked him to brew a pot of coffee. He correctly divined that I was not in a conversational mood, so he left me alone to watch the coffee as it dripped into the glass pot. I heard a noise behind me. It was Karen Koenig, a very contrite Karen Koenig.

"Hi, boss."

I surveyed her without speaking.

"I guess I'm fired, huh?"

"You can resign if you like."

"I don't blame you for being angry."

"That's big of you."

"Louie and I are in love."

"Congratulations."

"Are you going to quit helping Louie and Maria?"

"I don't know."

Karen clasped her hands and held them down in front of her.

"I'm sorry, Adrian."

"Me too. Karen, it is one thing for a client, or for Louie and his mom for that matter, to run a scam on me; it is totally different when it is done to me by my own secretary. We are dealing with some very brutal men. Not knowing all of the facts might have gotten me killed. We've worked together long enough for you to realize that."

Karen nodded sadly as she left the kitchen. I wanted to punch somebody. The coffee had barely finished brewing when Maria Kolakowski arrived. She was wearing a cotton blouse and a long skirt. Her hair was pulled back into a pony tail. Now that she was out of her bathrobe and hospital bed, I could see that even at seventy-four, Louie's mother had a slender, wiry build. I guessed her to be about 5' 3" tall.

"Would you care for a cup of coffee?" I asked.

"Yes, thank you."

I motioned her over to a small breakfast table by the window. We sat down across from one another.

"Suppose we start over."

"I would like that, Mr. LeBlanc."

"Adrian."

"Adrian, I would appreciate it if you would call me by my first name."

"Done. Now, will you please tell me what you are up to?"

"Where to begin? What I told you about my daughter's being kidnaped was true. I never pursued what happened to John after that. In fact, other than Joseph Jablonski, I never divulged to anyone what happened. When I brought my daughter home from that abandoned house, I called the neighbors and the police, telling them Katherine had gotten lost and finally found her way home. I warned Katherine to keep what had happened to her a secret and she did. I never gave the men who did it any reason to harm my family. After I stopped trying to discover what had happened to my husband, I grieved, Adrian. For years, I grieved for my husband. You have no idea what it is like never to have closure, and to be powerless to pursue answers. Then, last month, I found some of John's old files."

"You didn't find three boxes of diaries hidden behind the basement wall?"

"No. John did not keep diaries as far as I know."

"Where did you find the files?"

"In a file cabinet in the basement. John had several file cabinets that he kept business documents in. I went through them after he died, but never discovered anything of interest. I couldn't bring myself to throw them away, so they sat there for thirty years. Last month, I was concerned that water was seeping into a corner of the basement. I needed to move the cabinets in order to inspect the wall behind them. The cabinets were too heavy for me to move because they were full of papers. When I started emptying the drawers, I saw that one drawer was shorter than the others. When I removed the drawer, I found a compartment behind it that contained three files.

"One of the files included a notarized copy of Stan's will with instructions on how to dispose of his assets in the event of his death or disappearance. John had power of attorney to handle the disposition of the properties and funds. Milo Frankiewicz was to handle Stan's affairs in the event John was unable to. Stan had made provisions that insured St. Theresa'a Catholic School received the income from the factories in the event that he was absent more that two months without contacting John or Milo Frankiewicz. If he died or failed to contact John or Milo within six months, his estate was to be signed over to St. Theresa's school with the provision that nothing could be sold for twenty-nine years.

"There was also a detailed accounting of the value of Stan's properties and the trust fund he had set up for the school. There was over $150,000 in the trust fund alone. On paper, Stan's factories were worth over $3,000,000. That was a considerable fortune in 1963."

"What was in the other files?"

"One was a file with correspondence to Milo Frankiewicz. I'm afraid John and Stan were not happy with Milo."

"Because of his drinking?"

"It was his drinking, and Stan was upset with Milo's management of company funds. They had a huge argument in early November. Stan had threatened to fire Milo. One of the letters I found was addressed to a C.P.A. firm dated November 14, 1963. John was confirming that an audit of the companies' books was scheduled for December 1st.

"The last file was labeled 'Traitors'. It contained cryptic notes and dates that John had written. They appeared to relate to Stan's and John's search for the person who had given Castro the Bay of Pigs invasion plans. Some of the notes must have had something to do with the assassination plot. John had dates in 1961 written next to Michael Ungar's name. He also had a short list of names on one page including Wlosowicz, Mondragón, Ungar, Oswald, and Freemont."

"Oswald, as in Lee Harvey Oswald?"

"I don't know."

"How about Freemont?"

"There was a David Freemont who was the Special Agent in Charge of the Cleveland FBI office in 1963. I know because I tried to talk to him after John disappeared."

"Did he have any words of wisdom?"

"We never met. He promised he would look into John and Stan's disappearance. A few weeks later, he died in an automobile accident."

"Were there any other names?"

Maria Kolakowski pulled a folded sheet of paper from the pocket of her skirt and handed it to me. I unfolded it, then read the names written on it.

        Wlosowicz
        Mondragón
        Ungar
        Oswald
        Freeman.
        Guzman
        Turner

"Who was Guzman?" I asked, watching her face.

"I don't know. Maybe he had something to do with the invasion."

"How about Turner?"

"As far as I know John only knew a Kevin Turner, a journalist who was writing a book on the Bay of Pigs invasion. He contacted Stan and John about a year after the invasion. He wanted to interview people who had participated in the training and planning."

"Did they talk to Turner?"

"John told me they had, on the condition that Turner never used their names. Turner was interested in trying to document exactly what had gone wrong and who was to blame. Evidently, Stan and Turner occasionally exchanged notes."

"What happened to Turner?"

"He committed suicide in 1964."

"A lot of that was going around back then. What else was in those files?"

"That was it."

I contemplated the lady sitting across from me, wondering how she had avoided being institutionalized.

"What was all of this talk about $5,000,000 in hidden gold?"

"It was part of my plan."

"What plan?"

Ohio Salt

"When I read those files, all of the hurt, anger and fear I had suppressed for thirty years was released. I vowed that I would find the men who murdered my husband. So I planned. It occurred to me that the threat of exposure, and greed, would bring the guilty parties into the open. At the very least, it might persuade someone who knew something to talk to me. I also wanted to protect myself. I decided that my dying of a terminal illness would only enhance the story, and give me the excuse to be in a place where I was looked after."

"Oh?"

"Sister Mary Lipinski is the director of the Immaculate Heart of Jesus nursing home. I have been a volunteer there for many years; she and I are good friends. When I confided to her what I was engaged in, she agreed to let me use a room for several weeks. That way I would always have people around me. I kept the emergency buzzer under my pillow at all times.

"The first person I spoke with was Joseph Jablonski. Though I trusted Joseph, I was certain he knew more than he had ever told me. I called him and asked him to visit me at the nursing home. It is difficult to turn down the dying request of an old friend. When he came to see me, I showed him the files I had found. He read each file carefully. Something he read upset him. I asked what was wrong. Instead of giving me a direct answer, he told me about the contingency money Stan had entrusted him with, or at least the secret to the money's location."

"Did he tell you how much Stan had tucked away?"

"No, he only told me it was a lot, although to Joseph a thousand dollars was a lot. I asked him again if he would tell me what was bothering him. He told me something he had seen in the files was puzzling, that he needed to think. He promised he would call me when he was certain." Maria Kolakowski's eyes shifted to her coffee cup. "I think Joseph was old-fashioned regarding women. He did not believe we should be involved in men's work.

"I discussed everything with Louie. He told me that we needed your involvement because you are the smartest investigator he has ever met. He wanted to tell you everything. I was the one who decided to trick you into helping us. I didn't know you. I thought that the story of the hidden gold would induce you to look into the case.

Frank C. Dupuy

I apologize. I was wrong."

"Why don't you tell me the rest of the story?"

"I sent letters to Milo Frankiewicz, Stephen Wlosowicz and Michael Ungar, informing them that I had discovered John's diaries. I stated that I was dying and that I wanted their help in finding out what had happened to John and Stan. I wrote that in part of his diaries, John had alluded to a list of names he had compiled of the people who had betrayed the invasion, and names of people who were involved in the Kennedy assassination. I stated that I had not located the lists yet, that because of my illness I had been unable to read all of the material, but that I intended to read a little everyday. With luck, I would be ready to talk to them in several weeks. I also went into detail about how John had left directions to locate Stan's contingency fund of 1,000 pounds of gold."

"Did you mention Joseph Jablonski in your letter?"

"No, never. When he called me Monday morning, he asked me if I had gone to anyone. I told him you were going to help us, that you were a famous investigator he could trust. He promised me he would call you. That was the last time I ever spoke to him." Maria Kolakowski's lower lip trembled, then tears started flowing down her face.

"I am responsible. He was tortured to death because of my foolish scheme. I killed him." She placed her hands over her face and sobbed uncontrollably.

38

After Maria Kolakowski had finished her cry, I handed her several paper napkins. I couldn't locate any Kleenex. She dried her eyes.

"I am sorry. I seem to have made a mess of everything."

"Not necessarily. If you didn't mention Joseph Jablonski in your letter, then he must have called someone. Something he saw in the file prompted him to make a call. Whoever he called killed him, or had it done. Whoever it was wanted something he had."

"I never mentioned his name."

"Then you are not responsible." I walked over to the counter where I retrieved the coffee pot and refilled our cups.

"Was there any truth to your story about Stan Petrowski smuggling gold into this country before the war?"

"Yes, and later John helped Stan smuggle the gold into Cuba."

I sipped my coffee, then made a decision.

"Would you like to know what Stephen Wlosowicz told me?"

"Yes. Please, tell me."

So I did, not omitting any part of what the decrepit old giant had confessed.

"It was the details of the plot to assassinate John Fitzgerald Kennedy," Wlosowicz stated gravely.

"How did a Cuban intelligence officer know about a plot to kill Kennedy?" I challenged.

"When Stan and John met with Guzman, it was to purchase the identity of the person who had provided the invasion plans to Castro. Stan gave Guzman $10,000 for the traitor's name."

I couldn't restrain myself. "Who was it?"

"Claudio Mondragón."

I digested that information. "I thought Petrowski was looking for an FBI agent."

"Mondragón was only the conduit. According to Guzman, Mondragón landed in Cuba as part of a scout team about a month before the invasion. They were transported near the coast in a U.S. Navy submarine, then used a rubber raft to row to the beach. Mondragón murdered the three men in his team before contacting the Cuban authorities.

Guzman was present at his debriefing. Mondragón claimed that the invasion plans were supplied to him by a government agent. The Cubans were skeptical until he led them to the bodies of the men he had murdered. Guzman informed Stan and John that Mondragón claimed that U.S. government officials opposed to the Kennedy administration did not want the invasion to succeed."

"And the Cubans believed him?"

"Enough to permit him to make his rendezvous with the submarine. Castro knew that an invasion was being planned. Until then, he had not known when or where."

"Did Guzman name the government agent?"

"No. Guzman told them that it was his impression that the agent worked for the CIA, but he wasn't certain. However, it was not difficult for John and Stan to deduce that Michael Ungar was involved. After all, he was the FBI liaison agent, and Mondragón was his shadow."

"Did Guzman provide anymore details?"

"If he did, Stan did not confide them to me. What Guzman did do was offer to sell Stan the details of a Cuban plot to assassinate President Kennedy. He demanded $20,000 in cash before he would talk. Stan required proof before he would produce the money. Guzman provided them with the particulars of a failed U.S. assassination attempt on Fidel Castro. Kennedy had contacted a mafia capo to ask him to arrange for Castro to be assassinated. This was after the Bay of Pigs invasion. The scheme almost worked. When Castro learned about it, he was furious, and planned his revenge. Guzman was one of the planners."

"What happened?

"Stan had to arrange for a wire transfer of funds. They made plans to meet the next day. Unfortunately, someone murdered Guzman that night."

"Why didn't Stan and John go straight to the authorities and blow the whistle?"

"Because Guzman had stated that U.S. government officials were involved. They didn't know whom they could trust. Oh, Guzman did give them the name of one of the men in plot."

"Who?"

"Oswald."

"Are you telling me that this Guzman told Stan Petrowski that Lee Harvey Oswald was going to assassinate the President of the United States?"

"No. He only told them the last name as a teaser, to show he had hard information. He insisted on cash before he would provide any more details."

"What did they do?"

"After Guzman was murdered, Stan came to see me. He wanted to know if I had come across anything that might corroborate Guzman's story. He also asked me to provide him with any agency files on Guzman. Although we had nothing on an assassination plot, we did have a fairly thick file on Guzman."

"When did Stan come to you with this information?"

"In September, 1963."

"Did he say what he was going to do about Ungar?"

"Stan talked about a sting operation."

"Such as?"

"He was going to contact Ungar to tell him about his meeting with Guzman. His intent was to ask Ungar's help in investigating the assassination plot. He was also going to tell Ungar that he was meeting with a second defector to learn who had betrayed the invasion to Castro."

"Did he?"

Wlosowicz seemed to crumple. "I think so."

"What does that mean?"

"After my meeting with Stan, I researched the name Oswald. I had at least a dozen hits in our files. The most promising one was an ex-marine who had lived in Russia for several years. He was on an alert list because he had visited the Soviet and the Cuban embassies in Mexico City in October. I called Stan to arrange a meeting. I provided him with the information on Oswald."

"When did you and Stan meet?"

"November 10, 1963."

"What happened?"

"After I gave Stan the information, including Oswald's address in Texas, he said he was going forward with the Ungar sting. He also told me that he was going to notify a friend of his in the FBI office in Cleveland."

"Did he ask you to do anything else for him?"

"Yes, he asked me to officially notify my people that there was a Cuban plot to assassinate the President."

"Did you?"

"No, Mr. LeBlanc, I did not."

"Why?"

"Because his source was Guzman. If I alerted my people, the Petrowski/Guzman connection would be discovered, as well as my relationship with Stan Petrowski. Ultimately, it would come to someone's attention that Stan had been my source of information about Russian missiles in Cuba, and that I had been dishonest in my analysis. My big promotion had been based on that analysis. I would be finished."

"So what did you do?"

"Nothing. I did not learn until after the assassination that Stan and John had disappeared the day before. So you see, because of my career concerns I said nothing, and the President of the United States was assassinated."

We regarded each other in the dim, shabby room. I hoped that my face was not conveying my thoughts. Wlosowicz broke the silence.

"When the news flashed that John F. Kennedy had been struck down by an assassin's bullet, the enormity of what I had done consumed me. A year and a half later I suffered a nervous breakdown. Everyday for thirty years, I have lived with my sin. It was not only the President who died because of me. Stanislas Petrowski and John Kolakowski died as a result of my cowardice. If I had acted, those men would be alive today, or at least would have survived to see old age."

"Do you know who killed them?"

"No, but I can make an educated guess. I believe Stan contacted Ungar, telling him about the plot and the other informant. Ungar probably alerted his superiors, the ones who had condoned his supplying information to Castro. Ungar, or his accomplices, killed Stan and John to silence them."

"You mean people in the FBI sat on information about an assassination attempt?"

"Why not? I did. Ungar and his conspirators had considerably more at stake than I did. If I were to conjecture, I might imagine that Mr. Hoover would have been relieved to have the threat to his tenure eliminated."

"Have you been in contact with anyone who was involved in this?"

"No. When I received Maria's letter I panicked before it finally dawned on me that no information she might possess could harm me now. If, in the unlikely event she went public, I doubted that she could prove anything. I did not worry until I learned that Joseph Jablonski had been murdered. A crime that brutal made CNN. I was pondering what to do when I received a curious telephone call. It frightened me. I called a friend who owns this building. He is allowing me to hide here until this drama plays itself out, or I muster the courage to return to my house."

"What did the caller say?"

"It was a muffled voice. The caller asked to speak with Stephen Wlosowicz. When I identified myself the caller said, 'Be warned. Joseph Jablonski has died for your sins.'

"That's it?"

"That was all."

"Did you know Jablonski?"

"He often traveled with Stan. He functioned as his valet and general helper. Even though Stan was quite skillful with his artificial leg, he occasionally required assistance."

"Did Jablonski know about Guzman, Ungar, and the assassination plot?"

"I don't know. Certainly, he must have overheard things, but I do not think Stan confided sensitive information to him."

We spoke for another half hour, mostly going over details.

As I was preparing to leave, Wlosowicz pushed his chair back from the table. I hadn't realized until then that he was in a wheel chair. He caught my glance.

"I told you that I have circulation problems. My legs were amputated last year. Their sacrifice bought me a little more time." He hesitated. "I would appreciate it if you would contact me when you resolve this matter. I miss my house."

"How do I reach you?"

"Call my home number. It is call-forwarded to my cellular telephone."

"So, I went to the airport and took the next flight to Cleveland," I stated as I concluded my story.

"How horrible. That poor man." Maria Kolakowski shook her head sadly.

"That poor man has a lot to answer for."

She didn't argue with me; instead, she asked, "What are you going to do now, Adrian?"

"Set some wheels in motion, and hope that I don't get run over."

39

Monday

"So that's where we are," I concluded to a glum Collin Yates.
He shook his head. "It's a mess. You have a lot of supposition, but no evidence that will stand up in court."
"I will, and you're going to help me."
"How?" he asked warily.
"I want you to call J.C. Jensen to arrange a meeting in your office. Tell him that under no circumstances is he to let anyone know he is seeing us."
"Can I tell him why we are meeting?"
"No. Just tell him it's important, that he'll have to trust me."
"Are you always this high handed?"
"Only when serving the cause of justice."
Yates surveyed me, his features heavy with concentration.
"LeBlanc, you are a piece of work. I don't suppose that whatever you are planning will provide the D.A. with grounds to disbar me?"
"Trust me," I replied brightly. Yates was still glowering when I left his office.
My next appointment was not going to be fun. Informing a man that his son is an embezzler never is. I had phoned Harold Lipscomb last night asking him to invent some excuse to keep Harry, Jr. out of the office this morning. He grumbled some before promising he would. When I arrived at Newport Industries, the receptionist was expecting me. I was ushered into Lipscomb's office immediately. The man was a tad crabby.
"LeBlanc, you have my attention. Now, tell me what you have been up to."

Frank C. Dupuy

"Mr. Lipscomb, when you hired me, you asked me to do two things. One was to find out who murdered Gwen Hiltie; the other was to determine if your life was in danger. I am on the verge of learning the answers to both questions. Whether or not I do depends on you."

"What do you mean?"

"I mean I want you to trust me by not acting on the information I am about to give you."

"What are you talking about?"

I sighed. "Mr. Lipscomb, I am asking you to have faith in me, to promise that you will go along with me for the next forty-eight hours, no matter how painful things may become for you personally."

Lipscomb administered a long, hard stare. I was getting a lot of that lately.

"Very well, we'll do it your way."

"When Gwen Hiltie came to my office, she was driving a '93 Lexus registered to Ontario Enterprises. The apartment house she lived in is owned by Ontario Enterprises. When I asked for a list of your vendors, Ontario Enterprises was on there.

"Ontario Enterprises has two addresses, one on East 80th Street and one on Detroit. The East 80th Street address is an abandoned building. The one on Detroit is a secretarial service which provides accommodation addresses for people who work out of their homes. According to tho Ohio Secretary of State's office, Ontario Enterprises is owned by a J.B. Johnson. I sent a package to him at the secretarial service to see who would pick it up. Your son, Harold Lipscomb, Jr., was observed putting the package in the trunk of his Miata, and then followed to his house."

Lipscomb's face was a stony mask. He punched a button on his telephone.

"Betty, have Bill Plunket to come to my office. Immediately."

"Who's Bill Plunket?"

"He is the manager in charge of accounts payable." Before I could say anything, Lipscomb held up his hand. "The man is totally discreet. Not only that, he and Harry do not care for each other."

A few moments later, a narrow-shouldered man with a waist that was starting sag knocked on the door. Lipscomb did not introduce us.

Ohio Salt

"Bill, I want you to pull the file on Ontario Enterprises. I want to know what we purchased from them and how much we have paid them. I do not want anyone other than you involved. Understand?"

Bill nodded as he exited silently. Lipscomb stood up and started pacing. His hands were clasped tightly behind his back. Neither of us spoke. Four minutes later, Plunket knocked on the door.

"Come in. Well?"

"Ontario Enterprises has been a vendor since October of 1992. They supply miscellaneous tooling and supplies. To date we have spent $479,540 with them."

"Is everything in order?" Lipscomb barked.

"Not exactly, sir."

"What do you mean, not exactly?"

"Well, there don't seem to be any receiving documents in the file." Plunket was examining the carpet nervously. "The vendor inspection was done by Harry, and apparently, he established the account."

"Anything else?"

"The invoices come to Harry and he signs them."

"Thank you, Bill. Leave the file here. Do I need to remind you to keep this to yourself?"

"No, sir." Plunket almost ran out of the room.

Lipscomb crouched at his desk, slowly perusing the file. When he finished, he leaned back in his chair.

"$480,000 is a hell of a lot of money, isn't it?"

"Yes, sir," I answered, then asked, "What is a vendor inspection letter?"

"Last year, I initiated a site inspection program for all of our vendors we do over $100,000 with. People from our purchasing department are supposed to go to a vendor's premises to verify that they are who they say they are. The program is being phased in over a two year period. What Bill reacted to was an inspection report from a vice president. That is highly unusual, not to mention that there are no receiving documents in the file." Lipscomb began absentmindedly tapping his palm with a ball point pen. "Tell me about my son and Gwen Hiltie."

"Besides the fact that she was living in an apartment owned by your son and driving his Lexus, I don't really know anything."

"Is Harry involved in Gwen's murder?" Lipscomb asked. The sphinx might have displayed more emotion.

"I don't know. I intend to find out within the next forty-eight hours. The best I can tell you is that he may or may not be."

"Do what you have to do. I want to know the truth." His eyes locked onto mine. "All of it."

40

I wandered over to the well-equipped kitchenette where the coffee maker was located to refill my cup before returning to the spare office where I killed time by reading Yates's <u>Wall Street Journal</u>. A little after 10:00, a secretary arrived to announce that Mr. Jensen was in the lobby. I made it to Collin Yates's office about thirty seconds before J.C. Jensen was escorted in by Yates himself. When Jensen caught sight of me, his expression was not exactly cordial.

"This had better be good, LeBlanc. I have two pissed off detectives who claim that you are interfering with a homicide investigation. Not only that, I heard you just happened to find another mutilated corpse. Every time I talk to Collin, he asks me questions; when I give him answers, he counsels me to be patient. Well, I've been patient, and now I'm here for the secret goddamn meeting you called."

"J.C., I want you to know that I am grateful for your forbearance, and that you went to bat for me the night I discovered Gwen Hiltie's body. I also appreciate that you shared confidential information with Collin. If you will bear with me for a few more minutes, I have a couple of questions for you, then I'll tell you everything I know. After that, I will ask you to help me prove who murdered Gwen Hiltie."

"What do you want to know?" Jensen asked resignedly.

"Has the Sheriff's department made any significant cocaine busts lately? Specifically, do you have any large quantities stored as evidence?"

Jensen's eyes narrowed. "Yeah, the S.O. caught a pair of mules, a man and a woman from New York state, when they were pulled over on a DUI. The woman mouthed off to the officer, so the car was impounded. The deputies found four pounds of coke when they inventoried the vehicle. The case has been delayed because of their attorney's legal maneuvering. It should go to trial next month. Why?"

"The next time you inventory the evidence, you might check to see if it is all there, or if powdered sugar has been substituted for the dope."

Jensen started to reach for the telephone.

"I think it might be better if you waited for a couple of days before raising any red flags."

Jensen sat back in his chair. "LeBlanc, will you please tell me what in the hell you've been up to?"

"J.C., the day after I found the corpse in the Lipscomb cottage, I was retained by Harold Lipscomb, Sr. to find out who killed his mistress, Gwen Hiltie. Lipscomb does not want the affair to become public. I told him that might not be possible. His marching orders were for me to find the murderer."

My revelation did not improve Jensen's scowl.

"Ted Myers had financial problems. To solve them, he corrupted an OmniBank loan officer, thereby receiving 2.5 million dollars from a fraudulent loan application. About four months ago, it became known in business circles that Harold Lipscomb was going to be named to the OmniBank Board of Directors in June. Lipscomb and Meyers hate each other. Meyers was concerned that Lipscomb would have his loan audited.

"About that time, Gwen Hiltie returned to Cleveland after a three year sabbatical in California where she was probably into high class prostitution and drugs. When she came back, she looked up her old boy friend, Ted Meyers, the very person who had introduced her to coke. Meyers seized the opportunity, arranging to have Hiltie hired by Newport Industries. Her mission was to seduce Lipscomb to obtain enough dirt on him for Meyers to blackmail him. Meyers let the affair go on for three months because Hiltie was pumping Lipscomb, no pun intended, for all sorts of valuable business information.

"Apparently, Harold Lipscomb, Jr., Harry to his friends, fell victim to Mademoiselle Hiltie's charms. He owns the building she had her apartment in, and he owns the Lexus Hiltie was driving the day she came to see me. Whether Harry was simply smitten by her, or whether he was being blackmailed because she learned he was embezzling from Lipscomb, Sr., is yet to be determined."

Jensen's eyes bulged slightly. "The kid was embezzling from his old man?"

"Yes. About $480,000 to date, give or take a few shekels. Anyway, Hiltie still had a cocaine habit. The autopsy showed she had coke in her system when she was killed. Meyers swears that he only bought her an ounce one time after her return. Even an ounce is expensive as hell. It appears that all of Gwen's nose-candy was being supplied by her old lover from high school, who it turns out, was a woman. Hiltie went both ways."

Jensen exposed a larger area of his eyeballs.

"Hiltie's old high school flame was Sally Yuhas, as in Detective Sally Yuhas."

J.C. was now doing a credible imitation of a startled Mr. Magoo.

"Wait a goddamn minute, LeBlanc. Are you telling me that Sally Yuhas is a lesbian and that she was supplying Gwen Hiltie with cocaine?"

"Yes."

Jensen turned to Yates for help.

"I'm afraid there's more," Collin said consolingly.

"Jesus. Let's hear it." J.C. visibly braced himself.

"When I went to Hiltie's apartment, after Detective Fred Kules had searched it, I discovered that someone had taken a tape recorder that had been hooked into the telephone. It's a good bet that Hiltie recorded all of her conversations; she was probably planning to shake down everyone she could. I assume Kules told you that Hiltie's apartment had been ransacked?"

Jensen nodded.

"Cynthia Glicksman, the woman who has the apartment beneath Hiltie's, spends a lot of time watching her neighbors. She told me a tall woman visited Hiltie a few times. Interestingly enough, Sally Yuhas was not with Kules when he interviewed Mrs. Glicksman."

The stillness of the room was disturbed only by the incessant drumming of J.C. Jensen's fingers on the arm of his chair. With a final thump of his thumb, Jensen stopped wearing a hole in the furniture. He looked at Yates and then at me.

Frank C. Dupuy

"How much of this can you prove?"

"Just the embezzlement will stand up in court," I responded evenly.

"You still haven't told me who murdered Hiltie, either."

"You're right. I'm not certain I know. If you will indulge me though, I have a plan."

41

I inhaled deeply. The rich aroma of new Dodge Dakota 4X4 pickup truck drifted gently through my nostrils. Yes! I checked my rearview mirror to see if Carl Branner was still following me in the rented Ford Taurus. I had corralled Carl into accompanying me to the dealership. For the next twenty minutes I luxuriated in my new ride. After we reached my house, I parked the truck in the driveway and regretfully locked it. No way I was going to let anyone put bullet holes in my pristine toy. If lead started flying this evening, I wanted Mr. Budget's Ford to absorb the abuse.

Carl was quiet on the ride back to his house which provided an opportunity for me to reflect on the plan I had set in motion. After my meeting with Yates and Jensen, I had called Ted Meyers. He was still hiding out at Les Fazio's house. Meyers assured me that he would faithfully follow the script we had rehearsed last night when he called Detective Sally Yuhas. I hoped so.

My next call was to Harold Lipscomb, Jr. His secretary informed me that he was at one of the other facilities for the day. I gave her my cellular number, asking her to do her best to locate him. I told her it was urgent. Forty minutes later my phone buzzed.

"Adrian LeBlanc."

"This is Harry Lipscomb. What in the hell is so important?"

I hoped his testicles still ached.

"We need to talk."

"About what?"

"Ontario Enterprises."

"What's that?"

"Nothing your father needs to know about for now."

"You're not making sense." I thought I detected a quiver in his voice.

Frank C. Dupuy

"Suit yourself. I was prepared to be reasonable. I don't think your daddy is going to like it when he inspects the abandoned building at 805 East 80th Street."

"What do you want?"

"Tonight I want $10,000 in cash. In the next few days, you can sign over the apartment house to me, the one located at 2209 Lake Trail in Rocky River."

"I haven't got that kind of money."

"You have until tonight to get it. Take a loan out on the Lexus."

"I need more time."

"You have until 8:00 tonight. I'll meet you in the old factory parking lot on East 80th Street. If you're not there, I'll be in your father's office first thing in the morning."

"You son of a bitch."

"Hey, I'm not all bad. I sent you a bowling ball, didn't I? Be there at 8:00, by yourself, and Harry..."

"What?"

"Be on time. I don't like to be kept waiting."

I figured there was an eighty percent chance Junior would show. If he didn't, I might have some tall explaining to do to J.C. Jensen.

"Hey, boy! Are you deaf?" Carl Branner nearly shouted at me.

"No, so stop shouting."

"Ha! If you're not deaf, then you were in a trance. I asked you if there was anything you needed me to do this evening."

"Sorry. Not tonight. Tomorrow will be the day to see if we can raise the dead. I want everyone well rested for tomorrow evening."

"I may have to put saltpeter in Louie's potatoes, then. Those two are insatiable."

"Find out what kind of vitamins he's taking. I may want to buy some myself."

"Hmph."

It was a little after 2:00 when we reached Carl's house. My pager beeped as we were turning into his driveway. It was Patty Stone. I ducked into Carl's study to make a quick telephone call.

242

Ohio Salt

"Patty Stone."

"You paged, I responded."

"Harold Lipscomb, Jr. stayed at the Sandusky Sheraton six times between February 13 and April 6 of this year. The hotel faxed me the receipts. They showed that he paid for a single room."

"He's kind of cheap. I'm pretty certain he had company."

"Oh?"

"The poor dear was lonely."

"Ha! Men – you're all alike. I'll bet his wife didn't know he was lonely."

"Junior was simply being considerate. He probably didn't want to burden his wife with his problems."

"All men are pigs. You want me to mail you the receipts or what?"

"Fax them to my office today, then mail your copies along with your bill. Once again, you have astounded me with your professional abilities."

"Yeah, right. Are you ever going to tell me what you're up to?"

"Some day, if I ever figure it out."

My next call was to my favorite Cleveland detective.

"James Green."

I now knew he had a first name.

"Detective Green, this is Adrian LeBlanc."

"Yeah? What can I do for you?"

"I have a question I want you to ask the coroner for me."

"Why certainly, sir. Is there any other privileged information you want?

"Look, Green, you may not like me, but this is important. I need to know if there were any needle marks on Jablonski's hands"

"You think the old guy was on dope?"

"No. It's possible that someone injected Novocain into his fingers, at least some of them, before they were cut off."

"What are you talking about?"

"It's a long story. Find out, please. I'll meet with you tomorow to tell you what I've learned, I promise."

"OK, I'll ask, but you'd better have a damn good, long story."

Yeah, I thought, I'll talk to you tomorrow, if I live that long.

Frank C. Dupuy

42

> The secret to my military success is careful planning.
> Colonel George Armstrong Custer, 1876

I parked in front of the sagging gate at 805 East 80th Street. The battered padlock hung forlornly on a rusted chain. Reaching into my pocket, I removed a thin, rounded metal device that fit precisely between the shackle and the body of the padlock. Pressing down, I felt a slight resistance, then pulled. The lock opened. Quickly, I pushed the gate out of the way and drove through into the parking lot. I was ten minutes early.

"Testing, one, two, three, four, five. How am I doing?" I asked, staring down the street.

The brake lights of a van parked about two blocks away flashed once. The Adrian LeBlanc Show was on the air. Every time I moved, I could feel the pressure of the tape that held the transmitter microphone to my chest. J.C. Jensen had gone all out – he had even arranged for a SWAT team to cover me. Hopefully, they could tell the difference between Harold Lipscomb, Jr. and me if events took an ugly turn. I glanced at my watch. With a little luck, my perfect plan would expose the person responsible for Gwen Hiltie's murder. I waited.

Nothing succeeds like success. And nothing is more miserable than a perfect plan gone awry. Harry Lipscomb hadn't shown up. The concealed transmitter the police had taped to my body never had a chance to be used. The snipers with the night vision scopes never had an opportunity to be heroes. The whole damn thing was a flop. By 9:00 we called it off. I drove home slowly, feeling every inch the proverbial goat. I stopped by a bar on the way back to have a Bushmills and water. Then I had another one, just in case. I was fresh out of ideas and felt like the lowest layer of deep sea whale dung.

My home is located on six acres at the end of a long gravel lane I share with two neighbors whose houses are located closer to the paved street our lane intersects. My small kingdom is generously wooded and private. Jeannie and I like it that way.

As I neared my house, I could see the tail lights of my new truck reflected in the headlights. Maybe I would go for a drive in it, I thought, a quiet, protracted drive that might keep me from dwelling on what an idiot I was. The moment after I switched off my headlights, it occurred to me that the dogs had not run out to greet me. I sat perfectly still. Nothing. Slowly, I reached under the seat for the zippered vinyl case I had stored my revolver in, located it, and removed the pistol. Nothing moved. Where were the dogs? Screw it, I thought, better safe than sorry. The image of Joseph Jablonski flashed through my mind. The engine was still running. I shifted into reverse.

I don't think that I actually heard the shotgun; nevertheless, there was no doubt that my windshield exploded. Glass cascaded all around me. I lay down on the seat and floored the gas pedal. The Taurus's wheels spun in the gravel as they propelled the car backwards. Someone fired again. Pellets sprayed through the interior, shattering the rear window. The sedan careened about twenty yards before the rear bumper crushed into a tree. I was out of the car, scrambling madly away from the direction the shots had come from almost before it had stopped. With fear motivating me, I would have run half way across the next county if fate had not guided my foot into a shallow hole. My ankle twisted; I fell heavily to the wet, leaf-covered ground about forty feet from my car. Buckshot zinged through the leaves and branches around me. A sharp, searing pain traveled up my leg informing me that my running career was over for a while. I crawled to the base of a large tree, trying to blend in with the ground. A dark figure stepped out from the hedge near my front door. The bastard had been waiting to blow me away on my front steps.

"I think I got him."

Ohio Salt

A dark shape emerged from the side of my garage.

"Shut up, you damn fool!" the second figure hissed.

In spite of the cloudy sky, the three quarters full moon provided enough light for me to determine that one of the shapes was larger than the other, and they both held objects that glinted. Shotguns. The two shapes merged. I could hear a muffled conversation, then the shapes separated. The larger one was approaching the Taurus. His partner walked to my left where he could cover the area I was hiding in. I attempted to melt into the leaves. Hitting an indistinct target in the dark with a snub-nosed .38 revolver is not a recommended path to longevity, especially when you are facing two targets armed with scatterguns.

A stick snapped as the gunman advanced. I could hear each footstep. The car door moved. No light came on. One of the pellets must have taken out the dome light. I waited. The figure hesitated, then walked around the car. It stopped. I could almost sense that the man did not want to walk into the woods. Cautiously, he moved along the edge of the trees, angling towards his partner. The bastard was coming straight towards me. When he was about six feet from me he veered slightly and continued. I held my breath. He stopped about three feet in front of my position. He was between me and his partner. He turned to face his partner.

Combat rule number one: Never turn your back on your enemy.

Combat rule number two: It is a hell of a lot safer to shoot a man when his back is turned.

The muzzle of my pistol was less than two feet from his left buttock when I pulled the trigger. The muzzle flash was blinding. The man screamed, dropping his shotgun as he fell to the ground. He screamed again.

"I got him!" I yelled, hoping to confuse his partner.

The second figure hesitated. I crawled forward until I felt the shotgun on the ground. The figure in the driveway was about thirty yards from me. It moved. Boom! Boom! He was firing high by about a foot. Lying on the ground, I brought the shotgun up to my shoulder, sighted along the barrel as best I could, and squeezed the trigger. Flame erupted, destroying my night vision. I blinked. Whomever I had fired at was no longer standing. The man on the ground beside me was moaning.

"Please, I'm sorry. Don't kill me. Please. Oh, God, it hurts. I need a doctor. Please."

"Shut the fuck up or I'll finish the job," I hissed.

He shut up. His partner wasn't making any noise either. I had no way of knowing if he was hurt or merely waiting for me to expose myself. Something blurred my vision. I rubbed my eyes, feeling a distressingly familiar warm, sticky substance. I was bleeding. How badly or what from, I couldn't tell. Somewhere in my car was a cellular telephone. I was debating crawling over to look for it when I heard the siren. Thank God for neighbors who are thoughtful enough to call the police when they hear a gunfight taking place at the house down the lane.

The Hudson cop who responded later told me he thought he was looking for a couple of teenagers who had taken to shooting out mail boxes. I watched as the police car with lights flashing stopped at the head of the lane, evidently talking to the neighbor who had placed the call. They were taking entirely too much time. Jacking another round into the shotgun, I fired into the air. I could almost hear the cop's anguished call for back up. Shotguns in the night are a rather rare event in Hudson.

Within minutes two more units showed up. The three policemen conferred. One of them lost the toss; he proceeded to drive his prowl car slowly down my lane, using his spot light to illuminate suspect shadows. He was about twenty feet from a huddled form lying across the drive when he stopped. The other two officers had followed him on foot. Each had a shotgun at the ready. It was turning out to be that kind of a night. One of the cops on foot started forward as his two partners covered him.

"Be careful!" I yelled. "He has a shotgun."

A spotlight and two flashlights illuminated me. I was leaning against the tree with my hands above my head. I wasn't certain how bad I looked, but I knew that my face was sticky with blood.

"Stand up and keep your hands in plain sight," the cop by the car commanded.

"I can't. My ankle's twisted. The guy at my feet has been shot in the ass. He and the one in the driveway ambushed me when I came home. I live here."

Ohio Salt

"Christ! Is that you, LeBlanc?"

"Yes, and I could use some help. You ought to call EMS. How bad is the guy on the ground?"

Two of the police officers approached the unmoving figure with guns drawn. One of them kicked away the shotgun laying beside it. His partner found a pistol beneath a jacket.

"He's breathing," he pronounced.

"Help me, please, help me," pleaded the man beside me. "I've been shot."

The distant sound of the EMS unit siren heralded help was on the way.

A cop walked up to me. I recognized him as Bob Farley, one of the local constabulary with whom I was on speaking terms.

"You OK?" he inquired while shining a light on my complaining companion.

"I think so. I must have cut my face and my ankle's fucked up; otherwise, I'm fine. Do me a favor; take the ski masks off these assholes. I want to see who tried to kill me."

Farley frisked the man on the ground. He didn't find anything. A few seconds later, he tugged the ski mask off of the mystery man's head.

"You jackass," I groused, "You were supposed to meet me at the factory."

Harold Lipscomb, Jr.'s face was contorted with pain. "She said it might be a setup. She said you wouldn't expect us to be waiting for you at your house."

"Who's she?"

"Sally Yuhas."

Hudson Police Officer Bob Farley interrupted. "Would you mind telling me what's going on?"

Behind him I could see the EMS unit turning onto my lane.

"Actually, it's kind of a long story."

Frank C. Dupuy

43

The scene in the Emergency Room at Akron City Hospital was like old home week except that this time the young doctor, who was picking the glass out of my face, was from the Philippines. Otherwise, the cast was almost the same: J.C. Jensen, Collin Yates, and Detective Fred Kules. A rather confused Hudson detective, Ed Grible, stood on the side lines, silently listening. He had the good sense not to interrupt. Another piece of glass plunked into a disposable, green plastic container. The doctor carefully studied my face.

"I think we have removed all of the pieces. You were extremely fortunate that none of the glass pierced your eyes," he pronounced gravely.

I bit my tongue, figuratively, and merely nodded. I'm not certain that he would have appreciated "No shit, Sherlock."

"Can I change now?" I asked.

"Certainly, Mr. LeBlanc. Be careful when you remove your clothes."

He was referring to the fact that I had glass slivers all over me. Before I allowed EMS to transport me, I insisted on grabbing a change of clothes. Since there were no females present, I quickly changed into a pair of khaki trousers and a soft flannel shirt, gingerly putting as little weight as possible on my tightly strapped left ankle. The doctor had told me it was not broken, only severely sprained. What ever it was, it was swollen and hurt like hell. I barely managed to slip my left foot into one of the worn Converse sneakers I had brought from my house. There was a mirror on the wall next to a color poster displaying a cutaway of the human heart. I wondered if the hospital collections department had placed the poster there. The reflection staring back at me looked like hell. My worst wound was a gash near my hair line on the left side of my forehead.

Frank C. Dupuy

Ten neat sutures held it together. A small cut over my right cheek bone only boasted three stitches. Two butterfly bandages, one on my chin and one on my left cheek, had repaired the rest of the damage. I didn't count the half dozen small cuts that had been dabbed with antiseptic. The doctor had been right. I was lucky that the fragments had missed my eyes.

"How's Sally Yuhas?" I asked.

"She's in surgery. The doctors think she'll make it, no thanks to you. She has two buckshot in her stomach, two in her chest and one that penetrated her skull, not to mention a couple in her arms. You really did a number on her," J.C. reported matter-of-factly.

"Gee, I'm sorry. Next time I'll be more careful. What about Harry Lipscomb?"

"They're almost finished taking the slug out of his ass. The surgeon told me that the hollow point bullet made a hell of a mess. He's lost a lot of blood, but he'll recover." J.C. considered me quizzically. "Did you intend to hit him there or was that simply a wild shot?"

"It was a convenient shot. While he was hunting me with his shotgun, he turned his back when he was about three feet away. I reached up and plugged him where I thought it would do the most good."

Jensen nodded. "There's an office down the hall we can use. I am dying to hear you explain all of this."

We trooped down the hall with me limping like one of the marchers from the Spirit of '76. A hospital security guard was standing in front of an office door. When he saw Jensen, he opened the door for us.

"I put extra chairs in there, Mr. Jensen, and a coffee maker. I'll be outside if you need me."

Once again, I regarded J.C. in wonder. The man knows how to get things done. I found the coffee pot and poured some into a white Styrofoam cup. It actually tasted good. I found a chair and sat down, trying to ignore the four pairs of eyes boring into me. Jensen spoke first.

"You mind telling me what went down at your house tonight?"

"Lipscomb and Yuhas ambushed me with shotguns. They were supposed to have met me at the factory, but Yuhas figured it might be a setup. She told Lipscomb that I wouldn't expect them to be waiting for me at my house. She was right."

Jensen stood up, walked over to my chair, then leaned down to glare at me.

"LeBlanc, when we set up at that old factory this evening you told me that you were waiting for Harold Lipscomb, Jr., and that you were going to try to maneuver him into admitting that he had murdered Gwen Hiltie. You never said a goddamn thing about Sally Yuhas."

I sighed. It had been a long day. "I wasn't certain she was involved. I had Ted Meyers call her this afternoon, shortly after I talked to Junior. Meyers told her that he wanted her to pull me and the cops off his ass for the Hiltie murder. He said if she did, he would give her a tape Hiltie had given him of a conversation between Yuhas and Hiltie discussing cocaine. Meyers also mentioned to Yuhas that when he and I had spoken, I had informed him I had recovered a cassette tape with a conversation between Meyers and Hiltie that implicated him in the blackmail scheme. He added that he and Hiltie had discussed Yuhas supplying her with cocaine during the same conversation.

"If Lipscomb, Jr. and Sally Yuhas had acted together to kill Hiltie, I figured that my call to him and Meyers's call to her would flush them out. I was already certain Junior was involved."

Jensen's eyes narrowed. "How?"

"When I first met with Harold Lipscomb, Sr., he told me that he had received a voice mail message from Hiltie at about 2:00 PM on the day she was murdered asking that he meet her at the Sandusky Sheraton instead of the cottage. He gave me a handwritten copy of the message. She called him Harry and asked him to meet her there, just like the last time. Lipscomb told me he thought something was peculiar because she never called him Harry, and because they had never been to the Sandusky Sheraton.

"An associate verified that Harold Lipscomb, Jr., had stayed at the Sandusky Sheraton six times during February and March. I believe that Hiltie was trying to give Lipscomb, Sr. a hint that she was in trouble and that his son was the culprit."

"That's a hell of a stretch, LeBlanc," Jensen challenged.

"Not when you consider that Junior was providing Hiltie with a Lexus and an apartment. My suspicion is that Hiltie figured out Junior was embezzling from Daddy, then put the bite on him. She probably let him sleep with her to keep the arrangement on a amicable footing."

"How does Sally Yuhas fit into the picture?"

"She and Hiltie had been lovers in high school. The flame rekindled when Hiltie returned to the Cleveland area. Hiltie liked cocaine, which is an expensive habit. She told Ted Meyers that her old girl friend was supplying her with coke. As to what caused the falling out between Hiltie and Yuhas, who knows? My guess is that they had a lovers' quarrel, and Hiltie threatened to blow the whistle on Yuhas. When times were good between them, Hiltie may have told Yuhas about her dealings with Junior and Senior and about Junior's embezzlement. With one thing leading to another, Harry and Sally joined forces to eliminate a common threat."

Jensen tugged at his ear. "Even if you're right, it's too weak to take to court. I'll have a hell of a time convincing a jury beyond a reasonable doubt that they murdered Hiltie."

"Maybe. If you hurry up and procure a search warrant, you might find the tapes they removed from Hiltie's apartment, not to mention the diamond ring she was wearing when she came to my office. The lab techs didn't find the ring at the cottage."

Fred Kules's and J.C. Jensen's eyes met. "I'll call Judge Shoop tonight. He owes me a favor. By the time you get to Ashtabula, Fred, the warrants should be ready."

Kules was already headed for the door.

"With your permission, J.C., I'd like to talk to Junior. I have a feeling he might like to cooperate," I stated politely.

"That's out of the question," Jensen snapped.

"No, it isn't. With Detective Grible present, I want to ask Junior what he did with my dogs. I think I'm entitled to know that much."

"LeBlanc, you take everything to the fucking limit, don't you? All right. Detective Grible, I would appreciate it if you would accompany Mr. LeBlanc to inquire as to what happened to his dogs." J.C. was not a happy assistant district attorney.

Grible led the way to a hospital room that had a uniformed Akron cop sitting in front of it. Evidently, the cop recognized Grible.

Ohio Salt

"They wheeled him in about fifteen minutes ago," the cop reported, "He wasn't smiling too much."

Grible pushed the door open and entered the room. I followed. Harold Lipscomb, Jr. was lying on his stomach. The flimsy hospital gown did not hide the bulky bandage on his left buttock.

"Mr. Lipscomb, I'm Detective Ed Grible of the Hudson Police Department. Mr. LeBlanc wants to ask you a question."

I stood near the head of the bed so that Harry could see me.

"Go to hell, LeBlanc."

"Harry, that is no way to talk to the man who might drop the attempted murder charge against you."

"What do you want?"

"I want to know what you did to my dogs."

Lipscomb's features registered surprise.

"Your dogs?"

"Yes, my dogs."

"Sally cut the wire on the electric fence. They ran off."

My dogs are kept in the yard by an Invisible Fence system. They have electric collars that give them a shock if they walk too close to the underground wire that forms the perimeter. If the power fails or the wire is cut, the fence is inoperative.

"How did she find the wire?"

"Sally saw the sign in your yard that said your dogs were behind an invisible fence. She knows about those. She told me that there's a black box outside of the house that the wires go into. She said if we cut the wire, it kills the fence. She found the box, cut the wire and five minutes later your dogs were gone."

So much for my well-trained dogs. They bark, but would never bite anyone anyway. Hopefully, the mutts would come back in time for breakfast.

"Harry, Sally is going to be OK. She's in surgery, but is expected to recover. When she can talk, do you know what she's gonna do?"

"No."

"She's gonna call the D.A. to cut a deal, meaning she is going to finger you for Gwen Hiltie's murder. The cops are already searching her place and yours for the tapes and the diamond ring. When they find them, you are going to have a big problem. Oh, Ted

Frank C. Dupuy

Meyers also has a couple of the tapes that he is dying to turn over to the police. The way I see it, Yuhas will save herself from the death penalty by giving you up."

Junior's expression metamorphosed from sullen to seriously worried.

"Your father is my client. He hired me to find out who killed Gwen Hiltie. Well, I have. You and Sally did it because she was blackmailing both of you. The only problem is, Sally Yuhas is a detective and knows all of the angles. She knows that if she dumps on you first, she can avoid the death penalty. I can see it now. She'll tell the D.A. how you blackmailed her into helping you, how she stood by in horror as you tortured Gwen before finally ending her suffering by blowing her face off with a shotgun. Yep, she'll have you wrapped up in a neat package."

Harry Lipscomb's coloring blended nicely with his sheets. Despite the sixty-eight degree room temperature, sweat formed on his face.

"That's not true. It didn't happen that way."

"True or not, that's how Sally will sell it. That is, unless you want to get your licks in first. I can't get you off the murder rap, but I can guarantee you that the D.A. won't seek the death penalty if you cooperate."

"How can you do that?"

"By letting you talk to him. He's here in the hospital waiting for Yuhas to regain consciousness. I figure you have a few hours before she nails you for good. If you want me to, I can get him in here now, before he talks to Sally."

Lipscomb was perspiring heavily. "Get him, LeBlanc. I'm not going to die for something I didn't do."

I limped back to the office.

"J.C., Harry Lipscomb would like to talk to you."

44

Tuesday

Harold Lipscomb, Sr. was in a somber mood when he shook my hand. I had called him last night, giving him an abbreviated account of the festivities. He insisted that I meet with him at 8:00 AM. His eyebrows raised slightly when he saw my face as I limped into his office.

"Thank you for seeing me this morning, Adrian." Evidently, we were now on a first name basis. "How badly were you injured?"

"A little glass in the face and hands from when the windshield was shot out and a twisted ankle. I'll live."

He nodded. "Please, sit down."

A moment later, a secretary handed me a freshly brewed mug of coffee. I was receiving the royal treatment.

"I would like you to tell me everything, from start to finish. I need to know. I am arranging for an attorney to represent Harry."

So I told him, including Harry's confession to J.C. Jensen. I did leave out one of the more disgusting details. He listened intently without once interrupting. After I finished, he placed his arms on his desk and bowed his head. When he finally raised his head, he had aged ten years.

"Do you have a son, Adrian?"

"Yes, sir, I do."

"Then you can imagine my feelings at this moment. I am revolted by what Harry has done, yet I cannot abandon him."

"You already knew what he had done when you hired me, didn't you?"

Lipscomb started.

"How did you know?"

Frank C. Dupuy

"After you heard about the murder at your cottage, you figured out exactly what Gwen Hiltie had been trying to tell you when she left you that voice mail message. You just couldn't determine why he had done it."

"I was in torment. I had to be certain."

We sat in silence for a while.

"I'm sorry my son tried to kill you," Lipscomb finally said.

"It's not your fault. Sally Yuhas was the brains behind the setup. She used every trick she knew to pin the murder on me. If I had drowned in the river, they might have gotten away with it."

To make it look like rape, Yuhas had insisted that Harry have sex with Hiltie while she was still alive. That was the detail I had not provided to Lipscomb. Unfortunately, he used a condom containing a spermicide and the coroner picked up on it. I blushed when I thought about Yuhas manipulating me while I was unconscious to extract my semen to rub on the corpse.

"For what it's worth, I'm glad you weren't killed."

"Thank you."

When I left, Harold Lipscomb, Sr. was still seated behind his desk, staring into space.

45

My next stop was the Cleveland Police 4th District headquarters which is housed in a solid, dingy, brown brick building that appears to have absorbed the unhappiness of the people who have passed through its portals. It is not a cheery place. After convincing the police person behind the bullet resistant partition that I indeed had legitimate business with Detective James Green, she made a phone call, then motioned me to have a seat. A few minutes later, Detective Mullins, Green's morose partner, arrived in the lobby to retrieve me.

"Good morning, LeBlanc," he greeted, inspecting my face, "Looks like you had quite an evening. The news media is making a hero out of you."

I nodded. So far, I had ducked all of the reporters who were leaving messages for me to call them. I took my time following Mullins up the stairs. My ankle still hurt like hell. Finally, we arrived at a drab office that had about eight aging, gray metal desks crowded in it. Green was sitting at a corner desk blowing cigar smoke at a No Smoking notice posted on the wall. The contents of a police file were spread in front of him.

"Have a seat, LeBlanc."

I pulled a swivel chair from behind an empty desk and sat down.

Green cocked his head. "Nice stitches."

"Thanks."

He tapped one of the pages in front of him with a pencil.

"The coroner says that he didn't find any traces of needle marks or local anaesthetic in the hands or in the severed fingers. Now, I want to know why you asked."

I told him what I had found out about Mike Ungar and Claudio Mondragón, especially about Mondragón's interrogation techniques. Green and Mullins were disgusted.

"Jeez, that's cold," Mullins pronounced.

"Yeah," said Green, "cold as hell." Then he considered me speculatively. "I'm going to share something with you, LeBlanc, something that doesn't make any sense to me. According to the coroner, there's a good chance that Jablonski was unconscious when his fingers were cut off."

"What?"

"He was probably unconscious from the blow to the head he had received by the front door. Blood was on the carpet there, and the coroner found carpet fibers in the wound on the old guy's head. The coroner is guessing that Jablonski was knocked unconscious by the front door and dragged or carried downstairs, then tied up on the work bench. From the swelling in the brain, it's a wonder the old man didn't die when he was hit."

"What killed him?"

"Loss of blood and shock." Green mashed out the remnants of his cigar in a grubby ashtray. "You're supposed to be a hotshot investigator, LeBlanc. Suppose you share some of your wisdom with us lowly plodders." His eyes never left me.

I thought about it. Nothing fit. From the first I had suspected Ungar and Mondragón because of their involvement with passing information to Castro about the Bay of Pigs invasion. Jablonski's death had all of the earmarks of a Mondragón interrogation. I thought about it, and agreed with Green – it didn't make any sense.

"I haven't the foggiest."

"Uh huh," Green stated. "Well, just in case you develop any sudden insights, give me a call."

I promised him I would.

I had a late breakfast at a Bob Evans Restaurant and tried to concentrate on Green's information. One of my instructors at a federal academy had once admonished us to remember that "if the facts don't fit your theory, alter your theory to fit the facts, not vice versa." Back in the deep recesses of my shallow mind an idea was struggling to find its way into the light. I went to a pay telephone and called Carl Branner.

"Good morning, Adrian, you had us all worried to death. It's all over the news about your gunfight and how you solved that woman's murder. How are you?"

I spent several minutes assuring Carl I was fine before asking him to corral Maria, Louie and Karen so that I could talk to everyone on Carl's speaker phone. He gathered them; I killed another five minutes explaining that I was alive and well and providing details about the Hiltie murder. Finally, they were ready to listen to what I had to say.

"Maria, where are the files you found?"

Louie answered. "I gave them to Karen. She put them in your bank box."

"OK. Louie, I want you and Karen to go to the bank as soon as possible; take the files to Collin Yates's office. Play it safe. Make certain no one follows you. After that, come back to Carl's and wait for me to call you."

"You got it, Adrian," Louie said.

"Maria, I want you to call St. Theresa's to find out who at the church handled Stan Petrowski's bequest. I want to see a copy of the will and the amounts the church actually received. Call Collin Yates and tell him who you are. Between the two of you, I want you to arrange for me to see a copy of the will. If you could schedule it in a couple of hours, I would appreciate it."

"I will do that, but can you tell me why?" Maria Kolakowski asked.

"Later. If I'm right, I'll tell you this evening.

I was walking to my truck when my pager went off. I called the answering service from my cell phone. I had a message to call J.C. Jensen.

"Adrian, I called to let you know that we found the tapes in Sally Yuhas's house last night. One of them was a cat fight between Hiltie and Yuhas. Hiltie threatened to tell the Sheriff that Yuhas had been stealing cocaine from the evidence room. I believe that her habit had started to take its toll on Hiltie's stability. Anyway, we found about two pounds of cocaine in Sally's freezer. She had replaced the coke in the evidence room with powdered sugar."

"How is she?"

"Alive enough to ask for an attorney. She isn't talking. The doctors tell me she can be moved in about five days. They left the buckshot in her skull. Her surgeon said it would do more harm than good to try to remove it. In the meantime, she is under close guard at the hospital. I'm on my way to court to file charges on both of them for aggravated murder, kidnaping, rape, assault and attempted murder. The Hudson cops are going to meet with the Summit County D.A. to file attempted murder charges for last night."

"What kind of a deal did you cut with Harry Lipscomb?"

"After he retains an attorney, I'll let him plead to murder instead of aggravated murder; that way he avoids the death penalty and mandatory life imprisonment. He'll get fifteen to life on that alone. I'm not dropping the other charges."

"His old man isn't going to file charges for the embezzlement."

"The things a father will do for a son. Oh, that reminds me. Fred Kules is in hot water with the Sheriff. It seems that Sally Yuhas persuaded him to cover for her showing up late for second shift on the day of the murder. She told him she had personal business to take care of. Cops do that for each other, you know."

"That's the breaks. Did you find the diamond ring?"

"Yeah, Harry gave it to his wife as a surprise the day after the murder."

"Jesus. He better hope he spends the rest of his life in jail. If he ever gets out, she'll kill him."

"Probably. Listen, I would take it as a favor if you would let me buy you a drink next week."

"Thanks, J.C., I'd like that."

I spent the next hour sitting in a pew in St. Theresa's Catholic Church using the solitude to let my thoughts run loose. I was in the midst of formulating another surefire plan when my beeper vibrated. My answering service informed me that the documents I wanted were at my attorney's office. Thirty minutes later, I was examining Stanislas Petrowski's last will and testament.

"He was very generous where the Church was concerned," Collin commented.

"A good Catholic boy. I hope it did him some good upstairs. Did you and Maria find someone for me to talk to?"

"Yes, as a matter of fact. Father Leo Tschapanski at St. Theresa's has the original file and a copy of the will. He said you can

Ohio Salt

stop by at any time to review whatever he has."

"Good. In that case, I'm on my way."

Collin Yates held up a hand.

"Not so fast, Sherlock. How about confiding in your attorney as to what you are up to?"

"If my hunch is right, I'll be back in an hour or so to tell you all about it. Trust me."

Yates groaned, then shooed me out of his office.

The St. Theresa's rectory and business office had been built in the 1920s. Father Tschapanski informed me that the church and the rectory had been completed in 1926. When he insisted on showing me the church with its classic gothic arches and beautiful stained glass windows, I didn't have the heart to tell him that I had recently spent an hour sitting in it. He pointed out that everything had been kept in excellent repair by the parishioners, many of whom were contractors or were employed by contractors. He then led me outside to see the grotto Stan Petrowski had dedicated to the Virgin. I had to admit that it was magnificent. Polished basalt blocks formed the outside of the structure that housed a beautifully painted, larger than life statue of the Virgin. Standing in front of the statue, I was impressed by the feeling of peace and love that it exuded. Father Tschapanski correctly interpreted my expression.

"She has that effect on everyone. Count Petrowski special ordered it from Italy. Bernadinni himself created it." My lack of recognition spurred further commentary. "Pietro Bernadinni was one of the Vatican's foremost artisans. Very few of his works were ever imported into this country."

I made the appropriate noises. Finally, the good padre led me into his office.

"I have been at St. Theresa's for twenty-four years. I never had the opportunity to meet Count Petrowski, but his generosity has enabled us to keep our school open for all these years. Unfortunately, times being what they are, we will be forced to consolidate with another parish. It is a pity. We run a good school here."

He pointed to a thick manila folder on his desk.

"This is what you requested. Please, take your time. I will be in the back office if you need me." With that, he departed.

It took me ten minutes to determine that there was something seriously rotten in the State of Denmark. I compared the documents and shook my head. The bastard had almost gotten away with it. I went to the back office where I found Father Leo engrossed in a hunt and peck session with a word processor.

"Excuse me, Father, but I would like to speak with you for a few minutes."

He looked up from his screen, smiling sheepishly. "Computers are so wonderful. It is a pity I never learned to type. I use this machine to write my sermons because it has a spelling checker. I never learned to spell very well, either. What can I do for you?"

"Father, how well did you know Joseph Jablonski?"

His face clouded. "He was my friend. We had dinner together at least once a week and we shared an interest in chess. Joseph was a good and gentle person. I cannot imagine what kind of animals would maim and torture an old, harmless man. I am officiating at his funeral tomorrow."

"Would you like to help me catch the person responsible for his murder?"

Father Tschapanski's face lost its saintly glow as his features settled into hard lines.

"Yes, Mr. LeBlanc, I would very much like to help you."

"Very well, Father Leo. I have a plan."

46

Collin Yates stared at me incredulously. "You figured this out all by yourself?"

"Yes," I responded modestly, "I did."

He shook his head. "You are certifiable."

"I'll hold you to that in case I ever need to use it as a defense."

"Why don't you call the police? Let them handle it."

"Collin, we are talking about two murders that happened thirty years ago. The cops aren't geared for that kind of investigation."

"Well, the Jablonski case is certainly fresh. The man hasn't even been buried. They won't appreciate your interfering with a homicide investigation."

"Detective Green and I don't exactly see eye to eye. If I go to him, he might shut me down before I have the chance to get a confession. All I have is speculation."

Yates blew a prodigious quantity of air through his lips. "Remember what happened the last time you devised a foolproof plan? The one you used to catch Harry Lipscomb?"

"It worked. It just didn't work where I wanted it to."

"For goodness sakes be reasonable, Adrian."

"OK. You call Green for me. Tell him to be standing by near St. Theresa's at 8:00 tonight."

"But, you're not even certain that he will show up."

My pager vibrated. "Let me call my answering service, oh ye of little faith."

I was informed that Milo Frankiewicz had requested that I call him as soon as possible. I dialed his number.

"Mr. LeBlanc, thank you for returning my call so promptly. I understand you were at St. Theresa's today?"

Frank C. Dupuy

"Indeed, I was. I think I may have a lead on Stan Petrowski's missing gold and some of his papers."

"His papers?"

"Yes, company ledgers and perhaps a list of names of the people he was looking into before he disappeared. Maria Kolakowski gave me a copy of Stan's will and some other papers. I think Stan had a hiding place in the church. Father Leo hinted that his predecessor had some kind of agreement with Petrowski. Look, I'll tell you what. Father Leo has given me permission to search the church tonight. Why don't you meet me there at 8:00? I could use the help."

"I will be there, Mr. LeBlanc."

"Super. You can come in through the small door by the back parking lot."

"I know the door." He hung up.

Collin Yates was experiencing difficulty in containing himself.

"LeBlanc, that was absolutely the weakest piece of bullshit I have ever listened to."

"He called, didn't he?"

Yates threw up his hands. "Detective Green and I will be near the church at 8:00."

"Thanks, Collin. By the by, try not to get made." I left before he threw something.

My plan was received with more enthusiasm by Karen Koenig, Carl Branner and the Kolakowskis.

"Gee, Adrian, that's brilliant," Louie enthused, "It'll work for sure."

I had my first misgivings as I regarded Louie's beaming countenance.

"It sounds good, but will it stand up in court?" asked Carl.

"It depends on how much detail he divulges. I'll have everything on tape. If he supplies facts that only the killer would know, then we have him," I stated with more confidence than I felt.

"What are you going to do for backup?" Karen inquired.

"That's where Louie comes in."

"You can count on me, partner," Louie assured me.

I hid my qualms manfully. "I know I can. Now, here's what we have to do."

47

I love it when a plan comes together.
	Hannibal Smith, A-Team Leader

	The dogs ran out to greet me, at least as far as the limits of their invisible fence would allow them. One of my neighbors had snagged my furry fugitives while they were playing with her golden retriever. I had managed to repair the wire Sally Yuhas had cut without destroying anything. I spent about fifteen minutes playing with the mutts and promising them that Jules would be home tomorrow.
	I prepared a small salad, cooked some spaghetti, and heated a jar of sauce in the microwave. A glass of wine would have been perfect; however, I vetoed that idea. Tonight I needed to be at my best. After a quick shower, I changed into charcoal gray slacks, a dark blue shirt and a navy blazer. The outfit made me less of a target in poor light. I admired myself in the mirror, deciding that I was more than a match for any old arthritic attorney. None the less, I was carrying my .38 Chiefs Special and the Browning .25, just in case Milo Frankiewicz turned out to be feistier than expected. I put a fresh tape and battery into my recorder, a nifty little device I had purchased last year. It looks exactly like a Motorola pager and will even beep, if necessary. The microphone is extremely sensitive and the tape will run for ninety minutes. Thus fortified, I made my way to my truck and headed into Cleveland.
	At 7:55, I parked in the diminutive parking lot behind the church. If Collin Yates and Detective Green were around, they were doing a superb job of keeping out of sight. A porch light cast a feeble glow over the small door Father Leo had promised would be un-

locked. It was. I stepped into a dim corridor and switched on a three cell, machined aluminum flashlight. After a minute, I located a light switch and flipped it. Lights came on in the corridor. I pressed a button on my recorder. I was ready. The church itself was barely illuminated by a few lights that stayed on at night. They produced a spooky, surreal atmosphere that was enhanced by ghostly statues of saints set into the walls. I walked up the center aisle of the church, selected a pew and sat down to wait.

Footsteps echoed on the stone floor. I checked my watch. 8:09. I stood up to see Milo Frankiewicz shuffling towards me. He was wearing a dark three piece suit and a starched white shirt. I was willing to bet he had been wearing the same outfit for over forty years.

"Good evening, Mr. LeBlanc."

"Good evening. I decided to wait for you before starting my search."

"That was kind of you."

"Why don't we start over by the organ? Father Leo said that there are a lot of passages behind the pipes." I was referring to a massive pipe organ that had been donated in 1928 by a steel tycoon. Father Leo had given me a five minute history of the instrument and its importance earlier in the day.

"I don't think so."

When I turned to face Milo Frankiewicz, he was holding a sizeable revolver in his arthritic right hand. I noted that his grip was remarkably steady.

"Gosh, that is certainly an impressive revolver you are pointing at me," I said for the benefit of my recorder.

"Can it, LeBlanc," ordered a voice from the corridor. A moment later, Mike Ungar strode into view. He was holding a large automatic. I felt outgunned.

"Evening, Mr. Ungar," I greeted him, "Where's your little sidekick?"

"Here, asshole," declared a flat voice with a noticeable Spanish accent. Claudio Mondragón appeared from the shadows at the back of the church. He, too, was holding a large automatic.

"Hi, Claudio. Nice pistol."

"Shut up, dick head," he snapped. Claudio walked over to me

Ohio Salt

and patted me down with his free hand. He removed my Chiefs Special from its holster. He didn't pay much attention to my pager.

"He's clean, Mike." My respect for Claudio dropped. He had stopped looking for weapons once he found my revolver. Ungar holstered his automatic.

"You know, you're starting to be a pain in the ass, LeBlanc."

"How so?"

"You are dredging up old history that is better left alone."

"Oh, are you referring to the time that you and Claudio passed the Bay of Pigs invasion plans to Castro in 1961, or perhaps the incident in which you killed Mario Guzman in Mexico City?"

I didn't see it coming. Mondragón landed a solid punch on my right cheek that staggered me. It also ripped open my stitches. I blinked as lights danced in front of my eyes.

"That's enough, Claudio," Ungar snapped. I could feel blood running down my cheek. The entire side of my face was throbbing.

"You're not too bright, LeBlanc. Claudio has been set up on this church since 5:00. You didn't send anyone in and no one followed you. It appears you are all alone." Ungar was observing me with clinical detachment.

"I wasn't expecting to see your smiling face," I admitted truthfully. "In fact, I thought you and Milo here were at odds."

"No, not at all. We are partners in a treasure hunt. Milo assured me that you know where Stan hid his reserves. Maria Kolakowski is too ill to use the information John left her, and her son is too inept, apparently. Oh, there is one other little matter. I want John Kolakowski's diaries."

"Did it ever occur to you that Milo is setting you up? He wants to hang a couple of murder raps on you and Claudio."

"Shut up, LeBlanc." That was from Frankiewicz. I was being told that a lot tonight.

"It's true," I said.

Ungar's attention shifted from me to Frankiewicz.

"Cover him, Claudio."

Mondragón, who had been standing slightly behind us, pressed his pistol to Frankiewicz's head. Ungar reached across and took the revolver from him.

"I'm listening, LeBlanc."

Frank C. Dupuy

"In 1963, when John and Stan were gathering evidence on you and Claudio, they had problems closer to home. It seems that Stan's trusted legal advisor and treasurer, Milo, had been embezzling. In fact, he had stolen several hundred thousand dollars. His drinking problem was making him sloppy. Stan and John were about to audit the books. On the morning of November 21, 1963, they stopped by to talk to Milo, just before they headed to Dallas to see a man named Oswald, an individual with whom I believe you were acquainted. Anyway, there was probably a hell of a row; Milo murdered the two men who could send him to jail. With Stan and John missing, Milo became the executor of Stan's estate. He altered the will and supporting documents to reflect the diminished status of Stan's factories and fortune. He then proceeded to loot the rest of the money that was supposed to go to the church and ran the factories into the ground.

"End of story, except that thirty years later, Maria Kolakowski found some documents, one of them being an original copy of Stan Petrowski's will. She showed it to Joseph Jablonski, who read it and knew that something was wrong. The Church never received even half of the money Petrowski had left them. What does Jablonski do? He calls Milo, demanding an explanation. He tells him he has seen the will. Milo assures him it is all a misunderstanding; he even promises he will come over to show Joseph how mistaken he is. When Jablonski answers his door, Milo hits him in the head with the proverbial blunt object, almost killing him. He then drags Jablonski down to the basement where he stages a torture scene, just like Claudio used to do. In fact, Milo did his best to make certain I thought it was you and Claudio."

I paused to draw breath. "Milo told me a compelling story about how, shortly after Stan and John had disappeared, one of his children had been kidnaped, just like Maria Kolakowski's daughter. He implied that sinister forces responsible for the Kennedy assassination were behind the dreadful act. The only problem was, Maria never told Milo about her daughter's kidnaping. The only way he knew was because he had kidnaped the girl himself to stop Maria Kolakowski from pressing the authorities to look into John and Stan's disappearance. It worked.

"At least until Maria found documents that had been hidden

in a file cabinet for three decades and sent letters to the men she believed might know what had happened to her husband. After Jablonski calls Milo, Milo decides the timing is perfect to throw suspicion on the two men John and Stan had been investigating thirty years ago – two men who have a reputation for engaging in interrogation by torture. Exit Joseph Jablonski."

Mike Ungar's face could have been chiseled from granite. When I glanced at Milo Frankiewicz, I received a glare that was pure venom.

"Milo was worried that I was getting too close, so he calls you with a cock and bull story about a lost fortune because he needs help to deal with me. He knew that Stan didn't leave any money because he had embezzled it all thirty years ago."

The silence in the church was broken only by the four of us breathing. Milo Frankiewicz started to say something, then thought better of it after scanning Ungar's features.

"Where are Kolakowski's diaries?" Ungar grated.

"There aren't any. That was part of Maria Kolakowski's bluff to force the men who had killed her husband into the open."

"Bullshit, LeBlanc," snapped Claudio, "You know too damn much."

"I'm a good guesser, that's all." I tried to appear sincere and reassuring.

Ungar weighed me carefully. "Can you prove anything against Frankiewicz?"

"Right now, only the embezzling, and the statute of limitations expired on that some years ago. It would help if he would tell me what he did with Stan's and John's bodies."

Ungar motioned to Claudio. Mondragón smashed Frankiewicz across the bridge of the nose with his pistol. Bone cracked and blood spurted. The old attorney shrieked, grabbing his face with both hands.

"OK, you old cocksucker," Claudio snarled, "you tell me what you did with the bodies, or you and I go into the church basement where I take you apart a piece at a time." I've seen more compassion in the eyes of a cobra.

Frankiewicz got the message. "In my house," he mumbled through his fingers, "I buried them in the basement of my house."

Frank C. Dupuy

Claudio raised his pistol again.

"Don't hit me," Milo screeched. "I swear, I killed them in my house and I buried them in my basement."

Ungar raised an eyebrow.

"Works for me," I said.

"Hey, Mike, you're not gonna let this guy go are you?" Claudio was like a kid who had just had a butterfly taken away before he could pull the wings off of it.

"Come on, Claudio, let's get out of here. LeBlanc can't prove a damn thing."

With a disappointed shrug, Claudio Mondragón holstered his pistol and joined Ungar.

"Bastards!" Milo Frankiewicz screamed. He reached under his suit jacket, drawing a nickel-plated automatic. Evidently, I wasn't the only one to pack double pistols. His first shot hit Ungar in the back. Ungar pitched forward. Mondragón whirled, clawing desperately at his pistol. Frankiewicz shot him three times. I dove behind a pew as I tried to extract my tiny automatic from the small of my back.

"Freeze!" commanded a dark shape that sprang from the confessional. Milo twisted to confront a gaunt figure clad in a black suit, black trench coat and a black fedora. The figure was clasping a huge automatic pistol in both hands. Milo fired once. A sound like a 105mm howitzer filled the church as flame erupted from the dark apparition's weapon. Milo Frankiewicz's arms flew up as his body was propelled into a row of pews.

I poked my head over the back of a pew. Louie Kolakowski was the only thing standing.

"You OK, Adrian?" he called. Louie still held his pistol at the ready.

"I'm fine. How about you?"

"He missed me."

The door at the back of the church crashed open. Two figures came running into the church with pistols drawn. To my amazement, Louie calmly set his weapon down and raised his hands. I stood and raised mine also as Detectives Green and Mullins came panting to our rescue.

"What in the hell is going on, LeBlanc?" Green demanded.

Ohio Salt

"Milo Frankiewicz shot Mike Ungar and Claudio Mondragón. Louie Kolakowski saved my life by shooting Frankiewicz."

I hurried over to Ungar. He was still breathing, in spite of a rapidly spreading dark stain that was ruining the back of his tailored suit coat.

"Ungar's still alive. Call an ambulance."

Mullins was already talking into his radio. I pulled out my handkerchief and pressed it over the hole the bullet had made. I wondered if the ambulance would make it in time.

Frank C. Dupuy

48

Contrary to the doctor's prediction, Ungar did regain consciousness. Claudio Mondragón died on the way to the hospital, and Milo Frankiewicz was dead before he hit the floor. Louie's hollow point slug had hit him squarely in the heart. While we were in the waiting room, I asked Louie what in the hell he had been carrying.

"A Desert Eagle .44 Magnum. It's the most powerful automatic pistol on the market," he explained proudly. "They make 'em in Israel, and those guys know all about combat."

My ears were still ringing from the blast Louie's cannon had produced. "Christ, that's not a pistol, it's a crew-served weapon," I growled.

Louie beamed in acknowledgment.

After the cops had taken statements from us, I had been thoroughly reamed by Detectives Green and Mullins. They were only slightly mollified when I gave them the tape from my recorder. I wondered what they would make of the parts about the Bay of Pigs invasion and the vague reference to Lee Harvey Oswald. I decided I didn't care.

Father Leo Tschapanski, at my request, joined us at the hospital. I had a hunch Mike Ungar might be in need of his services. About two hours after we had arrived, a balding physician in a light green scrub suit approached us.

"Mr. LeBlanc?"

"That's me."

"Mr. Ungar wants to speak with you. I think I should tell you that he is in very serious condition."

"How serious?"

"He won't live much longer. The bullet did an incredible amount of damage."

Frank C. Dupuy

I followed the doctor down a hall, past a nurses' station and through a set of double doors into a large recovery room. Mike Ungar's bed was surrounded by several screens that partially concealed the monitors, respirator and myriad tubes that were connected to him. I had put a new tape in my recorder in the waiting room. I pressed the activation button. Ungar's eyes opened when I softly called his name.

"LeBlanc?" he asked in a hoarse whisper.

"I'm here."

"How's Claudio?"

"He didn't make it."

"I guess I'll see him in Hell then." Ungar's attempt at a small grin didn't come off.

"How about Frankiewicz?"

"He's dead."

"Good."

"How close to the truth was I?"

Ungar's eyes locked onto mine. "You're damn good, LeBlanc, but I'm the last one who knows what happened. Everything dies with me."

"OK. I have a priest in the lobby if you want to talk to him."

Mike Ungar's eyes closed. I thought he had slipped into unconsciousness. They fluttered open after a few moments. He appeared vaguely regretful.

"Thanks, but God already knows what I've done. I don't need to share it with anyone else."

"Is there anything you want me to do for you?"

His eyes closed again. "Yeah, there is," he finally murmured, "Have a drink for me. Johnny Walker Black."

"I'll do it, Mike. I promise."

His eyes opened again and found mine. "Thanks. Uh, LeBlanc?"

"Yes?"

"I did it." With that his eyes closed for the last time.

49

Wednesday

    I had accompanied Maria and Louie Kolakowski to Joseph Jablonski's funeral. I was surprised at the huge turnout. The old man had made a lot of friends during his years as the school custodian. As we were leaving the service, Detective James Green came up to us.

    "Mrs. Kolakowski?"

    "Yes."

    "I am Detective Green. I wanted you to know that we found two bodies under the basement floor in Frankiewicz's house. One of them had an artificial right leg."

    Maria Kolakowski grabbed her son by the arm.

    "Oh, thank God. Louie, they found them, they found them." She was sobbing into his shoulder as he stroked her hair.

    "It's OK, Mom, it's OK." Tears were running down his face, too.

    Green shifted uneasily on his feet. "We still have to positively I.D. the remains."

    Louie's mother pulled her head out of his shoulder. "Of course you do. I have all of John's dental and medical records at my house. I knew this day would come."

    I left the Kolakowskis to deal with Green. I had a feeling that I was not his favorite person. I was in my truck on the way back to the office when my pager went off. The answering service operator told me my wife had left a message for me to call home.

    "Hello."

    "Jeannie?"

    "Whom did you expect? Jules and I are home and the telephone has been ringing off the hook with reporters calling. Everyone wants to talk to you."

"It's a long story, Sweetheart. I'm on my way home now. I love you."

"Uh huh. I'll be here."

A great load lifted from my spirit. Jeannie and Jules were home. My world was complete again.

The cops must have been sleeping because I didn't get stopped for speeding. As I pulled up to the house, I saw Jules roughhousing with the mutts. He came running up when he saw the truck. I stepped out and gave him a huge hug. When I let go, his attention shifted from me to my truck.

"Neat truck! Gee, Dad, what happened to your face?" His gaze fluctuated between the cut on my cheek which now had four stitches in it and at the right side of my face was bruised and swollen, not to mention the other abrasions.

"I'll tell you when we go inside. I've had a lot of adventures lately."

Jules was hanging back as I limped to the house.
"What's wrong, son?"
"I kinda think you're about to have another one."
"Another what?"
"Another adventure."
"What are you talking about?"
"Uh, Mom's a little different, now that she has discovered who she is."
"What?"
My son sighed. "Trust me. You'll have to see for yourself."
Shaking my head, I entered the house.
"Jeannie," I called, "Where are you?"
"Upstairs."

I ascended the stairs and went into our bedroom. Jeannie was standing by the closet in a long, unbleached cotton dress and sandals. Her hair was gathered into a pony tail; a large crystal in a silver wire mounting hung from her neck. She was not wearing any makeup. My mind flashed back to the late sixties. Her eyes widened with concern when she saw my face.

"Oh, Adrian, what happened to you?"

Ohio Salt

"It looks worse than it is. I'll tell you and Jules all about it in a little while." I reached out and hugged her. "I missed you." I noticed that Jeannie's response to my hug was lukewarm.

She looked out of the window. "Is that truck yours?"

"Absolutely. The insurance company cut me a check for the old one."

"Does it have four-wheel drive?"

"Yes."

"Show it to me."

I struggled not to let my jaw drop. Jeannie has never had an interest in trucks in her life.

"Sure," I agreed as I led the way downstairs. I spent fifteen minutes explaining all of the features as she asked detailed questions. When I was done, Jeannie regarded the new Dakota thoughtfully.

"Nice choice," she finally pronounced.

When we reentered the house, Jeannie handed me a grocery list.

"Adrian, would you be a dear and go to the store for me? We are out of everything."

"Now?"

"Please, and take Jules with you. You two need to spend some time together."

I shrugged. "I'm on my way."

"Oh, take my car. I want to listen to the radio in your truck."

I stared at the woman in front of me. She looked like Jeannie, but she certainly didn't act like her. I wondered if her pod had matured while she had been in Lily Dale. I collected Jules and we drove Jeannie's car, a two-year-old Camry sedan, to the store. While we were shopping, Jules told me all about his adventures among the psychics. He had several readings that had helped him determine that his outlook on life had been affected by an unfortunate previous existence as an undertaker in Victorian England.

"It was a pretty depressing job. Now that I know what was bugging me, things will be better."

My mind began to melt from too much weird input. All I could manage to say was, "That's nice."

We spent almost an hour filling up a shopping cart. Jeannie's

Frank C. Dupuy

list had gone on forever. Jules and I drove home in silence as I tried to determine if I had actually entered the Twilight Zone.

The first thing I noticed when we pulled into the drive was that my truck was gone. The next thing that grabbed my attention was a letter taped the to front door. I read the first two lines, then turned to my son.

"Jules, will you please unload the car and put the groceries up for me?"

To my surprise, he said, "Sure, Dad." and started carrying in the food. I went into the living room, sat down on the couch and read Jeannie's letter. It had been written on Monday.

Dear Adrian,

When you read this, I will be gone. For sometime I have felt called to the wilderness in the West and have been taking camping and survival classes for almost a year. It wasn't until I went to Lily Dale to work with my spiritual advisor that I realized that I will not be complete in this incarnation unless I pursue my quest. Although I love you, our marriage in this life was a mistake. We have been together numerous times in the past, but this time we were supposed to experience other endeavors.

Please try to understand. This is something I must do. I have explained it to Jules and I believe he comprehends my reasons. Jules is much more spiritually enlightened at present than you are. Do not try to find me. My mind and spirit are committed to my new existence.

Spiritually yours,
Rachel, formerly Jeannie

My feeling of having entered another dimension was complete. The hastily scrawled postscript brought me crashing back to reality.

P.S., I took the truck.

50

May 3, 1994

    J.C. Jensen, Collin Yates and I were sipping expensive drinks at Morton's Steak House in Cleveland's Terminal Tower. Collin had insisted on paying for dinner and J.C. demanded the honor of buying the booze. I was feeling pleasantly wasted on Johnny Walker Black. We were on our third after-dinner round when Jensen asked me about Ungar.

    "Do you really think he assassinated Kennedy?"

    "Who knows? When he told me, 'I did it', he could have been confessing to the Bay of Pigs deal with Castro or even to killing Mario Guzman; maybe both."

    Collin Yates assumed his best cross examination demeanor. "Don't evade the question. Do you think Ungar killed Kennedy?"

    "That would be speculation, your honor."

    "So, speculate."

    I contemplated the rich amber liquid in my glass. I was drinking Johnnie Walker Black to honor the dying request of a man I hardly knew, a man who might have been a bigger traitor to his country than Benedict Arnold and John Wilkes Booth combined. For all of his sins, Ungar had not been a coward. I swirled the whisky in my tumbler.

    "When he was dying, he told the truth and he lied. The lie was that Ungar was the last one who knew what happened. He was covering for those who were left. The "I did it" was the truth, a final gesture to a man he had somehow connected with in his dying moments.

    "There is little doubt among the experts that Kennedy was shot by two gunmen, Oswald and someone else. If it makes you feel better, then yes, I believe that Ungar was the second gunman."

"Why did he do it?" Jensen asked.

"That we will probably never know. The conspiracy nuts have written dozens of books with dozens of theories. You can take your pick," I said.

Jensen and Yates exchanged glances.

"What about your interview with Stephen Wlosowicz?" Yates demanded. "He as much as told you J. Edgar Hoover was involved."

"Wlosowicz didn't tell the entire story, although he gave me a hint."

"What do you mean?"

"He told me Guzman thought Mondragón was working for a CIA agent."

"So?"

"Look, Wlosowicz wanted me to believe that his big sin was to sit on the information Petrowski had given him about the assassination plot. I think it was more complicated than that. Before Kennedy was elected, one of his stated goals was to get rid of the CIA. He regarded the Agency as a rogue organization that was dictating its own foreign policy without any guidance from the White House or Congress. As it turns out, he was correct. There has always been speculation that elements within the CIA conspired to kill Kennedy.

"It's probable that Wlosowicz set off some internal alarms when he pulled the Oswald file. If I were a speculator, I might speculate that Wlosowicz was visited by a few Agency heavies and told to mind his own business, or else. Knowing his ambition, they might have even dangled another promotion in front of him."

Jensen was frowning. "Mike Ungar was an FBI agent. How did he get mixed up with the CIA? I thought that Hoover and the CIA hated each other."

"There was a strong inter-agency rivalry. However, both were confronted by a young President who planned to eliminate Hoover and the Central Intelligence Agency. The cowboys within the CIA, the ones who liked to act without any supervision, and the Director of the FBI, had a common cause. Adversity makes strange bedfellows."

"My God, Adrian, you have a huge missing piece of the Kennedy assassination saga. The news media will go nuts when they hear the story," Yates enthused.

"What story?"

"The one you just told us. Any publisher worth his salt would advance a fortune for the rights to it."

"Then be my guest, Collin. As far as I am concerned there is no story, only some farfetched conjecture. If you want to run with it, you're welcome to my share of the publishing rights, fame and fortune."

Neither Jensen nor Yates had any comment. We lazed in our chairs for several minutes, enjoying the serenity of melting ice cubes.

Finally Yates broke the silence. "Beyond the shadow of a doubt, you are the most exasperating client I have ever had, Adrian. You never, ever tell anyone the entire story and," he paused for dramatic effect, "you are one devious, tenacious and hardheaded son of a bitch."

"Amen," declared Jensen.

They raised their glasses to me, and we drank.

Frank C. Dupuy

Epilog

May 15, 1994

    I was sitting in my office feeling sorry for myself. I had lost my wife, my secretary and my truck. Life sucked. I was on my second cup of coffee as I mulled over the events that had transpired since the night Ungar, Mondragón and Frankiewicz had died. Harry Lipscomb and Sally Yuhas were scheduled for trial in August. They were being held without bail for which I was thankful, at least in Yuhas's case.

    John Casimir Kolakowski and Count Stanislas Petrowski were buried with honors. The British military attaché had presented Maria Kolakowski with a British flag and the Polish Consul had presented her with flags for both men for their efforts to free Poland from the Communists. The President of the United States even sent a letter praising both men's contributions to the United States. Collin Yates had leaned on a hell of a lot of people to make that happen. Father Tschapanski conducted the joint service and Karen and Louie made no pretense about being in love with each other. They eloped after the funeral.

    I thought about Maria Kolakowski and the years she had endured not knowing what had happened to her husband and her harebrained scheme to flush out the bad guys after thirty years. In the old West, confidence artists would use shotguns to fire gold nuggets into the walls of worthless mines. This was known as "salting;" gullible rubes would pick the nuggets out of the walls believing they were being offered the opportunity to purchase a gold mine that would make them rich. In Maria Kolakowski's case, she had used nonexistent gold to salt her mine. Well, it had worked, in its own unique fashion.

Frank C. Dupuy

Someone knocked on my office door.
"Come in," I invited.
A UPS driver opened the door, and placed a weighty box on my desk. He had me sign a computerized gadget with a special stylus, then was on his way. I opened the box with my pocket knife. Inside was a letter and a heavy, brick-like object wrapped in layers of newspapers. It took me a moment to realize, after removing the wrappings, that I was gazing upon two ten pound bars of pure gold.
The letter was from Louie Kolakowski.

Dear Adrian,

By the time you get this, Karen, Mom and I will be in the Caymen Islands. I want to thank you for everything you did for us, especially teaching me how to investigate. Mom is a lot like you; she never tells everything she knows. As it turns out, Count Petrowski did have a hidden reserve of gold and Joseph Jablonski knew exactly where it was. He had hinted to Mom that the Virgin was guarding it. She told me this after Jablonski's funeral.

You know what a big deal the Count made out of building a grotto to the Virgin. I naturally assumed that he had hidden the gold in the grotto. Father Tschapanski and I spent a week probing that pile of rocks, but couldn't find a thing. Then, I remembered what you told me about never making assumptions.

Mom told me Joseph Jablonski was religious, but not a fanatic. It occurred to me that only a fanatic, or a nut, would build a scale model of a grotto to the Virgin in his backyard. You have probably guessed where this is leading since you and me think alike. Well, the gold was in his backyard under the Virgin, all 1,250 pounds of it, give or take a few ounces. It took Karen, Mom, Father Leo and me over two hours to load it all into a U-

Ohio Salt

haul truck.

As you know, Count Petrowski intended the gold to be used to fight communism, except that there isn't anything left to fight. So, we decided to honor his wishes to leave money to St. Theresa's Catholic school. I called your friend, Mr. Yates, and had him draw up the papers. Half of the gold was left as an anonymous bequest to the Church on the condition that it goes to St. Theresa's school and no place else. Otherwise, the money goes to the Salvation Army. Father Leo told me "You can bet your ass the Bishop will never let that happen." His words, not mine.

The whole pile is worth over $7,000,000. Just so you don't think I'm nuts, Mom and Karen and I kept half. Mom is pretty smart about smuggling so we should have our share banked in the Caymen Islands in a few days. Each bar weighs about 10 pounds. At today's prices, what we sent you is worth well over $100,000.

Well, I got to go. Thanks again for everything.

Your friend and fellow P.I.,

Louie

I hefted one of the gold bars appraisingly. Then, I gouged a corner of the soft metal with my pocket knife. No lead showed through.

Opening the telephone directory, I looked up the number of the Dodge agency. It was time to order a new truck.

Frank C. Dupuy

Coming Soon
From Agincourt Publishing

<u>Texas Cement</u>
by
Frank C. Dupuy

Adrian LeBlanc is involved in the most intricate investigation of his career as he tries to salvage a bank merger while unraveling a convoluted fraud scheme that has the FBI, the Mafia, and several bank CEOs all vying for a piece of him.

If you would like to know more about upcoming novels by Frank C. Dupuy featuring Adrian LeBlanc, visit us at our web site: Agincourtpress.com

Frank C. Dupuy

Ohio Salt

On the face of it, the anonymous letter writer knew what he was talking about. One thing I had learned during my banking days was that any loan or lease that goes bad within the first twelve months is almost certainly fraudulent. I also knew that banks do not like to acknowledge fraud unless they are forced to. I finished reading the document, then turned to face Cravitz.

"Roberta!" he barked again. The lights came on and the screen slowly disappeared into the ceiling. "Well?" he asked.

"If it weren't for the anonymous letter, you would probably have written this off as a bad deal and let it go. Now you have an allegation that a bank officer has participated in a multimillion dollar fraud. As soon as Howard Beal received the anonymous letter, he should have immediately turned it over to your security department for investigation, and security, per federal law, should have notified the FBI that it was investigating a major fraud."

Cravitz's did not comment. Instead, he asked, "Do you know who Buck Moody is?"

I racked may aging memory banks. "I believe he's a Texas banker."

Cravitz nodded approvingly. "He is the Chairman of the Board of Mustang Bank and Trust in Houston. Moody owns twenty-five percent of the stock, and, at the moment, is in full control of the board of directors." He paused for a moment as he considered me carefully. Non-disclosure agreement or no non-disclosure agreement, Cravitz was not happy about having to confide in me. "Do you know why Premier National Bank acquired National Trust Company?"

"I suppose A, because the price was right to acquire another 250 branches in a four state area, and B, because the Trust Department was relatively intact. I remember that our Trust clients included some of Cleveland's bluest blood."

"Precisely. National Trust had the largest and most profitable Trust Department in Northern Ohio. It controlled large blocks of old money. It was, and is, an extremely profitable operation."

Enlightenment was beginning to play around the edges of my brain. "Might I assume that your interest, if any, in Mustang Bank and Trust has something to do with the word Trust in its name?"

"You might, indeed. Buck Moody, over the last thirty years,

Frank C. Dupuy

has acquired a select Trust clientele that reads like a <u>Who's Who</u> of Houston society. It is an elite and profitable institution."

Cravitz hesitated, then leaned forward to skewer me with his blue-gray eyes.

"One," he rasped, "that we are on the verge of acquiring."

My features remained politely impassive.

"LeBlanc, we are at a critical time in our negotiations with Moody. One or two details need to be resolved before we close the deal. If everything goes as planned, we are scheduled to announce the merger on July 15th."

I had a question. "If Mustang Bank and Trust is doing so well, why does Moody want to merge with an out of state bank?"

"He would rather not merge with anyone, if he had the choice. Unfortunately, a number of institutions have decided that Mustang is desirable and have started to acquire stock. If Moody doesn't find someone he likes to cut a deal with soon, he will be vulnerable to an unfriendly takeover."

"What makes Premier so special? Why did Moody pick you?"

The blue-gray eyes shifted minutely. If I hadn't been concentrating, I would have missed it.

"LeBlanc, Premier National Bank is solid. We have a reputation for reliability and for being well-run. Buck Moody wants a partner that will not alienate his Trust customers. He is impressed by our Trust Department, feeling we share a common view of the Trust business. Premier has also made concessions. We will put all of our operations in Texas under the Mustang name, and retain Moody as president. Moody knows his clientele. If he merges with anything other than a first-class operation, his elite customers will go elsewhere."

Enlightenment blossomed. "And the last thing you need are headlines in the <u>Houston Post</u> announcing to God and everybody that one of Premier National Bank's leasing officers has committed a six million dollar fraud. Things like that scare the hell out of aristocratic Trust customers."

Cravitz held his emotions in check, but it was clear that he was unhappy.

"Yes," he agreed, "scare the hell out of them, and kill any chance of our ever acquiring Mustang Bank and Trust. If word of this leaks out, Moody will terminate negotiations with us in a heartbeat."

Ohio Salt

The seconds ticked by as we contemplated each other. Cravitz broke first. He had reached a decision.

"William Farrell speaks highly of you. He says you are discrete, and, I quote "devious as hell." Those are two qualities I admire. I want you to go to Houston to investigate this matter. Thoroughly. You report directly to me. When you are finished, I receive your written report and all of your notes. At the proper time, I will notify the FBI. Under no circumstances are you to contact any law enforcement agencies. Is that clear?"

I nodded noncommitaly. I wasn't agreeing to anything, yet.

"You received the anonymous letter on June 11th. Why have you waited a week to act on it?"

Cravitz pursed his lips. He did not want to tell me any more than he absolutely had to.

"Yesterday afternoon, Howard Beal received a telephone call from a Carl Ostermann. Mr. Ostermann was the sales manager for East Texas Diesel, one of the companies that supplied cement pumpers. He informed Beal that he was the letter writer, and if Premier didn't do something fast, he was going directly to the FBI. Our original intent was to sit on the letter until after July 15th."

Right, I thought, and continue to sit on it until hell froze over.

"What's Ostermann's problem?"

"He feels that his former employer treated him badly. I believe he also drinks. Beal informed Ostermann that an investigator would meet with him on Monday. He was assured that there was no need to contact the FBI."

I shifted in my chair. It was time to decide whether I was in, or out. Some decision. I had known I was going to take the case after Cravitz had shown me the second slide on the projection screen. Cravitz had known it, too. My concern was that the old bastard certainly hadn't told me the entire truth. I waited a little longer, just to make him wonder.

"Mr. Cravitz, what do you want the outcome of this investigation to be?"

"What I want, LeBlanc, is for this matter to be handled quietly and without any publicity. I want it put to bed. Do you understand me?" He did not raise his voice, yet the impact of his words was nonetheless powerful. Cravitz was asking a lot. In fact, he was asking the damn near impossible, and he knew it. This was his gambit to make me commit to how I proposed to handle the situation and to give him an idea of how much fallout there was likely to be.

"Tell me, LeBlanc, what can you do for me?"

"With a little luck, I can probably keep this from ever getting out in Houston, recoup most of your money, and prevent the FBI from having a fit that you didn't inform them of a major crime against your bank."

"Go on."

"At this point, you don't actually know if a crime has been committed, so you have no obligation to notify the Bureau. Frankly, that's the least of your worries, assuming Ostermann is telling the truth.

"On Monday, I'll interview Ostermann. When we're done, he won't feel much like contacting the FBI, especially after I point out he's part of the conspiracy. As the sales manager, he had to have been in on it. The bad guys probably cheated him, so now he's out for revenge. He hasn't considered he might go down with them.

"The case needs to be thoroughly documented. That shouldn't be too difficult. By next Friday, I will be ready to interview your leasing officer, Robbie Barton. The goal is to get a confession out of him and keep him on ice until after July 15th. When I'm finished, he can be suspended with pay, or sent out of town on a protracted assignment.

"With a confession and all of the documentation, you can probably persuade the local FBI office to accept jurisdiction. The victim, Premier National Bank, is in Cleveland, and ultimately, the loss took place in Cleveland. If the Cleveland office takes the case, and Barton rolls over, there is every possibility that the story will never get out in Cleveland, let alone Houston. Also, the same evidence you provide the Bureau will document your insurance claim."

Cravitz and I traded stares. He knew that I had presented a best case scenario, and that in the real world, best cases seldom occur. He also knew that if he didn't do something, his carefully nurtured merger would die when the first hint of scandal was

Ohio Salt

reported by the media.

"What do you need to get started?" he finally asked.

"I'll need Richard Freemantle to pull all of the files and review them with me. It would help if you can find me a downtown office to work out of. One that's away from the bank, but close enough to be convenient if I need something. I want a letter of introduction instructing your people to cooperate with me as your agent. All they need to know is that I'm a collections expert who is trying to recover as much of the bank's money as possible."

Cravitz did not write anything down. He could probably repeat our entire conversation verbatim if need be. I was also certain that the invisible Roberta in the next room was taking notes.

"Anything else?"

"Yes. I want a bank auditor to go down there with me. The Houston banks will cooperate better with an auditor than with a private investigator. Make certain that your audit department provides someone with a personality, someone other bankers will like to work with."

"Very well, LeBlanc, I will have someone for you this afternoon, however, the auditor is not to be informed of the merger, nor are any of our people in Houston. You and Freemantle are the only ones who are aware we are in merger negotiations."

I leaned back in my chair. "Mr. Cravitz, if you want the lid kept on your mess, I need your word that I'll have complete discretion in handling this affair, including spending money for information and outside services. I'm going to have to move fast, and I don't want to be second-guessed every step of the way."

Cravitz frowned. He wasn't happy giving anyone a free hand. "I must have one thing absolutely clear. Under no circumstances are you to contact any law enforcement authorities regarding this investigation. Is that understood?"

"Completely. Oh, you can cut me a check for $20,000. I'll let you know when I need more."

My client flinched slightly before nodding his agreement. He was, after all, a banker.

Frank C. Dupuy